Deep as a Tomb

By

Dorothy A. Winsor

Soft cover ISBN: 978-1-62432-024-8
eBook ISBN: 978-1-62432-025-5

BISAC Subject Headings:
YAF000000 YOUNG ADULT FICTION / General
YAF001000 YOUNG ADULT FICTION / Action & Adventure / General
YAF011000 YOUNG ADULT FICTION / Coming of Age

Cover art by Francesca Baerald

Please address all correspondence to:
Loose Leaves Publishing, LLC
4218 E. Allison Road
Tucson, AZ 85712

Or visit our website at:
www.LooseLeavesPublishing.com

Deep as a Tomb

Chapter 1

The tomb pulled at Myla like the sun coaxing a sapling toward the sky. She had to fight off a temptation to run rather than pick her way through the underbrush. She glanced over her shoulder to see if Kaven felt the tug too and found him scanning the trees to one side. As if sensing her gaze, he turned to her, hand raised to ward off a trailing bush.

Her heart lurched. "Don't touch!"

Kaven jumped away from the redthorn bush he'd been about to shove aside. Wiping his hand on his trousers, he frowned at the plant, a rare one, the Forest be blessed. Its scarlet, two-inch thorns gleamed with wicked hunger. "Thanks for the warning."

Myla's knees trembled. A scratch from a redthorn would swell and be sore for a week. A jab stuck its poison deep. People died of redthorn poisoning. She tightened her grip on the strap of her bag and pushed through the underbrush at a safer place, her scalp prickling as twiggy fingers snagged at her braid.

"Wait, Myla," Kaven said. "You're caught again." He moved close and slipped her hair from the grasp of a hawthorn bush. His warmth brushed her spine, and she smelled the leather of his jerkin, the faint tang of his sweat. Her breath stopped halfway through her throat.

When he held onto her braid, she gripped it and ducked around to look up at him. He dropped the braid to run the tip of his finger along the eyebrow she'd raised. Leaves fluttered, letting flashes of sunlight dance across his dark head. She stared at his mouth, spellbound, but she made herself brace her hands against his chest and step back. "Not now," she forced out. "Leaving an offering in a tomb is a sacred act."

"Kissing you is sacred to me," he said, voice husky.

"Still, not now. We have to get back to Lady Eran's before Prince Beran arrives." Myla handed him the sack of tomb offerings. "Hold this, and give me your cap." Like the sweet boy he was, Kaven surrendered the yellow knit cap he had tucked in his belt. She wound her braid around her head and netted the cap over it. "Now let's do what we came for." She grabbed the bag and set off toward the tomb where Lady Eran's husband slept among his ancestors. Once again, she felt as if she were rushing downhill. What was happening to her?

"I'm sorry." Kaven trailed after her. "It's just that the tomb isn't going anywhere , but you are."

"Not for four more months," Myla said.

"That's too soon."

The longing in his voice made her shiver. "I'll just be at our manor. That's an easy ride away." She swerved around another hawthorn.

"Too far," he said. When she stayed silent, he sighed and asked, "Do you think you'll be able to open the tomb?"

"I told you I'm not sure."

A manor's tomb was supposed to open to those of that manor's blood, but over the years, there'd been so much intermarriage that many families, including Myla's and Kaven's, had lost the power to open them, so it had never occurred to her that she could open her neighbor Zale's. She'd ridden there, intending only to leave flowers at the door, after Zale's old auntie had died. The auntie wasn't buried in their manor's tomb, of course, because no one could get in. Myla had prayed with her hands on the tomb door, her heart wrenched with pity for the poor woman wandering the afterlife away from the Forest, grieving its loss. Then the tomb door shocked her by opening.

Too bad she'd been stupid and told her father what had happened. Ever since, she'd regretted not entering Zale's tomb because sure as spring she didn't belong there, but she regretted telling Da even more because he'd gone on and on about how her opening a tomb would somehow gain him--not her, she noticed--more respect. Maybe today she'd open Lady Eran's tomb and see what one looked like inside. She'd keep that from Da for certain. Her breath sped up at both thoughts.

A bush with spear-shaped leaves sprawled across her path. She'd never seen one like it before, though that wasn't surprising. The Forest grew strange near tombs left unentered for too long. Giving in to her curiosity, she fought the force drawing her long enough to stop and look the plant over.

"What is it?" Kaven asked.

"I don't know." She pulled a scrap of cloth from her belt pouch, wound it around her hand, and snapped off a bit of the spear-leafed bush. When she sniffed the end, its scent pinched the inside of her nose.

"A tomb plant?" Kaven asked. "Has Steeprise Manor's tomb been closed up long enough for that?"

Myla lifted her gaze to a leaf canopy too thin to suggest life was thriving on Steeprise Manor. "Maybe." She wrapped the twig and tucked it in her pouch. She'd learn what she could about it later. Sometimes tomb plants were strong healers, like the tomb was trying to cure whatever had locked its people out. She resumed her hurried walk. "Da says I can open tombs because we descend from Jorn himself."

Kaven dismissed that notion with a flick of his fingers. "Can he do it?"

Myla snorted.

"That says it's not ancestry that gives you power," Kaven said. "Not his ancestry anyway."

"It makes my brother wild that he can't either."

"Why, Myla of Oak Ridge Manor," Kaven said. "I do believe you're gloating."

She tugged his cap to a jauntier angle. "I'm entitled."

"You are."

She had to gloat when the chance arose because the only thing Da told her was she was sixteen and knew nothing, so she should shut up and let him decide who to tell. Mostly she had, though of course she'd told Kaven. Then she'd been unable to resist telling Lady Eran when the woman was crying over being locked out from her husband. She'd begged Myla to come back and try to help once she'd had time to dig up a proper offering.

So today, when Kaven and Myla rode over, with Prince Beran's visit as an excuse, Eran slipped a lidded gold bowl full of herbs and dried flowers into the leather sack and handed it to Myla. "Bless you, Myla," Eran quavered. "I've been fretting because I'm too rotted old to make this trip any more and even leave flowers on the doorstep." Sometimes women chose to be buried in their own blood ancestors' tombs, but from the way Erantalked, Myla judged she wasn't one of those, and from the look of her, she'd soon lie at her man's side.

If Myla could open the tomb.

"Maybe you have the power from the medicines you try. I've seen you take them, chancy though that is." Kaven skirted a tangle of undergrowth.

"I only do it if I'm sure they're safe." Mostly. Sometimes the medicine books weren't as clear as a normal person needed.

"If it's the medicines, you could help every family that's locked out of their tomb," Kaven said. "Folks all over the Forest would be grateful."

A flame of happiness danced in Myla's chest, damped down only a bit by worry for the future. Four more months, and she'd see Kaven only when he visited. Da would like him, wouldn't he? Or at least like knowing Myla had someone. Like trees, people were stronger tied together than standing alone.

Ahead, something glimmered between the maples, and a warm breeze brushed over her, fragrant with the scent of rich soil and growing things. Her muscles eased, and the throb of her blood settled to match the throb of the Forest's life. She crept forward, setting her feet gently, and walked out of the trees into a clearing around a mound of earth covered in moss so green it glowed. The pull she felt let go as if she'd arrived where the Forest wanted her to be. At least she hoped so. She was about to find out if she'd gloated too soon.

Kaven soft-footed up next to her, lower lip caught in his teeth. His gaze flicked over the tomb and then into the trees, like he couldn't stand to look for too long.

Deep as a Tomb

Myla drifted around the tomb through air almost too thick to breathe. It pressed against her skin, heavy with the presence of old treasures, old life and death, and the Forest sheltering its own. Even the birds seemed to feel the power and fall silent. On the mound's north side, a stone frame appeared around a smooth stone door. Carved runes spidered up one side of the frame to the icon of Silvit and then ran down the other, spelling out Steeprise Manor's prayer. She wiped sweaty hands on her trousers.

Silvit save her. What had she been thinking? Opening that other tomb had probably been a one-time chance. She probably couldn't ever do it again. She pictured Da's face as he watched her fail and cringed. Then she thought of the ailing trees she'd glimpsed on her way here, and of Lady Eran's hopeful face. *Get hold of yourself, Myla. This matters to folks besides you.* She brushed aside a shriveled vine roped across the doorway, spread her fingers, and laid her palms flat on the door. When the cool surface hummed under her touch, her heart leaped. The neighbor's tomb had done that too. She began to read the runes aloud. With rising excitement, she ran through the prayer once and then a second time. The door still barred the way, but the humming bloomed louder and harder. Surely in another moment, it would slide open.

"What's taking so long?" Kaven said. "Can't you do it?"

Disoriented as if she'd been yanked out of a deep sleep, she wrenched her attention to Kaven. He shifted from foot to foot, darting looks every which way except at the tomb.

A flicker of movement flashed behind him. "Is someone there?" she asked sharply.

"Rot it!" a voice cried, and a man with a cloth tied over his lower face lunged out of the undergrowth, hand out, reaching for the bag holding Lady Eran's tomb gift.

"No!" Kaven threw himself between them, grabbing the masked man's arms. For a weird instant, they looked like they were dancing.

A second form moved among the trees, and Myla woke up out of the place where the tomb's spell had left her. Thieves!

She forced her frozen legs into life and ran.

Chapter 2

If Beran didn't want every tongue in the palace wagging about him, he obviously could never admit it, but he found the Westreach to be every bit as creepy as the howling storytellers said. Densely packed trees crowded right up to the edge of the road. Their shade lay chill on Beran's back and shoulders, and he clutched gratefully at the warmth of the horse beneath him. He'd fostered in every other part of his father's kingdom, and he'd never seen a place so full of shadowy, hungry life.

"I hate this," Nelas said from farther back. "I can't see a thing with all these trees in the way. I feel surrounded."

Beran rode near the front of the group with his bodyguard, Ander, so he had to twist in his saddle to see the compact, blond soldier glaring at the woods. He forced a grin that he hoped looked relaxed. "Don't you feel the power of the place?" He looked from Nelas to Jem, riding next to his friend, both of them leading pack ponies. Beran knew them because they were maybe eighteen or nineteen, only a couple of years older than he was, and so still young enough to live in the castle barracks. "You are both sad city boys. There's a wild way of life here you'll never see at home."

"That's what we're worried about." Like Nelas, Jem eyed the trees with loathing.

"They're trees," snapped Lieutenant Lith, who was leading the group. "Nothing with bark ever put a sword through your guts."

The woods closed in on the road dwindling behind them. Carl rode farthest back. He was older, forty maybe, and built like a boulder. Beran had seen Carl in the castle yard off and on. In truth, the last time Beran had seen him, he was drunk. But Beran didn't know him well, and this trip wasn't changing that. Carl looked straight ahead, as if he were riding alone.

"What's that?" Ander crowded closer, tucking Beran between him and Lieutenant Lith.

In the shadows under the trees ahead, a jumble of paving stones lay across the road. For a crazed moment, Beran pictured the trees heaving the stones into their way.

Lieutenant Lith prodded his horse toward the barricade. "See that, Beran? That's what His Majesty's road builders are up against. As fast as they lay the stones, the so-called True slap on their wolf masks, slink out of their dens, and rip them up." Lith's horse skittered, as if trying to get out from under the lieutenant's annoyance. "Bunch of young fools."

Lith started to squeeze his horse between a maple and the pile of stones, but Ander still frowned at the barrier. When Beran followed his guard's gaze, he saw a pair of beetle-black eyes peering over the stones, staring fixedly at the space between Nelas and Carl. "Is that a poppet?" Beran slid from his saddle.

The hard little eyes did indeed belong to a poppet, one with a crudely sewn body, twigs for arms and legs, and a shrunken apple for a head. The eyes were made from some sort of seed. Beran reached to take it, his gaze on the band of gold thread wrapped around its brow. A crown? He plucked the thing out of the stones to look closer.

"Wait! Let me." Ander was off his horse and next to Beran too late.

A note was pinned to the poppet's back. "Go home, grassland cub," Beran read, "before wolves eat your entrails." His fist closed around the poppet's body so hard that a seam burst and sawdust trickled down onto his boots. He deliberately relaxed his hand and gave the thing to Ander.

Ander read the note with narrowed eyes. When Lith sidestepped his horse closer, Ander handed the poppet up to him.

Lith read and swore full-throatedly, "Stone the whole stoning lot of them and their dogs and their grannies. Stone them all to the Eternal Nightmare."

He stretched to tuck the poppet, still leaking sawdust, into his saddle pack. "I'll see that the local magistrate gets this. Don't be too uneasy, Beran. As far as I know, the only things the True have attacked are paving stones."

"No need to involve the magistrate," Beran said.

"A threat is a threat," Ander said, his voice a little too loud.

Beran faced his guard, surprised yet again to find himself having to look down. "The king's advisors say the same thing Lith does. The True are just bored, well-off idlers who get a thrill from pretending to be outlaws. Throwing them in jail would only upset their powerful relatives. The king expects me to calm their fears, not make them worse."

"Lord Corin should know about this," Ander insisted. "I don't know what else your father could expect."

"I'm not going to whine to Corin or his magistrate about Westreachers in the first week I'm here." Beran leaned closer so only Ander would hear. "I'm making a good impression, remember?"

Ander's hands twitched in a move that meant he wanted to cuff a bit of caution into Beran, but he hadn't done that in more than a year, and Beran didn't expect him to start up again, with Lith and his men looking on. Sure enough, Ander drew a deep breath and settled for retying the leather band he wore across his forehead to keep his silver hair out of his eyes. "Let's go." He remounted, nudging his horse after Lith's.

Beran lingered, staring at the piled-up road stones. What did his father expect? Thien had been only nineteen and newly crowned when he rode into the hostile Forest and emerged two weeks later with a contract of marriage to the chieftain's only child and the promise of the region becoming a Rinnish province; he was not a man who thought small.

From the woods behind Beran came a high-pitched scream. "No! Let go of me!" He jerked around to face the sound, then sprang into motion.

"Beran, wait!" Ander's horse neighed a protest at whatever he was doing.

Beran tore through the underbrush, batting away branches that tugged at his clothes and clawed his face. His scabbard tangled in a bush. He yanked it free and kept going, but when the trees parted, a stream lay between him and whoever was screaming. He slowed for just an instant at the ravine's wide yawn, then lowered his head, ran toward the bank, and jumped, one leg flung out in front of him, pawing for the other bank. Water flashed past beneath him. His toes came down in mud, and his foot slipped. With every bit of muscle control he had, he threw his weight forward instead of back and landed on his hands and knees, his teeth skinning the edges of his tongue.

"Wait, Beran!" Ander called from not far behind.

"Get off!" the voice shouted.

Beran scrambled to his feet and hurtled ahead, barely noticing the loud splash followed by Ander swearing in a way he almost never did. Through the trees, Beran glimpsed movement. He burst into a glade to see a skinny man with a cloth tied around his lower face and both arms wrapped around a boy who faced away from him, hugging a leather bag to his chest. Stone the man. He was trying to grab the bag's strap.

Heart pounding, Beran drew his sword, the first time he'd ever pointed it at someone off the training fields. "Let go," he ordered, and was shocked at how calm he sounded.

The boy caught sight of him and snarled, baring gleaming teeth. "Rot you! I won't!"

The skinny man's eyes darted from side to side. The boy yanked the bag free and flung it away. Reaching behind him, he snicked a knife from the man's belt and drove it backwards into the man's thigh. The man shrieked, let go of the boy, and clapped a hand onto his leg. When Beran lunged toward him, he fled, limping, among the trees. Beran started after him.

"Stop right there." The boy blocked Beran's way, breathing hard and waving the blood-tipped knife. He wore a cap in one of the bright colors Beran had been told Westreach boys liked to display as they neared manhood. A small blue feather dangled from a leather thong looped around his left ear, swaying in time with the blade. "Where's Kaven? Did you hurt him?"

Beran dipped his sword so he wouldn't cut the kid accidentally. "It's all right." He spoke as soothingly as he would to a dog being dragged to the bath. "I'm not with the thief." Beran edged around the kid, frantic because even with a wounded leg, the masked man would hide himself quickly in all this creeping greenery. The interference with the king's peace sent heat flashing through Beran's gut.

"No? You just happen to show up and be going the same way?" The boy turned with Beran, keeping the knife between them. Their feet scuffed the two halves of a circle in the leaf litter. "If you're so clean, put your sword away, and tell me where Kaven is."

Beran slipped closer to the place where the thief had entered the woods. The boy's bag lay in his way. Beran nudged it with his foot.

"Don't touch that!" The boy leaped onto Beran's back and drove the knife toward his shoulder.

Beran dropped his sword, grabbed the boy's wrist, and yanked, sending the kid flying over his shoulder. He slammed the boy's back against his own chest and got hold of the little ingrate's knife hand. The stab-crazy idiot wriggled like a snake, his elbows and heels shooting lightning strikes of pain into Beran's ribs and shins.

"Stop it! I don't want your precious bag." Beran adjusted his grip across the boy's chest, trying to hold him still.

Something soft moved under his hand.

He stared at the fist around the knife. Each fingernail was painted a different color. Beran twisted the wrist until the knife popped free, then dropped his captive into the dirt as far from his sword as he could manage. He grabbed the red-tipped knife, and then, once the danger of being gutted was past, he looked from the tight trousers to the long dark braid that had fallen free of the cap.

"You're a girl."

"And you're scum," said a voice to Beran's left. A broad-shouldered boy of about Beran's age shot out from the trees, glaring. Under a leather jerkin, he wore a gold shirt and red trousers that made Beran blink. The missing Kaven, no doubt. Brown hair flopped across his forehead. His hands and booted feet seemed outsized, making him look like a mastiff puppy that hadn't yet grown into his paws. In one of those outsized hands, he held a knife of his own.

Did everyone here want to stab him?

"I ought to kill you for touching her," Kaven said.

Beran's face burned. "I didn't know." He side-stepped away until he could transfer the girl's knife to his left hand and retrieve his sword.

The girl climbed to her feet. "Are you all right? He didn't hurt you?"

"Him?" Kaven asked. "This is the first I've seen him. Who is he?"

"Put the knife away," a new voice said. Ander slid into sight and rested the tip of his sword a hand's span from Kaven's ribs. He was dripping and mud-smeared, but he was still the most menacing person in the clearing.

Beran felt a twinge of amused envy. Ander had clucked with concern when he bandaged a six-year-old Beran's skinned knee, and yet he could turn himself into this deadly threat. The odd thing was both sides were the true Ander. Beran had played enough royal roles to know how they could take you over. More than he could say, he admired how his guard managed not to lose track of himself.

Kaven's hand wavered, but a glance from Ander kept him from doing something unutterably stupid. He sheathed his knife.

Smiling approvingly, Ander lowered his sword. With a hand Beran saw trembling from clear across the glade, the girl reached for her bag half-buried in a pile of rotting leaves.

"Have I missed the introductions?" Ander asked.

"This is Kaven. We're not on your manor, are we?"

Kaven shook his head, thank the Powers. Westreachers were territorial as hornets.

"And this is who? His sister?" He thrust the knife into his belt. No way was he handing it back to this wild girl.

She gave a shaky laugh. With her dark hair and flushed face, she was quite pretty. Her brows slanted like bird wings. Her mouth was wide, her nose slightly arched. On the other hand, her eyes gleamed with nasty-spirited enjoyment. "Sister? Oh, no. I'm Myla of Oak Ridge Manor."

Beran pawed through the clutter in his memory, unearthing the manor names he'd learned. Oak Ridge was held by Lord Talun, maybe? Beran sighed. The impression he made on Talun would depend on whether he wanted this girl back, which right then Beran wouldn't have sworn to.

"A thief attacked her, Ander," Beran said. "He ran that way. He might still be around."

"Let me check," Ander said. "Wait for Lith." He moved in the direction Beran had pointed, and when Beran made to follow, he said, "Wait. I mean it." Beran reluctantly stopped where he was, while Ander slid off, scanning the undergrowth, sword raised again. Beran could hear him, so he was only searching nearby, making sure the thief wasn't lurking, ready to jump out and attack Beran.

"Ander," Beran called, "he was running away."

"Wait," Ander called back.

"And you are?" No way Kaven could sound that rude without trying.

"Beran of Rinland." Kaven's face changed the way people's always did when they first learned who he was. Beran swiveled to where Lith should be arriving. They were wasting time.

"King Thien's heir," Kaven said stiffly. "We should have known. As it happens, we rode to Steeprise Manor to meet you."

Presumably stabbing Beran hadn't been part of the plan, then. Presumably.

"Shall we bow, Your Highness?" Myla cocked her head.

"It's not necessary." He smiled coolly. "We're on 'intimate' terms."

She flushed. Kaven looked ready to commit whatever the princely equivalent of regicide was.

"Moreover, both bowing and 'Your Highness' are inappropriate," Beran said. "I won't be named King's Heir until this fall."

Kaven had turned to follow the sounds of Ander's search, but he focused on Beran long enough to say, "That's right. The king's council has to accept you. I hear our Lord Corin might object."

Beran had heard that too. So had his father. Beran put on his court face, the one that said he was politely interested and wasn't, of course, thinking anything critical about whoever was running his mouth. "That would be Lord Corin's right, but perhaps he and his people will get to know me better while I'm visiting my grandmother."

"You take that to be a good thing?" Myla asked.

Deep as a Tomb

Ander reappeared as the thunder of pounding feet drew close, and Carl ran into the glade, sword drawn, with Lith, Jem, and Nelas at his heels. Their soaked clothing explained their lateness. Lith's eyes skimmed Beran, assessed Myla and Kaven, and came to rest on Ander, who said, "All over before I arrived."

A picture flashed into Beran's head of himself presenting Lord Corin with one of the thieves Beran had been told were plaguing Corin's people. If Beran wanted to make a good impression, that would do it. "It's not really over." He nodded toward Myla. "A man tried to steal her bag. We need to go after him." He took a step in the direction the thief had gone, but he was the only one who did.

"Did you know him?" Lith asked Myla.

"He was masked," Myla said.

"Like a wolf?" Lith asked. "The road's torn up back there. Could it be—"

"It wasn't a wolf mask, just a cloth," Myla interrupted. "So it wasn't the True. That bunch is harmless, but there've been thieves around." She tossed her braid off her shoulder. "You're King Thien's soldiers. What are you doing about them?"

Beran was beginning to see why the Westreach was such a stone in his father's shoe. They didn't want the king to interfere until they did. Still, she had a point. "The thief can't have gone far. We should go after him." He took another step in the right direction. "Lith, we need to search."

Lith exchanged a look with Ander, then put his sword away. "We need to get you safely to your grandmother's. Under the circumstances, we'll skip Steeprise Manor. Nelas, you take word of that and the thief to Lady Whatever Her Name Is."

Beran felt his temper rising and paused to be sure he could sound cool-headed.

Kaven spoke first. "We can take word to Lady Eran. Our ponies are there, and it's time for us to go home."

"If you're going our way, you're welcome to ride with us," Lith said. "Just in case the thief is still around."

Myla aimed her answer at Beran, not Lith. "Didn't I say? Kaven and I are fostering at Lady Isadia's."

"My grandmother's?" Beran blurted.

"Is there more than one Lady Isadia in these parts?" She widened her blue eyes like she'd never seen sin.

Beran scraped up every bit of what he'd learned watching his father politely put people in their places. "How nice."

Ander sounded as if he might be choking on something.

Lith said, "Go with these two, Nelas. Meet us back where we left the horses. There's a bridge across that stream?" he asked Myla, who nodded.

"Near the house." She shouldered her bag. "Let's go, Kaven."

As straight-backed as any court lady, she marched away. Bits of leaf clung to her trousers, and Beran couldn't help noticing how they outlined her legs and backside. Kaven glared at him as if he knew what Beran was thinking. He probably did. He was young and male too. He settled a possessive hand in the small of her back and walked behind her, blocking Beran's view. Nelas flashed Beran a grin and went after them.

Tipping his head in the same direction, Ander waited for Beran to move. "We'll take the bridge this time."

"No." Beran had finally managed to reach cool determination. "I want to track the thief. She stuck him pretty hard, so he might still be around."

Ander gave Beran the same assessing look he'd been subjected to repeatedly as the King's Council prepared to name an heir. The council nearly always named the king's oldest son, but they didn't have to. When lords like Corin played power games, the challenge to a potential heir was a strong move. Surely Ander understood the stakes here.

"The king is concerned about thieves in this part of the Westreach," Beran said. "They add to the unrest. I'm supposed to learn what I can while I'm here."

"But not chase them down on your own," Ander said.

"It was one man, and the girl took his knife. He ran when he saw me."

"You don't know what other weapons he had," Ander said.

"We can't leave a thief loose to do more damage." Beran drew close and murmured to Ander while Lith, Carl, and Jem held back. "I need to make a good impression on the people of the Westreach, Ander. Catching a thief would do that, you have to admit. I'm *not* going to pass up this chance."

Ander rubbed a hand over his jaw. "We don't chase him for long, and you do what I say." He raised his voice so the rest of them would hear. "Show the lieutenant which way he went, Beran."

Ignoring Lith's eyeroll, Beran hastened to where the thief had vanished onto a faint path. He started along it, but Ander caught his arm and jerked his head for Carl to lead the way. Beran pushed up close to Carl's back, trying to hurry him along. As if the trees themselves were against him, a branch whipped at his face. He flung up his arm to ward it off and nearly ran into Carl, who'd come to a stop. He peered around Carl and found the path had split.

While Beran jiggled one leg, Carl searched a few yards down the left trail and then the right. He straightened from the crouch he'd been in and came back. "I don't know."

"We should—" Lith started.

"Carl, you and Jem, go right," Beran said. "Ander, Lith, and I will go left." Carl looked past Beran at the lieutenant, a soldier waiting for orders though not from Beran. "Go," Beran barked. With a shrug, Carl started down the right-hand path, trusting Jem to follow, and Beran wasted no time going left. He was unsurprised when Lith slid past him into the lead, but then prickled with annoyance when Lith made only a half-hearted search for signs of someone tearing through in a hurry.

"Beran," Ander finally said, "we need to gather Jem and Carl and go back to meet Nelas." Lith immediately stopped and turned back.

The gurgle of flowing water had been growing louder, most likely from the same stream Beran had jumped. The noise of it broke into a splash. Lith snapped to face it, but Beran pushed past him and ran, with Ander close behind.

"Carl! Jem!" Lith shouted. "To me!"

Beran rounded a stand of thorny bushes and halted. Two yards below, the stream rushed past. Muddy ruts cut through the bank. Someone had skidded down into the water. Beran twisted to scan the stream in both directions. Nothing. No one.

"He could have gone either way," Lith said as he jammed to a halt next to Beran. "We'll never find him."

"We should follow the stream for a while," Beran said.

"Which way?" Ander asked.

"Either. Both."

Carl and Jem panted into sight, swords drawn.

"He's gone," Lith said. "We're done here." The others sheathed their weapons, but Beran looked downstream again.

"No, Beran," Ander said. "We're not going to catch him today, and we need to be on our way if we're to reach Lady Isadia's before dark."

Beran hesitated, then slid his sword into its scabbard. "We'll come back here tomorrow and search some more. Lord Corin's not been able to learn anything about them. Our running into one was lucky."

Ander laughed and slapped his shoulder. "Is that what you call it? We'll come back if you like. Wait here with the lieutenant while I take care of a personal matter, and we'll be on our way." He strode off toward the bushes.

"You'd better watch out, Ander," Jem called. "I hear there are wildcats ready to attack a Rinlander with his trousers down."

Ander made a rude gesture over his shoulder and vanished in the undergrowth.

"Stone it." Lith dropped to one knee to tug on a broken bootlace. "Do you have twine, Jem?"

Jem began to dig through the tangle of odds and ends he always had in his pockets.

Fidgeting with his signet ring, Beran continued to scan for signs of the skinny thief. The stream burbled along, threading the trees that stretched in all directions. A bird he didn't recognize trilled a heart-piercing song. He shifted uneasily, the back of his neck prickling with the sense that the forest was watching him, guarding itself against him. He'd been told Westreachers thought of the forest as a fierce, living creature, embodied in the great cat Silvit. At home, that seemed ridiculous, but here, among the trees, Beran understood. The trees, stream, and birds were all connected to one another, and none of them needed—or wanted—him.

He glanced in the direction Ander had gone. His guard was taking a long time. Beran hoped their food hadn't made him ill. If it had, they were all going to feel it. He walked a few yards that way, following a game trail. Lith looked up from his boot long enough to point at Carl, who drifted to the trail's start, keeping an eye on Beran.

"Ander?" Beran called.

No answer.

Beran went a little farther. "Do you need anything? Water? Wet leaves?" He grinned. "Poison ivy?"

Ander didn't answer.

Uneasiness writhed in Beran's gut, a squirm that didn't come from bad food. He trotted farther down the path. "Ander?"

At the foot of a maple, something silver was tangled in a heap of black leaves. Beran blinked. The silver turned into Ander's hair. The black leaves became his uniform. Beran lurched to his knees, heart thudding. Ander's open eyes stared at nothing. His face was purple. When Beran shoved his arm under Ander's shoulders and lifted them, Ander's head lolled back like the head of a doll whose owner dragged it by one leg. Then Beran saw the leather strap twisted around Ander's neck. He tore at it, ripping the nail on his right forefinger, a blessed instant of pain rather than terror. He yanked the leather loose and held up the band Ander always wore to hold his hair back.

"Please, please." Beran shook him. "I took it off. Talk to me, Ander. Talk to me!"

Chapter 3

"Lith!" Carl shouted from far away in a different world but somehow close enough that his scarred hand touched the side of Ander's neck. Beran slapped it away.

One part of Beran's brain screamed at him to stand up, draw his sword, and protect himself if the killer still lurked nearby. Or better yet, get out of there, run into the arms of his father's soldiers. But he couldn't leave Ander. For Beran to do that, Ander had to be dead. And he couldn't be dead. He couldn't.

But if he were alive, Beran reasoned dazedly, *he'd smack me for not moving.* A fist squeezed his heart. He stood up, drew his sword, and left the thing that used to be Ander lying in the leaves like trash. His guard would have been proud of him.

Lith and Jem scrambled into sight and ran to where Carl still crouched. For a reason Beran didn't remember, Lith wore only one boot.

Beran looked away, staring at a bare spot in the dirt. His eye caught, and he woke up to the realization that he was staring at the marks of two men, one of them limping and probably leaning on the other. On its own, his hand contracted on his sword, and he followed, moving as quickly and quietly as he could. In the undergrowth, some small animal scurried out of his path, as if it felt how much he wanted to kill something. A shape moved next to him that he vaguely recognized as Carl. Not far ahead, a horse whickered unhappily.

Deep as a Tomb

With vicious glee scalding through his veins, Beran hurtled toward the sound. Hoofbeats tapped slow, then faster. He tore after them, but he couldn't run fast enough. They drew away and faded.

"Here's where they were." Carl pointed to churned leaf litter, then followed the deep gouges the galloping horses had left. Hope swelling again, Beran hurried after him. Maybe Carl could track the stoning murderers. The marks led along a deer path and came out onto the king's road. Beran spun one way, then the other. He wiped the sweat from his eyes with his sleeve and looked again, but he still saw nothing, and, of course, the road wouldn't show tracks. There was no way to tell which direction they'd taken.

"Nothing we can do," Carl said. "Not now, anyway."

No, not now. Before maybe, if Beran had been paying attention, but not now.

"Come. We'll go back." Carl waited until Beran turned and trudged ahead of him through a blurred world. He went only a few yards before nearly running into Lith and Jem. He stopped, blinking them into clarity.

"There were two of them." Carl jerked his thumb over his shoulder. "They took the road."

Lith's face was grim. "Go get Nelas and our horses, Jem. Bring that snippy girl and her boyfriend too if they still want to travel with us. Move."

Jem took off at a run.

"I'm sorry, Beran," Lith said.

Sorry. Well, yes. Beran waited dumbly until Lith stepped aside to let him go on his way back to Ander. As Beran stood staring at the body one more time, a fly settled on Ander's open eye.

"Stone you!" Beran swung his sword, as if he had a prayer of hitting the filthy thing, as if it mattered if he did. He crouched, closed Ander's eyes, and smoothed back his hair. Then he waited, fists clenched, his torn nail pricking his palm like he could take all his pain into his hand and pull it out of his heart.

19

The tramp of horses signaled Jem's return. He came into sight, followed by Nelas, each leading a string of horses. Myla and Kaven came too, with their Westreach ponies. The animals snorted and balked at coming too near. The stink of death must already be in the air, though Beran couldn't smell it.

Myla breathed a soft *Oh!* and dropped the reins she held, leaving Jem to grab for them before her pony realized it was loose. Beran wanted Myla gone, her and Kaven both. They lived in this place that bred wild animals and killer men. They had no business anywhere near Ander.

"This is all wrong." Kaven's voice was high and breathless. "It must have been an accident."

"No." Beran said. "This was murder." He opened and closed his fists, daring Kaven to disagree so he'd have an excuse to hit someone. "And since Ander was my guard, it was also treason."

Kaven blinked at him, face ashen.

"Jem, get Ander's cloak from his pack," Lith said.

"I'll do it." Beran clucked to Ander's nervous horse and unwound the thong closing the saddle pack. Ander had been wrapping himself in his cloak to sleep, so it lay on top of his belongings, neatly folded to display the row of tiny red birds his wife had embroidered around the neck. Last winter Beran had warmed himself at the fire in their castle rooms watching Lyren's hand rise and fall. He breathed in and out and grabbed the cloak.

Lith crouched to unbuckle Ander's belt, but Beran elbowed him aside and fumbled with the metal clasp. The body was still warm. Vomit burned in Beran's throat.

"Why don't you wait with them?" Lith said gently, nodding toward Myla and Kaven. "Carl and I will wrap him." He picked up the cloak Beran had set aside.

"I said, I'll do it." Beran snatched the cloak back, shook it out, and laid it next to Ander. He slid his hands under Ander's shoulders and took hold. "Someone get his feet."

Carl crouched. "On three." They moved Ander onto the cloak and wrapped it around him, covering his face. Beran secured the bundle with Ander's belt and headband.

Lith led Ander's horse under a dip of branches, but the animal danced away when Carl and Beran approached with the body. Whispering in its swiveling ear, Lith laid a soothing hand on its neck. Beran's heart twisted. Ander had ridden that horse for four years. It always ran toward Ander when it saw him, and now it didn't want to be within ten yards of him.

He and Carl laid the body face down across the saddle. Beran was still fussing with the balance when Nelas approached, carrying the rope they'd been using to picket the horses at night. He stopped a couple of yards away, looking at Beran sideways.

"No." Beran stood next to the horse, one hand on the body. "I'll hold him steady."

Nelas raised an eyebrow at Lith, who shrugged, then skirted Beran to reach his horse. "Carl, you walk by the horse's head and keep it moving," Lith said. Good choice. By now, Carl was the only one brave enough to come near Beran. Everyone but Carl and Beran mounted, Lith leading Beran's horse and Jem leading Carl's.

With the first step Beran took, he stumbled over a tree root. "Stone trees," he snarled. Myla sent him a shocked look.

"Just keep putting one foot in front of the other," Carl said without turning around.

"Shut up," Beran said.

They began the long walk away from where Ander used to be alive.

Dusk had set in by the time they followed the dirt track off the new road to the gates of Green Valley Manor, where Beran's mother had lived as a girl. He'd never been there before, but it looked like all the others they'd seen on their way into the Westreach. The wooden house lay wide and low with painted blue and gold sun rays fanning out from every doorway. Along the roof pole sprawled the usual carving of a giant cat-like creature with its mouth open in a snarl. Its long body was painted green, and its claws clutched the roof on each side, gradually shifting shape until they looked like roots. Silvit, the mythical animal Westreachers revered as the forest's embodiment and guardian. Beran's shoulders tightened. What kind of place revered a deadly animal?

One of Isadia's men-at-arms kept watch at the gate. "Who—" he started.

"It's all right," Myla said. "It's the prince."

A woman stood in the house doorway, a slim-skirted shadow against the firelight inside. At the sound of Myla's voice, she hurried into the yard. Beran hadn't seen his grandmother in the three years since his mother had died, but in the fading light, she didn't look much changed. Her dark hair had wider streaks of wine red, one of the bright colors a trick of the blood substituted for gray in Westreachers as they aged, like leaves at their most colorful near the end of their lives. But she still looked much like his mother with high cheekbones, gray eyes, and a narrow nose.

Isadia spotted him among the dismounting men and hurried toward him, arms extended. "Beran! At last. Be welcomed, and take shelter. I was beginning to think you'd been delayed and decided to stay the night with Eran at Steeprise Manor." She wore no shawl against the evening chill, but when she hugged him, her body still radiated the warmth of the house. Beran endured her embrace, helplessly stiff, until she stepped back, gripping his shoulders, a pucker between her brows. Then her gaze went past him, and the delight faded from her face. Beran turned to see Carl and Lith with Ander's wrapped body between them.

"What happened?"

"It's Ander." Beran's voice broke. "We need a place for him to lie."

Her fingers tightened, then let go. "I'm so sorry. Come. We'll put him in the solar." She hurried toward the house, calling orders.

Beran nudged Lith aside to take Ander's shoulders, and he and Carl carried their burden through the Hall into a room lined on two sides with windows, showing only their ghostly reflections against the night. A woman hastily scraped benches and looms out of the way while Beran adjusted his increasingly awkward hold on the body. Men rushed in with trestles and boards to make a table. They laid the body on it, as two more women came in, carrying basins of water and towels.

"Come into the Hall, Beran," Isadia said. "I want to know what happened."

"Lieutenant Lith can tell you." Beran frowned at a woman undoing the headband he'd tied around Ander's ankles.

His grandmother tugged gently on his arm. "They have to make the body ready, child. Come." When Carl shoved him through the door into the Hall, Beran glared at him, but Carl ignored his resentment and went out into the yard. His grandmother guided him to a pair of high-backed benches near the larger of the room's two hearths. She sat, gesturing for Beran and Lith to sit too. "Now, tell me."

Beran's tongue lay like lead in his mouth.

Lith waited a moment, then began telling her about hearing Myla and chasing down the thief. As he spoke, Myla came through a back doorway with bowls of soup. She offered one to Lith, who took it, and the other to Beran. When he shook his head, she hesitated, then set it on the bench beside him, but the smell made him gag until he pushed it farther away. Kaven came in behind her with mugs. He offered one to Beran, and that Beran took. Myla settled gracefully to the floor at Isadia's feet, while Kaven leaned against the back of the bench behind her. They both listened to Lith as attentively as if the story were new to them. Polite little snots.

Carl came back in and went past them to the solar, carrying Ander's pack. Beran shifted on the bench, wondering how long the women were going to take.

Having finished his tale, Lith turned to Myla. "That's the end, but what's the beginning? How did you get into trouble in the first place?"

Myla licked her lips and glanced at Kaven, who studied his ale, ashamed, maybe, that he hadn't been the one to save her. Beran understood that feeling well enough.

"We, Kaven and I, were out for a walk," Myla said. "We'd been waiting with Eran, but she needed to rest. She's really sick." Myla looked at Beran's grandmother, who nodded, her face pulled down by sadness. "We wanted to leave her in peace and work the kinks out of our muscles before we had to ride back, so we took a walk, and two of them just jumped out of the trees at us."

Several servants had been working as they spoke, bringing in gear from the horses or laying out food and drink on a side table where Nelas and Jem sat. The room was quiet, and Beran realized everyone was listening because they'd begun muttering among themselves.

"Thieves," a maid said with a tremor in her voice. "And so close to us. Lord Corin needs to do something."

"We never had trouble like this before King Thien gave away trees he didn't own," a man-at-arms said. He shot a sudden glance at Beran and pressed his mouth shut.

Beran bit back hot words about fools who tore up roads, murdered travelers and rejected the wellbeing a good ruler was trying to give them.

When Carl and the women finally came out of the solar, Beran sprang to his feet and went where his thoughts had been. Ander lay on his back, dressed in his formal uniform, his silver hair, still wet from being washed, now the color of pewter. His hands were clasped on his chest, holding his sword. The night air blew in through the open windows. Scented candles burned on the side tables, but for the first time, Beran smelled what the horses had smelled in the woods. Death squatted in the room like a toad.

When Lith spoke, Beran jumped. He hadn't heard him and Isadia come in.

"With your permission, lady, we'll bury him wherever you suggest tomorrow," Lith said.

"No," Beran said. "He has a wife, and he's going home to her. You'll need a cart. Can you loan him one, Grandmother?"

She opened and closed her mouth. "Of course."

Lith's brow furrowed. "Beran, I understand the wish, but we'll be here for a few days to rest and get you settled. He won't…keep."

Keeping didn't enter into it. Ander wasn't here, but the thing that was here would be precious to Lyren. "I'm settled. You can go in the morning."

Lith clawed a hand through his hair. "Even with a cart, the unfinished part of that road will be a struggle. And if it rains, the mud might as well be glue."

"That's a good reason to leave early then."

Lith sent an entreating look toward Beran's grandmother, but just then a maid appeared in the doorway. When Isadia glanced her way, she said, "The prince's bed is made up, my lady."

24

Deep as a Tomb

"You're tired, Beran," Isadia said. "Get some sleep, and see what you think in the morning."

"I already know what I'll think in the morning, and tonight, I'm standing vigil for Ander." Beran went to stand at Ander's head. Family should stand vigil, but right now, Beran was all Ander had.

For a moment, no one spoke while Lith and Isadia both studied him. Lith touched Isadia's arm, and they left the room, but Beran heard them murmuring together just outside the door. They went away, leaving him as alone as he'd ever been in his life.

Footsteps sounded, and Jem came in, freshly shaven and wearing a clean uniform. He nodded and took up a position at Ander's feet, his stance mirroring Beran's. Beran drew a shaky breath and settled down to keep watch.

The room filled with silence and memories.

When Beran's mother died, he was among strangers, a week into fostering on a lord's manor in the Basket. Ander had been the one to break the news. Then he'd barred the door until Beran could put on his court face and bear the weight of a hundred curious eyes. When Beran was eight, his tutor had delivered a scathing lecture on the problems a prince created by having children outside marriage. Beran had no idea how babies were made and was worried he'd do it accidentally, which of course, was what his tutor had warned him against. It had been Ander who realized what he was fretting about and explained sex in terms frank enough to leave Beran reeling. He'd believed it only because it was Ander. Ander had given Beran his first lesson in swordplay. He made Beran clean up after himself when he threw up because he drank too much. Beran was the person he was in large part because of Ander, who had protected Beran as his prince, but treated him like a boy who had things to learn before he could grow into a good man.

Some of his grandmother's people still prowled the yard. He heard the faint sound of hammering and men calling to one another. The night wore on. Nelas replaced Jem, and then Carl replaced Nelas. None of them spoke, but Beran was grateful for the company. When Lith came to take Carl's place, servants were moving in the Hall, stirring the fire, sweeping the floor, setting up the trestle tables, and taking dishes off the shelves for the morning meal.

Beran went to the doorway, moving stiffly after having been still so long, and beckoned to a freckle-faced page. It was early enough that the boy still had a pillow mark on the side of his face. "Would you fetch writing materials for me, please?"

The page trotted off, and Beran went back into the solar. Lith had watched without comment as Beran left his place. Now he said, "You don't have to do this. I'll report. That will be good enough."

"It won't." Beran moved a second candle near a clear space on a side table. The page came to the doorsill and stopped, staring round-eyed at the body. Beran took the parchment, pen, and ink and sent the boy off, obviously happy not to have to come in.

Beran set parchment in the space he'd made. Then he sharpened a pen, unstopped the ink, and began to write to his father. As king, Thien needed a clear account of what the thieves were up to. As a father, he needed to know Beran was unhurt and hadn't acted foolishly. Or maybe that last bit was part of what he needed to know as king. It wasn't always easy to separate his different roles. Beran struggled for a while, then decided to just lay out what he knew. The simply worded truth was usually best with his father anyway. He blew on the letter and set it aside to dry.

Then he set out another piece of parchment. He held his pen a finger's width away from it for so long that ink rolled off the point and made a huge blotch. He gritted his teeth, took a clean sheet, and wrote to Lyren. Afterwards, he wasn't even sure what he'd said, but it was done, and Beran didn't look at it again. He dripped candle wax on both folded letters, pressed his ring into the seal, and handed them to Lith, who wore an expression Beran couldn't focus on enough to read.

While he was writing, a gray dawn crept up outside the windows. Four of his grandmother's men appeared in the doorway, carrying a coffin. Abruptly, Beran remembered the hammering he'd heard in the night, and his head swam so he had to lean against the table.

"Come." Lith steered him one way around the body while the men maneuvered the coffin the other way. "I want to eat before we go."

They went out into the Hall, where Beran sat on a bench near the open door to the yard and took deep breaths.

When the men carried the coffin out, he followed. They slid it carefully into a cart that had been rolled up to the doorstep. Beran shook the cart's back gate to make sure it was securely fastened, then walked around it to look at the wheels. The cart stood between him and the doorway when he heard Carl's voice and looked across the coffin to see him and Lith coming out into the yard.

"Sir, I ask you again to reconsider," Carl said. "You know I'm not fit for this duty."

Carl sounded desperate to avoid whatever Lith was ordering him to do. Beran bit back the urge to tell them to keep their minds on the need to get Ander home.

"Should I assign Jem or Nelas?" Lith said. "He'd run them over and not even notice he'd done it."

Beran came around the cart. When they saw him, they hushed. Carl blew out his breath and looked away.

"The cart's ready," Beran said.

"Good." Lith straightened his uniform jacket. "Carl will be staying on as your new guard."

Beran opened his mouth but snapped it shut before saying he didn't want a new guard. Given what had happened to Ander, his father would have Lith's head if he went home and said he'd left Beran unguarded. And even if a killer weren't loose in the Westreach, he had to have a guard. He'd always had one. He'd always had Ander.

"Very well," he said.

Lith looked relieved while Carl stalked away, evidently unhappy in his new role. Beran couldn't bring himself to care.

Jem and Nelas came into the yard while one of Isadia's men tried to hitch a pack pony to the cart. It fought so hard they finally brought Jem's horse around to try between the traces instead. At last, they rode out through the gates with Jem driving the cart. Beran watched until they vanished among the trees, taking his last glimpse of Ander with them.

His grandmother had come out into the yard to bid his escort farewell. "Bed now, Beran," she said. Beran turned toward the house, picking each foot up with conscious effort. He couldn't remember ever being so tired. She guided him through the Hall and down a corridor to a small room with two beds. "You're sharing with Kaven."

Wonderful.

Beran set his sword on a chest at the foot of the bed she pointed to, then dropped his belt, pulled off his boots, and fell flat. He was asleep before his grandmother was out of the room, but in the moment of insight between waking and sleeping, he realized what he had to do. Ander kept Beran safe for years, but Beran had failed to even notice when someone killed Ander within a hundred yards of where he stood. Beran owed him. He and Ander had been going to look for the thieves. Beran would do that, just as they had planned. He'd make the local magistrate look, too, pulling royal rank if he had to, though his father had explicitly told him to be careful of that in the Westreach. But he'd do it, because when they found the thieves, they'd find Ander's killer.

And then Beran would kill him.

Chapter 4

Myla slid from her pony, plucked her bag from the saddle, and turned to Allain, the man-at-arms who'd accompanied her on her visit home this morning. When she'd said she meant to go home, Isadia wouldn't let her ride alone. Kaven had gone off to visit his own family, so Isadia sent Allain. Sapless as it made Myla feel, she was relieved to have him. When the thief had seized her, she'd been too fired up to be frightened, but in bed that night, she'd closed her eyes and once again struggled in the thief's grasp, waking herself up with her shaking.

"Miss?" Allain raised an eyebrow.

Myla shifted from foot to foot. The five months she'd spent at Isadia's told her a well-run manor would offer him food and drink, but Da didn't like strange men-at-arms in the house. She planted her feet firmly. Da had specifically sent her to Isadia's to learn to run a manor. She handed Allain her reins. "The stable's around that way. Ask someone to point you to the Hall. Be welcomed and take shelter." She smiled. "Oak Ridge makes good ale."

His face relaxed into a grin. "In that case, take your time." He clucked to the ponies and set off around the corner of the house.

She glanced at Silvit, stretched along the roof, eyes fixed on the trees beyond the stone wall. Did the cat also keep watch over what happened under his long belly? "Tell me you scared Galen out of doing anything stupid," she murmured. The one eye she could see kept looking straight ahead. Not encouraging.

She passed out of the sunlight and into the shadowy Hall, her nose immediately filling with the scents of her childhood—smoke from the chimney that never could be coaxed to draw right, the breakfast bacon, the breeze that blew through the Forest and drifted in the open windows. From a side door, a maid emerged, carrying a fistful of candles. At the sight of Myla, she stopped so fast she stumbled. "Miss Myla! We didn't know you was coming."

"Just for a visit, Daera. To see my father and brother and leave some medicines." Myla held up the saddle pack.

Daera's brows drew together. "Lord Talun and Galen are in the study with Lord Zale."

Zale was the neighbor whose tomb Myla had opened. Maybe Da had decided to tell him.

"They're not to be disturbed unless it's important." Daera clutched the candles in both hands, plainly trying to work out whether Myla counted as important. "I could maybe knock."

"No," Myla said hastily. "I'll see them when they're done."

Daera looked relieved. Myla didn't blame her. She'd hesitate to disturb Da, too, if he told her to leave him in peace.

"One of Lady Isadia's men came with me," Myla said. "He'll be in soon. See that he's comfortable and has some ale."

"But—" Daera began.

"He's a guest," Myla said, pleased with how much she sounded like Isadia. Ignoring Daera's squeak, Myla went down the hallway and was halfway to the back door before noticing she'd shortened her stride in an effort to move quietly. Kaven laughingly called that her "mouse creep," and she'd thought she'd broken the habit, but now she was setting her feet softly again. In her head, she argued with Kaven. *I'm not timid. Da asked not to be disturbed.* Still, once she was out the door to the yard, she deliberately stretched her step. Her whole body warming, she crossed to the building holding her herb room. More than the house, her herb room was home. When she was twelve, she'd even asked for Da's leave to move in and sleep there. He'd told her not to be stupid.

She pushed the door open, then froze on the sill. The familiar smell of herbs and medicines met her like a friend, but she'd left every leaf and jar in its right place, and the room look like a storm had blown it apart. Heart pounding, she took a single step inside. A quick sweep of her gaze around the room told her the shelves of medicines were untouched. Only her books lay everywhere—open, closed on bent pages, and even flung on the floor. She knotted her hand on the strap of her bag. Who could have had the gall to do this? Everyone at Oak Ridge knew the books were precious because they were old and rare, most herbals having been destroyed during the long-ago Blight War. The famous northern herbalists had made some dark medicine that accidentally killed a third of the trees, and in return, scared people had burned every bit of written herb knowledge they could find. Every housewife could make the common medicines, but the ones in the herbals seemed gone.

And then Myla found the books. It was pure luck she'd stumbled across them in the Oak Ridge attic one rainy afternoon when she was ten. She'd accidentally broken the leg off a wooden horse Galen was carving and fled up the attic ladder. Lying on the rough boards and looking down, she saw her brother run past, to her relief, never thinking to look up. And then, like a fool, she felt dizzy at how high she was and had been afraid to climb down. So she backed away into the low space littered with broken furniture and trunks of clothes in styles from a hundred years ago. Rain pattered on the roof, one of her favorite sounds. She would just poke around for awhile until she felt braver.

When she opened a crate behind a pile of frayed rope and found a heap of old books, she couldn't quite believe it. Da wasn't one for reading, and Galen hadn't touched a book since his tutor quit. Poor man. The book on top felt warm, almost alive in her hands, like it had been waiting for her touch. Careful of the ancient parchment, she opened it to the first page and read: "The Forest provides. It takes a child to see beyond looking, to risk a first step and weave the web of life back into being."

She turned a page and found a drawing of a wood violet so lifelike she could almost smell it. Words in the old script described a way to crush the plant and make a tea. Scanning page after page, she found wonderful drawings of plants. The words were hard to read, though, except for those around the picture of the violet.

To Galen's malicious glee, a servant eventually had to carry her down the ladder because she was too afraid to descend on her own. The servant also carted the books down, and Myla set to work the next day, starting with the violet tea, which was supposed to sharpen eyesight. After that, she found the words easier to read. By the following month, she'd seen for herself how the medicines they described made people whole again. The books deserved respect, not the chaos she saw in front of her now. Every servant at Oak Ridge knew how much she valued her books. None of them would drop one to the floor like this. That didn't leave many possibilities for who would.

"Blight him," she muttered.

Teeth clenched so hard her jaw hurt, she put her bag on the table and started picking up books. She smoothed pages, brushed dust off the wooden covers, fastened the straps that held them shut, and tucked them one by one into a row on their shelf. Under the stool, she found the book she wanted to consult. She flipped the parchment pages until she spotted what memory said she would—a drawing of spear-shaped leaves like those on the plant near Steeprise Manor's tomb. She squinted at the faded words scrawled underneath.

"Daera said you'd come," said a voice from the doorway. "I might have known you'd miss playing healer and come straight here."

Myla shot her brother a look meant to turn his guts to gruel. "Did you do this, Galen?"

"Do what?" He sauntered in, hooked the stool closer with his foot, and sat down. His dark hair was long enough to brush his shoulders, and fuzz shadowed his chin. He might be growing his hair and beard on purpose, but he might also just not be bothering to trim them. Galen could be lazy about things like that. How did he expect to attract a mate if he looked so shabby?

"Did you toss my books around?" She emptied her bag of medicines.

"They're not yours," Galen said. "They belong to Oak Ridge, so I have as much right as you to look at them."

She scoffed. "You've never so much as peeked at a page before. What were you looking for?"

"Nothing." His hair swayed to hide his face, but the hollow in his voice gave him away. She'd heard him at twelve trying to be brave and telling their father "nothing" was wrong with an arm that turned out to be broken, and at fifteen saying "nothing" when Da asked what he'd been doing with their grandfather's sword.

"You wanted to know if they explained how to get into tombs."

"They're nonsense anyway." He pulled the page with the spear-shaped leaves closer. "'Summer the mud and burn the fear.' What in Silvit's name does that mean?"

She seized the book. "'Simmer the mixture until it turns clear.' See?" She slid her finger over the words.

"So you say." Galen shrugged. "I think you're making it up."

"If the books said how to get into tombs, don't you think I would have told you?"

"No. You like being special. You like having Da dote on you."

"Dote on me?" She took a step back, then snapped the book shut and tucked it in her bag. She'd have more time to study it once she was back at Isadia's. "How can you say that? You're the future lord here. You know he'd rather it was you who could open the tombs. He probably told you to look through my books."

"Don't be stupid. Da would rot if there were something in those books that let just anyone open tombs. That would cut down on the specialness of his special daughter."

"That's ridiculous."

He shrugged. "So why are you honoring us with your tomb-opening presence?"

"Mostly I wanted to see you. Are you running with the True, Galen?"

He tipped the stool onto its back legs, elaborately casual. "Why do you ask?"

She groaned. "You have to stay away from them. The prince suspects they killed his guard."

"What are you talking about? I mean, I heard the prince had arrived." His mouth quirked in a satisfied smile. "But no one killed anyone."

"They did," she said. "What's more, they—or someone—attacked me and tried to take the tomb offering I was carrying."

"What?" The stool thumped upright. He sat stick straight, scruffy jaw sagging.

"Someone attacked me, and the prince and some of Thien's soldiers drove them off, and then one of them killed his bodyguard. The road there was ripped up, so the head soldier for sure thought it was the True. I could see it in his face when he asked about them."

"It must have been the thief gang. They've robbed at least one traveler. Maybe they were after the prince, but he was surrounded by too many soldiers, and you showed up, dangling goodies under their noses. The True wouldn't kill someone." His eyes narrowed. "Wait. You were carrying a tomb offering? That was near Steeprise Manor. Did you tell Lady Eran you could open her tomb?"

Every possible answer fell out of her head. Then she realized what he'd said. "Wait yourself. You know the True tore up the road near Lady Eran's, but you're not one of them?"

He waved his hand like he was shooing a fly. "I heard it from a friend. Did you spill your precious secret to Lady Eran?"

"Miss?" Daera hovered in the doorway.

Myla jumped, glimpsing Galen doing the same thing. How much had Daera heard? It surely didn't matter. The only thing Daera ever said to Da was "Yes, my lord."

"What is it?" Myla asked.

"Lord Talun wants you."

Galen started to rise, but Myla leaned across the table and put a hand on his wrist. "Thank you, Daera. Tell him I'll be there right away."

Daera hesitated. "He's in his study." She turned away slowly, probably unhappy to return to Da without Myla in tow.

Myla waited until she was gone. "Galen, you have to stay away from the True. It won't matter if they didn't kill that guard as long as the prince believes they did. And he's saying the death was treason."

Galen jerked out from under her hold. "What do I care what some grassland prince is saying? We're going to run him and all the other grasslanders right out of the Forest."

Even for Galen, that sounded daft. "What are you talking about?"

Galen pushed to his feet. "Ask Da. Maybe he'll tell you now that you're special. Come on," he said when she was slow to move. "Unless you want to keep Da waiting, of course."

That got Myla moving sure enough. She followed her brother out the door.

Chapter 5

Da hadn't sent for Galen, but he dogged Myla's steps anyway. No matter what he knew, he wasn't about to miss anything Da might tell her. Either that or he wanted to see Myla's reaction to whatever was going on. She knocked on the study door.

"Enter," her father snapped.

The latch slipped under her suddenly sweaty fingers. She tightened her grip and opened the door on her father pinning a sky-blue butterfly to a display board. His collection had grown during the time she'd been at Isadia's. Rows of dead butterflies ranged all over the wall, scraps of red, yellow, orange, and purple. They were beautiful, and they'd never fly again.

At the sight of her, Da straightened and looked down the arched nose he and Myla shared. "You took your time. I don't know what kind of willfulness Isadia indulges, but when I send for you, I expect you to come."

"Sorry. I was cleaning up the herb room."

Galen tensed, but Da didn't blink, so he probably didn't know about the damaged books and wasn't interested enough to ask.

"Sit. You too, Galen." Da moved to his desk.

She beat Galen to the chair, ignoring his scowl as he dragged a stool up from the corner. As Da settled in his own chair, he barked a cough that must have torn at his throat. "I brought home a syrup that will help that. Shall I get it?" She started to rise.

"I'm not that desperate," Da said. "Ale with honey is all I need." He sipped from the cup at his elbow, set it down, and pressed his fingertips together. "It's fortunate you're here today," Da said, "because we need to be sure of some things before Zale will agree to our plans."

"Not surprising," Galen murmured.

"Plans?" Myla asked. "Is this about his tomb? If Lord Zale wants me to open it again, I'd be happy to do that."

Galen snorted. "You are so enchanted with yourself."

Their father gave the same dismissive wave Galen had given in the herb room. "When he wants that, he'll have to ask." He cleared his throat and sipped honeyed ale. "At the moment, though, we have bigger things to deal with. Pay attention, and don't waste my time."

Wouldn't dream of it. If he wanted, she'd be happy to go back to Isadia's right now. *High and mighty talk,* whispered a voice in her head. *Care to say that out loud?* She shuddered.

"Which tombs are you sure you can open?" her father asked.

"Sure? Just Zale's, I guess." The hum of the Steeprise tomb door pulsed through her fingers. She blanked the memory from her mind and hoped it was wiped clean off her face too.

"You're certain about what happened at Zale's?" he asked. "You're not exaggerating? Because Zale can't get in there, and neither Galen nor I could open it when we tried."

"I'm not exaggerating." The fingers of her right hand dug into her thigh hard enough to hurt.

"Can you open our tomb? You know I can't, and when I had your brother try, he couldn't either."

Galen's face went red, and Myla quickly looked away.

"I don't know." She'd never even gone to mourn anyone at the Oak Ridge tomb. Her mother had died when Myla was born and, when the Oak Ridge tomb wouldn't open, she'd been buried in a graveyard at the edge of the meadow where the tenants who'd died since were also buried. At night, Myla sometimes heard Silvit howling his grief for his tombless dead.

"She's tried other tombs, though," Galen broke in. "She was messing about with Steeprise Manor's tomb when thieves found her."

"What?" Da jerked upright.

Tromping on the urge to slap her brother, Myla resigned herself to repeating the whole story. By the time she finished, Da's breathing had grown loud.

"Did you open it?" he asked.

"I didn't have a chance."

He dragged his hand down his face, stretching his cheeks. "I told you to keep this secret, Myla. You took a stupid risk, and we'll be lucky if that old biddy Eran doesn't flap her tongue to everyone she knows."

"I asked her not to tell."

"And of course, she'll listen to you." He sprang to his feet and paced, his shoes slapping the floor. "The thieves killed someone? They've grown bolder and bolder. I told that fool of a magistrate he needed to do something, but he's as useless as Corin. Doubtless they both know it's grasslanders coming down that road Thien is so eager to build. They don't want to chance crossing the so-called king." He stopped in front of a long-tailed, deep purple butterfly, rubbing the back of his neck and thinking.

Myla hunched in her chair. *Mouse*, she heard Kaven tease. Easy for him to say. Galen wasn't so much as twitching, so she wasn't the only timid creature in this room.

Their father turned. "Well, thanks to Myla's boasting, we'll have to organize more quickly, but perhaps that's not a bad thing."

"Organize what?" she asked as her father resumed his chair.

Da leaned toward her. "Myla, I'm sure you think the same way I do about Thien and the trees he's given away as if he owned the Forest. He thinks it's the same sort of place as the farmland around his city—somewhere that exists only to grow what he needs."

Da had gentled his voice. Myla couldn't remember him ever doing that before, not with her. He was talking to her almost like he cared what she thought. Hard as she wished to believe that, the voice in the back of her head whispered, *Don't be stupid. He won't even take your medicines.*

"Thien is wrong," she said, and couldn't help a flush of pleasure when Da nodded approvingly. "The Forest owns itself. We're part of it, caring for it as it cares for us." Families and their tenants lived on manors rooted around their tombs, but the manors still belonged to the Forest. Thien called the lands between the manors "uninhabited," but animals lived there. The Forest lived there.

"These roads are wrong too," Da said. "They let grasslanders come in where they don't belong, and then they let those invaders carry away the trees. Even Corin is wrong as lord. *Lord*, mind you, not chieftain. Thien appointed him, but the very Forest rejects him when he can't open the Black River tomb."

Myla chased away the thought that Da couldn't open Oak Ridge's tomb either.

"Now we here at Oak Ridge descend from the northern lords, from old rulers, from Jorn himself," Da said. "The old chieftains' ancestors threw them from power, but even during the Blight War, the ability to open a tomb gave you the right to the land around it. The law actually still says a land dispute can be settled by that test, though as far as I know, it's been decades since anyone has asked for it." He clasped his hands on the desk and set his face in earnest lines. "So what would it mean if you could open any tomb?"

Myla stopped breathing. "You can't be serious," she forced out.

"I knew she'd be too sapless," Galen said.

"Hush." Da kept his eyes on Myla. "The Forest owns itself, of course. But with grasslanders swarming in, it needs better guardians than it has. We could provide the care the Forest needs if we had the rule of it in our hands."

"You'd never be able to make a claim like that hold," Myla said. "The other manor lords would never sit still for it."

"We'd leave them on their holdings," Da said. "After all, someone needs to run things. We'd call them 'stewards' or some similar title."

Myla felt breathless at how he fluffed away the notion that other lords might resent his claim.

"What I thought," Da said, "was that we'd name you chieftain."

"Chieftain? Me?" Her mind blanked and then, astoundingly, flooded with pictures of herself choosing good for the Forest, spreading healing to its people. And Kaven. If she was chieftain, she could keep seeing Kaven even if it turned out Da didn't like him.

"The chieftain has always been a man." Galen reeked of outrage, so Myla guessed Da hadn't shared that part of his plan with her brother.

"Myla knows she's not really fit to govern," Da said, "but she could have the title, and that alone might rally manor holders who resent how Isadia and Arthan handed their daughter and the Forest over to Rinland. Not an animal in the Forest would have given away territory like that."

Myla swallowed a sudden ache in her throat. *Stupid.* Of course Da would never really let her rule, not over him anyway. "Lord Corin wouldn't agree. King Thien wouldn't. Like you said, no one gives away land like that. And they have soldiers, men-at-arms. There'd be war, and how could you ever hope to win?"

"If we can work out certain details, Zale will help. He can call on at least eighty men, and others would join us if they thought we had a chance of winning. They respect strength. And they need those tombs open, not just to bury their dead, but as a place to pray for healthy trees and many children. For now," Da said, "we need to know more about what you can do. Have you tried to enter Isadia's tomb?"

"Of course not. Isadia trusts me. I'm her fosterling."

"You can't afford to be squeamish. That tomb is the chieftain's. If you can enter it, that would go a long way toward establishing your claim. Try it, and send word of what happens. And what about this grassland boy? What's he there for?"

"Boy? Oh, the prince. He said something about people getting to know him better so Corin will vote for him to be heir."

"Oh yes. People getting to know him, not him getting to know them. He's doubtless as ignorant of the Forest as his father is. Watch him. Undercut him with people he tries to impress."

Myla hadn't yet made up her mind about what she thought of the prince. She pitied his obvious, pole-axed grief for his guard. She'd glimpsed him standing vigil in the solar the previous night, hollow-eyed and lost in his own head. He was good-looking too, with that dark hair and those gray eyes. But he'd cursed the tree he'd tripped over. And he'd been rude to her and Kaven, like he thought he was already in charge of things. Maybe he wouldn't be good for the Forest. Maybe, like Da said, she'd really be saving the Forest if she helped wrest it from Rinland's control. But start a war? Blood-freezing stories were still told about the Blight War. She became aware of her father watching her intently, as if waiting for the right moment to snare her in one of his nets. She dropped her gaze and tried to look submissive, which wasn't hard, given how many years she'd had to practice.

"It's almost time for dinner," Da said. "Afterward, we'll see if you can open Oak Ridge's tomb." He picked up his pen.

Myla sprang loose from her chair and followed Galen out of the room.

Galen scowled at her. "Don't let it go to your head. You couldn't do any of this on your own."

"Just you remember what I said about the True."

He turned his back on her and swaggered off to the yard.

She watched him go, hopeless that she'd dented his thick head. Should she let him stab himself in the foot? She sighed, then trotted through the Hall and into the family wing. Her own room lay there, and she paused to peek in and see it dusty and empty. It smelled faintly of the herbs she'd left for Da and Galen in a box that hadn't been moved. She closed the door without regret and went on to Galen's room, wrinkling her nose against the sour sweat and dirty clothes. She'd have to wash her hands after touching anything in here. With one finger, she lifted the lid of Galen's chest. The Forest be thanked. She wasn't going to have to search after all. The wolf mask lay on top of the pile of unlovely belongings.

Rot Galen. He was such a fool.

She helped herself to the mask, hid it in a shirt she'd leave in the laundry, and headed out the yard door, meaning to spend what time she could in the herb room. The house felt too much like a trap she'd just triggered. She needed to at least pretend to herself that she had choices.

As she crossed the yard, she spotted Allain sitting on a bench outside the kitchen, mug of ale in hand. He stood when she approached.

"You don't want to come into the Hall?" she said. "Dinner will be ready soon."

A look flitted across his face that might have been pity. "Lord Talun asked me to wait for you out here."

Heat rose into her cheeks. "I'm sorry."

"It's too fine a day to be inside," Allain said, "and you spoke no more than the truth about the ale." He lifted the mug in salute. "A credit to the lady of this manor."

She turned quickly toward the herb room. Lady of this manor. A title even less likely than chieftain to reflect Myla's power.

Chapter 6

When Beran awoke, green-tinged sunshine slanted through the window of an unfamiliar room. Where was he? Memory sliced through the fog in his head. He was in the Westreach, and Ander was dead. His throat swelled, and then his last thought before falling asleep came roaring back.

Find the man who killed Ander.

The pain in his throat eased. He would hunt that man down and kill him. Kill? He'd never killed anyone. Did he really mean to do it now? Something fierce growled in his chest. Yes, he did.

He rolled to sit on the side of the bed, rubbing his head in an effort to scrub away the grogginess. Someone had left a tray of food and ale on a narrow table under the window. At the sight of it, his stomach rumbled. He lurched to his feet and padded to it in his stocking feet, still thinking. The tray held flat bread and a bowl of some soft white cheese. He drank, then spread the cheese on the bread and ate.

A vision of Ander's body floated into his head. He shoved it aside. What did he know that would help him find the killer?

The man had turned up near where the True had left a note chirping happily about dining on Beran's entrails. Myla had protested that the True were harmless, but that didn't sound harmless to him. Corin's men were having trouble finding the thieves, which might be because they weren't looking hard enough at the True. From what Beran understood, the True came from powerful families, and Corin wasn't eager to upset them. Beran chewed on more bread and cheese, tapping his signet ring against the rim of the mug. The ring's carving of the Tower of Rinland flashed in and out of the sunlight.

While he'd stood vigil the previous night, someone had unpacked all his gear. The wall pegs on his side of the room overflowed with shirts and trousers. The pegs on the other side held two sets of clothes in the green and gold of his grandmother's manor, plus a small collection of bright but shabby stuff that was presumably Kaven's, since it matched what he'd worn yesterday. Wherever Kaven came from, he wasn't well off. Because Kaven was Isadia's fosterling, she was responsible for clothing him, but he must be clinging to what he'd brought from home. Too stiff-necked to admit his need, probably. As a fosterling, Beran had roomed with hostile jerks before, but never a poor one, since fostering was mostly a way for well-off children to meet people and learn skills they couldn't learn at home.

Myla's voice came through the open window. "I'm sorry I ran and left you, but I had to save the tomb offering. Thank the Forest they didn't hurt you. Did you tell your family?"

"Yes," Kaven said. "Myla, you shouldn't go back there. It's not safe."

Their conversation faded. The window looked out over a vegetable garden. A path ran along the edge of the house and then meandered through the cabbages and carrots to a postern gate. Judging from the treetops visible over the wall, an orchard lay just outside. Leaves rippled in the wind, showing undersides the silver of Ander's hair.

Beran gave his ring a hard thump on the mug and drained it. He didn't bother sending for hot water, but washed in what was in the pitcher and put on clean clothes. When he picked up his belt, the skinny thief's knife clattered to the floor. He scooped it up and eyed it thoughtfully. It was as long as his hand and looked not much different than a hundred other knives he'd seen. Still, someone had owned it for a while. The leather wrapped around the hilt was worn and sweat-darkened, but a blue strip circled above the crosspiece. Maybe someone would recognize it. The idea of catching the man with his own weapon made Beran's body buzz with satisfaction. He shoved the knife back into his belt, retrieved a letter, and set off to find his grandmother. He would ask her to send for the magistrate, today if possible.

To his right, the corridor ended in a door open to the yard where a pair of small children were spinning a top. So family quarters lay at that end of this wing. He turned the other way and passed the closed doors of what were probably more bedrooms for the single men in his grandmother's household.

The corridor emptied into the Hall. The door to the front yard stood open, and Beran glimpsed more fluttering leaves. Out there, someone was singing about love. Inside, the only people were his grandmother and a strange man sitting near the fireless hearth. Signs of the Hall's normal life were everywhere. A lute was propped in a corner, and a toy horse lay abandoned near a child-sized stool. In the light of day, everything looked clean and innocent, as if Ander's death had been tidied away.

"Beran," his grandmother called, "come join us."

For the stranger's sake, Beran put on his court face. No sense airing grief or guilt in front of someone who might use it against him. He crossed the room to kiss his grandmother's dry cheek. She smelled of the soap that had been on Beran's washstand and the same violet scent his mother had used.

"How are you after some sleep?" Brows drawn down, she scanned his face.

"Better."

She inclined her head toward the man sitting across from her. Long-jawed and strong-nosed, he wore a dark shirt and leather jerkin. In his lap lay the poppet the True had left for Beran. "This is Halid of Little Lake Manor," Isadia said. "He's our local magistrate. I thought he should know about Ander's death."

"Good." Beran returned Halid's bow, then sat next to his grandmother and leaned forward, elbows on thighs. Bless Isadia for recognizing how important this was. "Shall I tell you what happened?"

"Lady Isadia has already done that," Halid said. "It sounds like your man stumbled on one of the thieves and tried to seize him."

"I agree. What do you know about them?"

"They've been robbing houses and travelers since the road came through a year or so ago."

Beran waited, but Halid seemed to think he'd already said something meaningful. Beran pointed to the poppet wearing the gold thread crown. "That might mean the True are involved."

"Not likely. The timing suggests the road invited the thieves in from elsewhere. It lets all kinds of outsider riff-raff stroll right in where they don't belong."

"Did you read the note?" Beran asked.

"Yes, but, I tell you, we didn't have thieving until the road was built."

Something in Halid's tone made Beran suspect the man counted him— and certainly Ander—among the strolling riff-raff, which maybe meant Halid saw neither the thieves nor Ander as his to worry about. "Wherever they're from, they're here now, so you need to do something," he said sharply.

Halid stiffened. On the bench next to Beran, his grandmother shifted, but said nothing.

Beran handed Halid the knife. "Myla took it from the thief. Do you recognize it?"

Halid turned the weapon over and gave it back with a shake of his head.

"So what are you going to do?" Beran asked. "I need to know because I intend to take part."

"No need to involve yourself," Halid said. "Lord Corin's offered a reward. It's only a matter of time before we hear something."

"So, until then, you're doing nothing?"

Face flushing, Halid rose and brushed sawdust off his trousers. "I advise you not to interfere with Lord Corin's plans. Lady Isadia, I'll be on my way." He strode toward the door, with Isadia trailing.

Beran rose when his grandmother did, but stayed near the hearth, afraid that if he did as manners required and went with Halid, he might boot the man's backside out the door. He stared at the circlet, the chieftain's symbol, carved over the mantle, its ends twisted together to form a graceful leaf. He could insist that Halid act, but what would be the point? The man was useless. Besides, now that Beran thought of it, he liked the idea of tracking down the killer on his own.

The problem was that antagonizing Corin would be bad for Beran. As far as he knew, Corin's objection to his being named heir wasn't personal. Beran had never even met Corin because he sent representatives to the king's council meetings rather than coming himself, and even those representatives tended to go home with no warning, saying living in the city made them sick. The current representative had privately said Corin didn't think Thien understood the province and didn't believe Beran would either. That feeling had strengthened when Thien ordered the roads built and granted land and timber to people not from the Westreach. This visit to Isadia was supposed to convince Corin that Beran was taking the trouble to learn about the Westreach, not finding fault with the way Corin hunted the thieves.

Beran slid the knife back into his belt. His father would be angry if Beran ruined his chances of being named heir. The king's peace would be in real danger, as the throne became a prize for someone else to seize. For a moment, Beran's resolve wavered. He was of the royal family of Rinland, even if he was never named heir. His personal feelings always, *always*, had to give way before that fact. It would be wrong for him to let his grief lead him away from acting for the good of Rinland. And yet, what about justice? What about Ander? He met his grandmother on her way back from the door.

"Beran, I know you're upset, but you need to leave this to Halid and Corin. You can't interfere."

Without answering, he handed her the letter. The Tower of Rinland marked the front of it, the way it did his life, he thought bitterly. Well too stoning bad. "From my father."

She held it by one corner as if it were a dead rat. For reasons neither had ever explained, she and his father weren't enthusiastic about one another. Beran had occasionally been tempted to ask what had happened, but had always hastily backed away when he saw how they reacted to any mention of the topic.

"I thought I'd look around outside," Beran said, "maybe get to know Kaven and Myla better." Or at least know better what they and any of his grandmother's people knew about the thieves. Because no matter what it meant for his own hopes, the inescapable truth was that Ander died because Beran pressed him to go after the thief. Beran would avoid offending Corin if he could, but he'd hunt down the cockroach who killed Ander.

47

"Good idea." She seemed relieved. "If you want to know the Forest, getting acquainted with those two will help. Kaven's family has had a manor here for ages, and Myla can teach you things you'd never learn in the city."

What a scary thought.

"Don't roam too far, though," Isadia said. "We'll have supper soon." As if to prove her point, two serving men began setting up trestles. At the mention of food, Beran's stomach growled again, apparently forgetting he'd just eaten.

The yard outside the front door was mostly empty this late in the afternoon. The man singing of love turned out to be the gate guard. He paused to scrutinize the thief's knife, failed to recognize it, and took up his song again. Beran went on around the house, ignoring the evil-looking cat stretched along the roof. A wild animal was just the right symbol for this cursed place where no one cared that a good man had been murdered.

Following the sound of voices, he went through the garden and out the postern gate. At the end of a row of apple trees, he found Myla and Kaven picking raspberries.

"So was your father glad to see you?" Kaven asked.

A strained look crossed Myla's face. "Yes." She looked ready to say something more, but must have heard Beran coming because she turned.

Kaven wore the cap Myla had worn when Beran first saw her. Myla had on a narrow-skirted, Westreach-style gown, slit up the sides to ease walking. Beran's grandmother and her women wore them too, with high, soft, leather boots underneath, but Myla's feet and legs were bare. Beran stared at the expanse of shapely calves flashing in and out of sight.

"Did you want something?" Kaven glared. "Other than the obvious?"

Beran's face grew warm. "Of course not."

Kaven flung a handful of berries into the basket on the ground between him and Myla and took a step toward Beran. "Are you insulting her?"

"No!"

"Oh, because groping her wasn't insulting?"

"Hush, Kaven," Myla said, to Beran's relief. "We're very sorry about your guard, aren't we, Kaven?"

Kaven took a deep breath, then evidently decided he'd rather stay on Myla's good side than keep baiting Beran. "We are. It…it surprised us. The thieves have never killed anyone before."

"They're obviously grasslanders," Myla said, "coming down that new road."

"Magistrate Halid's very words," Beran said. "But if the roads are the issue, then someone should be looking at the True since they're the ones ripping the roads up."

"Maybe," Kaven said at the same moment Myla said, "It's not them." The two of them exchanged a look. "It's not the True," Myla said again. Kaven lifted his gaze to the whispering trees.

Beran breathed in and out, trying to settle his temper. No matter how much it galled him, he needed this irritating pair's help. "This is the knife you took from the thief. See the bit of blue? Do you recognize it?"

Myla shook her head.

Kaven took it from Beran and hefted it. "It's a poor excuse for a weapon. The balance is off." Before Beran could stop him, he drew his arm back and threw it. It spun toward a maple, but whooshed past it and vanished in the thick greenery. "Oops. Sorry," he said.

"You fool! I need that." Muscles tight with fury, Beran ran toward where the knife had vanished. "Help me look."

As he poked through the bushes, he heard the two of them doing the same thing a short distance away. It was good they stayed away because, even before Beran came outside, he was ready to slug someone, and Kaven's mouth was one big target. He shoved past a gray-twigged bush. The undergrowth was thick here, and a dark-green stream cut through the area. Beran hadn't heard a splash, but if the knife had gone into the water, they'd have a hard time finding it. They'd searched until Beran was ready to wade into the water when he spotted a metallic gleam in a bush. He prodded the leaves apart and found the knife, snared in its branches. "Found it."

Myla and Kaven came to join him.

"You want the thieves gone?" Beran held up the knife. "This is going to lead me to them. Unless an idiot throws it into a tangle of this cursed forest, of course."

Myla's mouth dropped open. "Idiot? Cursed?"

"You've got it back," Kaven said. "I don't know what you're still mad about." He stomped away toward the house.

"You are rude and irreverent and Rinnish." Myla's voice rose on each word.

"*I'm* rude?" Beran stored the knife safely in his belt. "Unless 'Rinnish' is another word for reasonable, I don't know what you mean." To his astonishment, she kicked dirt onto his shoes. He jumped back. "What's that for?"

Ignoring him, she traced a big toe along a squiggle in the dust. Her toenails were painted like her fingernails, each a different color. She crouched and crept toward a patch of long grass. Her hand darted out for something Beran couldn't see. "Here," she said.

Without thinking, he put out his hand, and she dropped a writhing black snake across his palm. A yell jumped out of his mouth and he flung it away, realizing only at the last instant that it was a harmless water snake. "Is that supposed to answer me?" he choked out.

"I think that's a 'reasonable' conclusion." Myla dodged around him, heading back toward the raspberry canes.

Beran was waiting for his heart to slide back down into his chest when a voice called, "Myla! Beran! Come to supper."

He stalked back into the Hall, where several dozen people were gathering behind the trestle tables. Isadia beckoned to Beran from the room's head. When he started toward her, though, Carl rose from one of the benches and grabbed his arm. People seated nearby turned to look.

"What is it?" Beran asked. Myla and Kaven were already seated with his grandmother. Sweet Powers. He was going to have to be polite. He should have told them they had to bow to him when he had the chance.

Deep as a Tomb

"You went outside the manor walls without me," Carl said in a low voice. He shook Beran's arm and waited until Beran faced him, apparently wanting to be sure he had Beran's attention. "Don't do that again."

Beran scoffed. "I was in the orchard." From the time Beran was three, his father had given Ander complete authority over Beran's safety, and Beran had grown up expecting to obey his guard. Usually anyway. But Carl was being ridiculous.

Carl tightened his grip painfully. "Don't do it again," he repeated, then let go and dropped onto the bench with his back to Beran.

Isadia beckoned more peremptorily. Beran was keeping the servants waiting. With an exasperated look at the back of Carl's head, he took his seat. Thank the Powers Isadia was between him and Myla, who sat on her left, and Kaven, who sat beyond Myla.

At his grandmother's signal, the servants brought out platters of some kind of meat rolled in flat bread and giant mushroom caps filled with a mashed orange substance. Carrots, maybe? Beran served his grandmother and then himself. The meat had an odd aftertaste. He decided he was happier not knowing what it was. Mostly he loved Rinland's rich, changing landscape and her varied people, but you could have too much of a good thing.

His grandmother chatted to him, naming the people seated in the Hall. Then she turned to him and grew grave. "You've had an unfortunate introduction to the Forest, Beran. But once you've had a chance to see more of it, I hope you'll realize there's a wildness and power here that's hard to resist."

Wildness and power? He had to give her those. He even remembered marveling at them on the road. But that was before Ander.

Behind Isadia's back, Myla and Kaven had their heads together, whispering. Kaven's face softened when he looked at her, and Beran judged him to be a lost man. He wondered what his grandmother thought about that. In Beran's experience, when a household had fosterlings, the lord or lady usually smacked romance down hard. Getting to know well-born girls from elsewhere was part of why there was fostering, but the Powers forbid you actually cozied up to one of them. As the king's son, Beran had been taught his body belonged to Rinland, whether on a battle field or in a

51

marriage bed, even if he was never named King's Heir. He believed in that duty, but the lords he stayed with had probably ferreted out any girl he had ever kissed and reported it home. He watched Myla cover Kaven's hand with her own. Any kissing she engaged in wouldn't be with Beran, which was surely a relief. He had more important matters to deal with.

"Isadia?" Myla's voice drew his grandmother's attention. "I promised Lady Eran I'd go back tomorrow with medicine."

"That's not a good idea," Kaven said quickly.

"Good idea or not, I'm going," Myla said.

Kaven looked up at the ceiling and shoved away the brown hair that had flopped into his eyes. Beran almost felt sorry for him. Not quite, though. Myla might be difficult, but Kaven was still lucky. Even without kissing, a friend's presence eased the loneliness that came from constantly moving around and living with strangers.

"That's kind of you, Myla." Isadia scanned the table where her men-at-arms sat. "You shouldn't go alone though."

"I'll go with her." Beran wanted to take another look where Ander had died. "Which means Carl will come."

"I'll go too," Kaven said, not altogether surprising Beran.

"You should be quite the jolly party," Isadia said.

That would be one word for it.

Chapter 7

Myla stepped out into the morning to find Kaven and Carl already waiting. Kaven's face lit at the sight of her, and happiness sprouted in her chest as she handed him the small bag of medicines for Lady Eran. He hooked it to her saddle while she turned to Beran's guard, who stood a little apart, scanning the trees beyond the manor walls. "Isn't it a beautiful day, Carl?"

He shifted his gaze to her, then looked around at the clear sky and summer-leafed trees. "It is." He sounded faintly surprised.

Myla had spent long stretches of her girlhood by herself. Visitors to Oak Ridge wanted to see her father, not her. Mostly, that had been all right. She'd had the trees and birds and other animals for company. But Carl struck her as the most alone person she'd ever met, trapped on his own inside a cocoon of misery so thick he aroused her healer instincts.

Kaven touched her sleeve. "Myla, you shouldn't do this. Carl and His Princeliness can take the medicines."

"I promised." Eran needed the medicines, but only Myla could deliver the access to Steeprise's tomb that Eran really wanted, and Myla wasn't going to be talked out of going. The idea of opening another tomb made her blood race. She swore she felt the pull of the tomb all the way from Isadia's front yard. She took a moment to revel in the memory of opening her own family's the day before, enjoying again the excited look on Da's face and the stricken one on Galen's.

Beran hurried out of the house, carrying a long, leather tube. As he hooked it to his saddle, she glimpsed the Tower of Rinland stamped on its side. The symbol was all over his belongings, like he had to remind other people of who he was. Not that he needed it. He might not know it, but he was used to being deferred to. His clothes were unmarked and grasslander dull, but he wore his sense of himself in his skin.

Kaven linked his fingers to boost Myla onto her pony, but before she could lift her foot, Beran spoke. "Have you seen the thief's knife, Kaven? I left it on the table in our room."

Kaven straightened. "You think I took it?"

"No." Beran frowned. "Not until you said that."

Kaven walked toward Beran, his fists opening and closing. "Accuse me of thieving again, and I'll knock your head off, prince or no prince."

"You could try." Beran shifted to the balls of his feet with an eagerness that scared her.

"Stop it!" Myla cried. Silvit save her from battle-hungry men here. She had enough of them at home.

"Let's try not to flood the yard with bravado, shall we?" Carl slid between them, facing Kaven but backing toward Beran so he had to shuffle away.

Kaven almost certainly couldn't see around Carl, but he jabbed a finger in Beran's general direction. "Someone needs to tell him he's not king yet."

Carl looked over his shoulder. "You're not king yet," he said pleasantly. Beran blinked, then laughed, and his stance eased. "All right?" Carl asked Kaven.

"I don't have his knife," Kaven said.

"You could have just said so," Beran said.

Face pink, Kaven turned to help Myla mount. With one foot in his hands, she paused to give him a kiss on the cheek, and his frown faded as he lifted her the rest of the way. Carl nudged Beran toward his horse, and they set off for Lady Eran's with Kaven and Myla leading, and Beran and Carl twenty yards behind.

"Looks like Carl doesn't want to have to break up any more fights," she said.

"Sorry," Kaven said. "I shouldn't have let Rinnish Boy get to me."

"It's all right." She'd not seen Kaven so touchy before, and in the back of her head purred the satisfying suspicion that he was jealous. At supper last night, he'd pressed to know what she and Beran talked about after he'd left the orchard. The morning felt full of possibilities. Her skin tingled at the touch of cool, green-smelling air. Under her good mood, though, worry gnawed.

After opening both Zale's tomb and the one at home, she had no doubt she could open Lady Eran's, and the closer they rode to it, the stronger the urge grew to dive into its mysteries. But what about Da's plans for rebellion, all of them hinging on her power to open tombs? She pictured arrows buzzing through the oaks and maples, bodies bleeding in the grass.

"Kaven, does your family have tales of the Blight War?"

He looked around at the trees. "You know we're north descendants, so some of my ancestors were targeted. My grandfather told me an old story that when one of their manors was under attack and the family and tenants crowded into the house for safety, the attackers burned it with everyone inside." He stood in his stirrups to touch a maple leaf. "What put the Blight War in your head?"

"My father was talking about it yesterday."

"Telling your family's tales?"

"Not really. Da just says our northern ancestors were the rightful rulers."

"They were, but they grabbed for too much power," Kaven said soberly. "They did a lot of damage."

"Power's not always bad. Da says we have to be able to stand up for ourselves and our people."

Something in her tone must have showed she was troubled because he quickly said, "He's right about that. When do I get to meet him?"

Her pony shied, and she forced herself to relax her suddenly tense muscles. "Da is…busy with something right now. Maybe afterwards." Assuming there was an afterwards. "When do I get to meet your mother?"

"Soon. She says I talk about you a lot." He grinned at her. "Come on. Let's show the boy prince how to ride." He urged his pony into a gallop.

"No fair!" Myla bent over her pony's neck and sped after him, washing her worries away in the wind that made her feather earring tickle her neck.

When they neared Steeprise Manor, Kaven slowed his pony and glanced back at Carl and Beran, as if making sure they were too far away to hear. "Listen, Myla, when you go to Eran's tomb, take me. I'm worried someone will hurt you, and I'd never let them do that. You know that, right?"

"Of course, but the thieves will be afraid to go back to the same place." She felt like she was floating, buoyed yet again by her surprise that this sweet Forest boy was courting her. She'd been less astonished by Zale's tomb opening than she was by love. Not that Kaven had said "love" yet, but then neither had she. The thought of saying it made her chest swell with the same mix of wonder and fear as the thought of entering a tomb.

A few moments later, they rode through Lady Eran's gates, with Beran and Carl trotting to join them. As they dismounted, a boy ran to take their mounts. Myla lifted her medicines down and started toward the front door, Kaven at her elbow.

"Wait, Myla. Would you take this?" Beran held out the leather tube. "Tell Lady Eran I'll be along soon."

Myla was reaching to take the tube when Carl stepped between them, jaw set. Startled, she drew back.

"Where do you think you're going?" Carl said.

"To the place Ander was killed." Beran cleared what sounded like a clogged throat. "I want to see if we missed anything. I know you'll go too, of course."

"No."

"Excuse me?"

"You're not wandering off into the woods." Carl planted his booted feet wide apart and leaned over Beran.

"Are you saying you're not capable of guarding me?" Beran frosted his voice with an awe-inspiring amount of ice.

"I'm saying you're going inside." Carl jerked his head toward the house.

"Ander would have allowed it."

"Ander is dead." Carl's words spidered out like a vine, filling the yard, crowding out any other words Myla might have said or even thought.

Beran grunted like he'd been punched in the stomach. "If you're saying that's my fault, I already know it."

"I'm saying go inside."

By then, Lady Eran had appeared in the doorway. "Be welcomed and take shelter," she called.

Even from where she stood, Myla saw Beran quiver. Then, still clutching the tube, he brushed blindly past her, bowed to Lady Eran, and went into the house. Carl sank onto a bench by the door, looking exhausted. He dropped his head against the house wall, but his eyes still shifted constantly, keeping watch for the Forest only knew what.

All sympathy for Carl had drained from Myla's body. "That was mean. Anyone who's spent an hour with him can see he's grieving."

Carl barely spared her a glance. "Anyone who's spent an hour with him can see he's been so sheltered he has no sense of danger. Don't encourage him."

"Myla, Kaven, won't you come in?" Lady Eran's wrinkles deepened with her smile as she leaned on her cane and waved them into the house. Myla spun from Carl and followed Kaven inside to find Beran near the hearth, stiffly accepting the greetings of two men.

She recognized Lord Naeth from his visits to Isadia. His family had owned Hilltop Manor forever, and Naeth looked old enough to have ruled it since the week after its tomb erupted from the Forest floor. Wrinkles webbed his skin, and his bony body looked like it was being dried out to be preserved for the winter. Every hair on his head had gone dandelion yellow.

"Myla, Kaven, do you know Lord Adon?" Lady Eran said in far too neutral a voice, indicating the other man. "The king granted him land just west of here."

Adon bowed over his round belly, the ends of his long moustache sweeping forward. "I call my manor Adon's Wood."

Kaven coughed, probably swallowing the same words Myla was struggling not to say. The land had been here first. Its name should come from itself, not from the person who ruled it. And a manor without a tomb was no manor at all. What did Beran's father think he was doing? She glared at Beran and was annoyed when he seemed not to notice. A smug grasslander, that's what he was.

They all sat on benches around a low table holding Lady Eran's spindle and basket of wool. The room smelled of the roses heaped in a bowl on the mantle. Despite the warm day, a fire blazed, and a blanket slumped in the rocking chair drawn up next to the hearth, though Eran had abandoned it to sit with her guests.

Reminding herself why she'd come, Myla perched, bag at her feet, ready to spring up the moment Lady Eran signaled. She'd see what she could do for Eran, whose lips and fingernails were blue enough to be worrisome. Then she'd be off to open a tomb. Her breath quickened at the thought.

Beran still looked shaken from his encounter with Carl, but Adon started in on him anyway. Myla judged him to be the kind who couldn't resist talking to a prince.

"I hear you ran into the thieves, Beran," Adon said. "It's a disgrace they're still loose. I told Magistrate Halid it had to be the True. They've no respect for property. Look what they do to the king's roads. But Halid's about as useful as my goatboy in stopping them."

Beran licked his lips, but Myla saved him the trouble of struggling to speak.

"The True?" She rolled her eyes and hoped Galen had taken the loss of his mask as a sign to stay away from the road wreckers. "Oh yes, it's them. Roads and robbery are exactly the same. The thieves just got them confused because they start with the same letter."

"You don't know what you're talking about, little girl," Adon said.

"The 'little girl' stuck a knife in a thief," Beran said.

Myla flicked him a surprised look. He was obviously getting hold of himself. His stunned expression was vanishing behind an emotionless mask, but the mask was cracked just enough to let his dislike for Adon leak through. She'd expected him to side with the landowner his father had sent.

"It's not those arrogant True donkeys." Naeth spoke in a quavering old man's voice, but Myla recognized the shrewdness in his blue eyes. She'd thought before that Naeth had probably been devastatingly good-looking when he was twenty. "It's Rinlanders coming up the road."

"My father says the same thing," Myla said.

"Whoever they are, I mean to find them," Beran said. From the tube in his lap, he slid a rolled parchment that opened into a detailed map of the central stretch of the Forest. He spread it out on the table, anchoring one side with Eran's spindle and the other with the wool basket. Myla craned her neck to see a small X marking the road near Steeprise Manor—the place where the True had torn up the road and left the poppet. "Can you mark the places there've been robberies," Beran said, "and where the True have been active too?" He pulled a pen and bone ink tube from his belt pouch.

Silvit save them. She'd told him the True weren't involved, but he still hadn't let go of the notion that they and the thieves were the same, and that one of them had killed his guard. Myla had to admire his fierce search for revenge, but if he kept on this way, Galen would be in trouble, and while Galen was a creeping, tattling sneak, he'd never kill anyone. He'd never watch someone else commit murder and still be able to smile in the smug way he had yesterday. He'd curl up and hide. If he still had his stuffed lamb hidden away, he'd clutch it.

Naeth and Adon leaned over the map. Adon uncorked the ink and drew an X. "The road was barely built when they tore it up here, and one of my own men was robbed right there."

"Magistrate Halid doesn't want Beran to interfere," Myla said, "but Beran thinks Halid doesn't care, so he's going to take over, maybe even get help from the king."

Beran's head jerked toward her. He gave her a sharp-eyed glare.

She smiled brightly. Undercut him, Da had said.

Naeth waved a spotted hand over the map. "You'd do more good telling your father to set guards where that road enters the Forest."

"I don't speak for the king, of course," Beran said.

"I don't know why you people are all so against the roads," Adon said. "Kaven, your Uncle Rickard sold off half his trees this year. Paying debts your grandfather left, I hear. And when a manor needs money, it needs the road. Rickard wouldn't have wanted to move that much wood on the dirt lanes you people were using."

A muscle jumped in Kaven's jaw. "My grandfather left no debts." Myla itched to slap Adon. She knew how much Kaven had loved his grandfather.

"I heard different," Adon said. "I know for sure Rickard was mighty worked up when the True went to work near Sweet Stream in the spring. And then, of course, the thieves robbed his steward, which didn't help." When Kaven shook his head, Adon shrugged. "I must have heard wrong then, but Rickard still wanted that wood shipped. And cutting the wood is hard enough, given how clumsy Westreachers are sometimes. I've had three men cut with their own axes. Every one of the superstitious fools said Silvit made him do it."

If that wasn't a sign of the Forest's feeling about Adon, Myla didn't know what was.

"Myla?" Lady Eran touched Myla's arm and spoke low. "If you're willing, maybe you could show me the medicines now."

Relieved to be away from the squabbling men, Myla grabbed her bag and followed Eran from the Hall. Kaven's voice rose behind her. "With respect, Lord Adon, you need to stop talking about things you know nothing about."

Lady Eran led her along a hallway ending in a door propped open to the kitchen yard, where head-bobbing chickens scratched at the dirt. Eran opened the door to what, judging by the rune-carved marriage bed, was her room. The familiar leather bag of tomb offerings rested on the dressing table. Eran offered it to Myla.

Myla gently urged Eran onto the stool and loosened the drawstring of her bag of medicines. "Let's take care of you first." She took out a flask and the packets of herbs she'd picked out that morning. The drink in the flask used an extract of goldbark tree root, which Myla had been lucky to find because, even in the Forest, it was rare. "Drink this now, and I'll explain how to use the dried stuff."

Deep as a Tomb

Eran drank the tincture in three swallows, then thumped the flask onto the table, cutting off Myla's explanation of the packets. "Yes, yes. I understand."

Myla gave in and took the bag of offerings. "You'll remember not to tell anyone I can get into tombs? My father's afraid the thieves might try to make me open one so they can clean it out."

"I'll remember. The Forest bless you, Myla." Eran's color was already better. For the hundredth time, Myla marveled at the power hidden in the Forest.

When she cracked the door open, the corridor looked empty, but the chickens were squawking at some invader. She slipped to the open yard door in time to see Beran vanish through the postern gate, having apparently decided what Carl didn't know wouldn't trouble him, which was a lovely, green thought, but Silvit save him if Carl found out. Still, she could hardly blame Beran. Carl had been too high-handed.

She looked back toward the Hall. She should get Kaven, but her face grew warm at the thought of Adon and Naeth winking and smirking if she and Kaven left for a "walk." She'd be fine on her own.

She gave Beran time to get away, then followed him into the woods where the pull of the tomb hit her again. Certain of the way, she broke into a trot until the clearing opened before her, and she once again walked into the presence of a Forest tomb. The moss blanketing it glowed with life. She circled it, eyeing the trees nervously but seeing no sign of thieves. She'd told Kaven she wasn't worried, and mostly that was true, but a little part of her brain shook with the memory of the man grabbing her. The heat of his breath over her ear and neck., irt had blackened his fingernails and the darkened the creases in his hand.

At the tomb door, she crammed thoughts of the thief back into a dark hole in her memory and slid the strap of the bag onto her shoulder so she could lay both hands flat on the cool stone of the door. What would it be like inside? Da had been in too big a hurry to let her enter their tomb, and of course, she hadn't gone into Zale's either.

She swept her gaze once over the prayer carved on the doorframe. Dusting the last little bit of a yellowed vine from the doorway, she drew her awareness in close and sank into the words carved so many years gone that no one knew how long ago it was. "We are the Forest's children. We lie in its arms and trust in its care."

The door trembled, then slid silently sideways, as she'd been sure it would. Well, mostly sure. The passage was so dark she couldn't see more than two yards. Lady Eran had said there would be light inside. Myla cursed her own stupidity. She'd seen the darkness inside her family's tomb. Why hadn't she brought a torch? She teetered on the doorsill, but she couldn't turn back now. Heart beating like a butterfly's wing, she walked out of sunshine into earth-scented shadow.

Fire sprang to life and ran down the passage walls in lines about hip high, making Myla smother a startled cry. She'd never seen anything like this and couldn't imagine describing it to someone in a way they'd believe, which might explain why Eran hadn't tried. Cautiously, she stretched a hand toward the fire, then jerked it back when she felt the heat. She took a step, then looked back at the door, sweat dampening her armpits at the thought of it closing behind her. She scooped up a handful of small stones from the floor and wedged them into both lower corners of the doorway. It would have to do.

She started along a stairway, which sloped down and curved to the right. The light faded behind her and ran only a few yards ahead, flaring as she approached, so she moved in a world that stretched only a few steps either way. Every few yards, the passage turned, forcing her to creep when she wanted to run. The light strips stopped unfurling. Dismayed, she halted, then saw a glow ahead. She darted forward to find the strips wrapping around a circular room, maybe five yards wide. In its center stood three stone coffins, their sides carved with runes, their tops heaped with irregular shapes she couldn't identify under a thick layer of dust.

Breath stopped by the knowledge that these were the oldest coffins in the tomb, she tiptoed closer and squinted to identify the dusty offerings. A leather ale flask, maybe? A bowl, a knife, some sort of carved animal? Dust pinched the inside of her nose, and she pressed her finger under it, like the dead would mind if she sneezed.

She turned to the altar under the faded painting of Silvit. Because she'd never been in a tomb before, this was the first time she'd seen one of the altars where folks left offerings when something was wrong in the Forest, which meant the cat was unhappy. From the bag, she pulled out a fist-sized cake made of herbs that Silvit was said to like best, not much different from the herbs the barn cats liked, really. She put it on the altar. "Bless this manor, Silvit, and all the living and dead who dwell here."

The coffin belonging to Lady Eran's husband was in a lower room, reached through one of the six doors leading off this one. To herself, she carefully repeated the directions Lady Eran had given her. She'd heard fright stories about folks becoming lost forever in a maze of tomb passages.

She took the door across from the bottom of the middle coffin and picked her way down stone steps, the light unrolling before her. First door on the left, up a short flight, across the circle, down. She emerged in yet another circular room and knew she was in the right place when she saw the single coffin holding the tall, blue vase Eran had said would be there. Dust had settled on it since Eran's son had died, and no one else had been able to open the tomb, but its color still showed.

Myla unbuckled her bag and drew out Erin's gold bowl, set it down next to the vase, and lifted the lid. Some of the bright-green mix caught in the lid, and she wiped it out with her fingers, then rubbed them together over the bowl. For a moment, she smelled only dust and earth. Then the scent of pine and roses and herbs drifted around the room. The gold bowl was costly, but to Myla, the real offering was what the bowl held because the power of the Forest was here, the power of Silvit. Myla inhaled, then breathed out, whispering Steeprise's prayer one last time for Eran's man.

She hesitated, then added another prayer. "Silvit, if you can, help keep me and the ones I love safe."

Leaving the bowl's lid on the coffin, she turned to go, then had to put her 'and on the wall to steady herself against her suddenly swimming head. Maybe the air was bad down here. There were stories about that too. She took one step and stumbled to her knees, jolting them on the stone floor. Her face flamed. She gasped, pressed her hands to her pounding temples, and closed her eyes.

Colors flashed behind her lids. Dream forms rippled alive. Silvit leaped. A doe screamed. Was Myla predator or prey? She was a tree with sap rising and leaves cupped to hold medicines. She pulled up her roots and tried to run, but the path ran two ways and she couldn't choose. She finally managed to cry out, and when she did, her eyes flew open. She had to get out of there before she was smothered.

Both hands on the wall, she hauled herself to her feet and up the stairs. Across now, yes? Or should she go left? Her heart pounded so hard she choked. If she lost her way, she could run from room to room forever. She made herself picture the way she'd come, but was sure she'd remembered well only when she saw Silvit's altar.

Her galloping heart slowed, and as she took a moment to breathe, she frowned. There was no cat cake on the altar. Was she in the wrong place after all? Something rattled, and she whirled to see pebbles pattering down the steps.

Instantly, she thought of the thieves, and the fierceness of the predator she'd just been flooded her muscles and heart. "Rot them! Silvit, rip them to shreds!" She grabbed the knife off the coffin. Before she could move, a solid shadow swept up the stairs. She made out a huge, brown-gold cat, then heard a man cry out.

She raced up the stairs to where the leaves of a flourishing green vine stood out against a dark blue sky. As the door thudded shut behind her, she saw a man lying on the ground, face turned away. She ran toward him, knife clenched, just as Carl and Kaven burst into sight.

"Are you all right?" Kaven cried, wrapping an arm around her heaving shoulders. Carl ran to the fallen man and rolled him onto his back.

Ashy-faced and limp-limbed, it was Beran. At Myla's feet, a giant paw print was pressed into the earth. Her throat closed. What had she done?

Chapter 8

Pain pounded at the back of Beran's skull. From far away, he heard Carl's urgent voice. "What happened?"

"I don't know," Myla cried. "Really, I don't."

"Weren't you with him?"

"No. I was gathering herbs and heard him cry out."

"You're sure you're not hurt?" Kaven asked. "You're shaking."

"I'm fine," Myla said. "Stop asking."

Beran sucked air and forced his eyes open. Carl's face loomed over him, drained of all color. He grabbed Beran's shoulders and shook. "Talk to me."

"Don't," Beran said. "I'm all right." Apart from feeling like he'd been kicked in the head by his horse.

Behind Carl, Myla scuffed her toe over the ground before Kaven pressed her to his side. His bow clutched in his other hand, he scanned his surroundings, mouth set in an angry line. Myla, flushed and breathless, leaned on him. When she caught Beran watching her, she twitched and tucked something out of sight behind her back.

Carl released Beran's shoulders. "What happened?"

Good question. Beran touched the sore spot on his head. "I'm not sure. I saw a shadow. An animal, I think, some sort of wildcat."

Kaven lowered his bow. "Silvit," he whispered, "trying to send you home."

"Don't be ridiculous," Beran snapped. Westreachers spreading that belief was all he needed.

"It wasn't the thieves?" Carl frowned and felt the lump Beran had just probed, sending pain flaring under the callused fingers. "How'd you get the bump?"

Beran jerked his head away. "I said *don't*. I think I hit it when I fell." He stared at his left sleeve. A long tear gaped open over a scratch, too shallow to bleed but stinging nonetheless.

Carl spotted it and grunted. "Someone should have told me there were wildcats here."

Beran drew a deep breath. "I'm not hurt. An animal startled me so I fell. It wasn't Silvit," he added emphatically. He struggled to get his knees under him, and Carl grasped his arm to haul him to his feet. Carl loosened his fingers, but kept them near, so he must have felt how shaky Beran still was.

Carl glanced over his shoulder at Kaven and Myla. "Go on to the house. We'll be along." He waited for them to vanish in the greenery on the path before he shoved his face close to Beran's. "It never occurred to me that you'd lie and sneak behind my back," he said in a low voice. "I thought you had more honor."

Beran stiffened. "I owe it to Ander to catch his killer, and you were keeping me from doing that. I never lied."

"You sure as spit deceived me." Scowling, Carl gestured for Beran to move. Beran stalked ahead of him, concentrating on not swaying. When they reached the manor yard, they found Kaven and Myla waiting, the stable boy hovering nearby. Carl snapped his fingers. The boy took one look at him and scuttled off to fetch their horses.

"I'll tell Lady Eran we're going." Myla pulled free from Kaven and hurried into the house.

"Would you bring my map, please?" Beran called.

A moment or two later, Myla emerged carrying Beran's map tube and the bag with her medicines. She gave him the map with a hand as filthy as if she'd been digging among the ashes in a fireplace. He frowned. What had Myla been doing? What was it he'd seen her hide? He eyed her bag, sure whatever it was lay concealed inside.

Adon strode behind her, followed more slowly by Naeth, with Lady Eran on his arm. Even holding one another up, the two old people looked as tottery as Beran felt. Not Adon, though. To Beran's annoyance, he was as unshakeable on his feet as he was in his opinions. "This is an outrage," Adon said. "The thieves should be hung for treason."

"They should, but this was an animal," Beran said firmly. To his relief, the boy returned, keeping their horses between him and Carl. Beran bowed to Lady Eran. "Thank you for your hospitality." They all mounted and rode out the gates, heading for home.

Myla and Kaven rode ahead, which was fine with Beran because he wasn't sure he could keep arguing that Silvit was a myth. Kaven leaned toward Myla, as if trying to talk to her, but she looked straight ahead, only occasionally spilling a short answer. Carl rode next to Beran, grim-faced, which probably meant he hadn't finished what he had to say, though Beran was stone sure he'd finished listening to it. He hated to admit it, but Carl's accusation of lying stung. Others had to be able to rely on his words. When he spoke, they heard Rinland. Or they would one day, if the council named him heir.

If his solo exploration had given him some insight into who Ander's killer was, he wouldn't care about Carl's judgment, but he was as baffled as he'd ever been. He'd searched the place where Ander had died and the path the killer had taken afterward. He didn't find much, but in front of where Ander's body had lain, a bush still looked crushed. Beran imagined the scene. Ander had found one thief hiding, probably the one they'd been chasing, the one Myla stabbed. While Ander's attention was on that one, the other jumped him from behind, slid his worked leather headband down to his throat, and twisted. None of it would have taken long, or Ander would have called out.

Or maybe not. Maybe he'd wanted to keep Beran away from danger and struggled in silence. Beran hoped that wasn't true. He hoped Ander trusted Beran's strength and training and loyalty enough to want him at his side.

He dragged his sleeve under his nose. He was wasting time. He should get moving to hunt down the killer who'd twisted that headband and left Ander in the dirt. Beran was sure his father would say he should leave that to Magistrate Halid and avoid offending Lord Corin, that he should think of his own future and, more importantly, Rinland's. He'd say a court face that hid feelings from others wasn't always enough for a prince. Sometimes he needed to hide his feelings from himself so he could do what Rinland needed. Sometimes he needed a court heart.

But Beran couldn't do it. He wouldn't do it. Not for this. Not for Ander.

He headed back to Lady Eran's at an angle that would take him there more quickly, but he went no more than two hundred yards before the trunks parted, and he walked into the presence of what could only be a Westreach burial mound. Details from his tutor's lessons floated around in his head. Westreachers traditionally buried their dead in these mounds, but fewer and fewer of them could get in because the tombs were tied to the manor holder's blood, and generations of intermarriage had finally created enough change in that blood's character that the tomb entrances didn't respond. According to Beran's tutor, legends floated through the Westreach of a way to fix the problem, but it had been lost in the flow of time.

He circled to the north where the entrance should be and was startled to find the doorway open. He took a single step inside before…before what? Before a shadow had swept over him and knocked him down? Silvit? Despite Kaven's claim, that sounded daft to Beran. It must have been an animal hiding in the tomb.

He had no intention of letting the fuss over his encounter with an animal distract him from hunting down Ander's killer. He looked at Myla, riding ahead, and thought again of the moment when she'd hidden something. He was almost sure he'd glimpsed a knife in her hand, one she evidently didn't want him to see.

That evening, Beran paused in the Hall doorway. Fires danced in both hearths, and his grandmother and several of her women sat near the larger one, their spindles dropping and being drawn up again. Her men-at-arms and various other servants were gathered a short distance away, sipping ale and chatting. Two of the men-at-arms were casting knucklebones for a scattering of coins. Another man plucked at the lute and sang a story of lovers who'd pledged to one another and been forcibly parted to the pain of all involved. The stable master was showing the page how to mend a bridle. Seeing them together, it was hard to miss their resemblance. The boy leaned against his father's thigh as casually as if it were part of him. With a twist of pain, Beran resisted the urge to creep closer and hear what they had to say to one another.

Carl stood near them, though not near enough to count as with them, but now he shifted his eyes from them to Beran. Except when Beran had to lie down or fall down after dinner, Carl watched him like a jailer, including when Beran dutifully invited him on a short trip to the orchard. He'd held his tongue, but was still obviously hot, and just waiting to be sure Beran hadn't broken his skull to let him know just how hot.

Isadia's gaze caught on Beran. She beckoned.

He set the sack he carried behind the stacked trestles, nudged it out of sight with his toe, and went to see what she wanted, Carl's gaze prodding him all the way.

"How are you?" she asked. "Is your arm bleeding?"

"It was just a scratch. It's nothing."

"You're not dizzy?"

"Not at all."

"If you are, the one to tell is Myla. She has a gift with medicine."

Beran glanced across the Hall to where Myla and Kaven were shoving a high-backed bench around in front of a window open to the starry night. "Good idea." He had questions for Myla that had nothing to do with his head.

Myla plunked onto the bench and pointed to the side table holding a bowl of raspberries. Kaven loped off to fetch the fruit.

Beran slid into the spot next to Myla and spoke softly. "Myla, did you take the thief's knife?"

69

"No. Why would I?" She sounded genuinely startled. "You think we're all thieves?"

"What's wrong with you?" Kaven must have hustled back because he was close enough to hear that last bit. "You accuse me and then Myla. Like you have any right." His face flamed scarlet, and the dish in his hand shook hard enough to send a berry rolling off onto the floor. "You grasslanders come here and steal away the Forest, and you have the root-rotting nerve to call us thieves. Don't you think I care about honor just as much as you do? Don't you think I hate thieving just as much?" His voice rose as he spoke, and to Beran's astonishment, his chin trembled as if he were about to cry. The rest of the room fell silent as people turned to look. In the hush, Kaven glanced around, shoved the dish into Myla lap, and stomped off toward his and Beran's room.

Myla rose. "Kaven?"

As if he hadn't heard, he vanished down the hallway.

Beran frowned after him. "He's touchy about the thieves."

"Wouldn't you be?" Myla whirled to face him, spots of color in her cheeks. "Oh, wait. I forgot. You're the king's son, and you're rich. No one's going to accuse you of thieving."

"Actually, Kaven just did." Beran suspected the chances of a friendly chat were thin, but he pressed on anyway. "I know you had a knife, Myla. If it was the thief's, you might want it for the same reason I do, so you can find the owner. I understand that, but I need it back."

Her voice shook, but she kept it low. "I don't have your knife. Now get away from me." Clutching the bowl of berries, she shoved past him and went to offer some to Carl, who'd been slouched against the wall, studying the doorway through which Kaven had disappeared. He straightened as Myla thrust the bowl toward him, and his arm bumped it, sending it crashing to the floor where it shattered. Myla gave a dismayed cry.

"Sorry," Carl said. Both of them stooped to reach for bits of the mess.

While everyone's attention was on the mishap, Beran retrieved the sack from behind the trestles. He'd given her a chance to cooperate, but he'd suspected she wouldn't. He'd have to carry out his other plan, underhanded as it felt. He slipped through the doorway into the wing that housed his grandmother and her women, including Myla. He'd asked the little page which room was Myla's, and the page had been innocent enough to answer.

Beran glanced through the open doorway of the first room, scattered with benches and looms. Night poked fingers around the edges of the window shutters. When he recognized the solar where Ander's body had lain, his throat threatened to close. *Keep your eye on the target*, he told himself fiercely and moved on, taking and lighting one of the candles waiting around a lantern glowing on the side table.

He was sure he had the right room, but he knocked and waited before ghosting inside. For a moment, he stood just inside the doorway, letting his eyes adjust and settling his uneven breath. *It's for Ander. I have the right. Stone it, I have the duty.* He forced himself to get on with invading Myla's privacy.

The room matched the one he shared with Kaven, right down to having two beds, though Myla had the room to herself at the moment. The bed with the rumpled covers had to be hers. The place looked like a storm had swept through, leaving a litter of shirts, stockings, and carelessly dropped feather earrings. It smelled of the herbs on the table that rose like a neat island in a sea of storm debris.

He set the bag down, held up the candle, and opened the chest at the foot of her bed. Plunging his hands through jumbled layers of clothes, he found several narrow-skirted gowns, apparently packed away in favor of the trousers hanging on the wall pegs. The chest also held her linen underclothes, which he handled only enough to be sure they weren't wrapped around a knife, and then tried to blot out of his mind. This was not the time to let himself be distracted. He moved on to the pockets of the trousers and the toes of her high boots. The books were herbals, all of them old, judging from the pages' crumbling edges. One of them had a forget-me-not pressed between two pages. Beran was willing to bet that that had come from Kaven.

He looked around. What had he missed? The beds, maybe? Setting the candle on the floor, he dropped to his knees and looked under the one Myla used. His heart jumped. Something wrapped in fur was wedged into the rope web supporting the mattress. He tugged the bundle free, feeling something long, thin, and very knife-like under the fur. Breath quickening, he sat on his heels and peeled back the wrapping. His instant's triumph turned to confusion. It was a knife all right, but no line of blue showed at the base of the flaking leather handle. If he had to guess, he'd say it was an antique with a curved crosspiece and blade design he'd seen only in the old weapons in the castle armory. What was it doing here? Why would Myla hide it?

His hand tightened around a lump in the fur wrapping, and he turned it over. A wolf's snout and empty eyeholes leered back at him. *Wolves will eat your entrails.* For a moment, he forgot to breathe. What was Myla doing with a True mask? Was he living with one of the people threatening him?

His mind raced to make sense. Myla scoffed when anyone accused the True of thieving. She defended them. Could that be because she was one of them? All the talk called them "sons" of wealthy manor holders, but he saw no reason a girl couldn't shove a pry bar under a paving stone. Did that mean she was part of the thieves? No. That made no sense. A thief had attacked her. If she was True, then the thieves and the True were two different threats.

He stirred that around in his head: Assume the True and the thieves were different. Despair tightened his gut. If that was so, then he couldn't find Ander's killer by going after the True. That made it even more important that he find the thief's knife, because hunting down its owner was the only potentially useful path open to him.

He twisted his signet ring and thought, recalling Kaven's shaking voice and distressed face when he defended himself against suggestions of thieving. Maybe he'd been so shaken because he really was associated with the thieves. Kaven had been in a better position than Myla to take the knife. But Kaven would never hurt Myla, so would he be part of the group that went after her? Not likely.

Beran scanned the room as if it would cough up some inspiration. He needed a way to draw the thieves out into the open. In the meantime, he wasn't about to leave the mask in Myla's hands. Despite her hostility, he'd seen no sign she was dangerous to him. Besides, he had to admire her sharp-tongued willingness to stand up for the Forest in the same way he stood up for Rinland. Any interest in the True was more than likely a momentary impulse he could try to head off. It occurred to him that his father would give his grunt of startled laughter if he knew Beran was thinking critical thoughts about someone else's impulsiveness.

He pictured the page in the Hall leaning on his father's knee. If Beran had ever been that relaxed around his father, it was long ago, before his mother's death certainly. He'd once tried to count the days he'd spent time alone with his father in the three years since she died. He'd come up with thirty-four. They'd not often been home at the same time, and when they were, Thien was busy. The last time Beran had seen his father was when he'd come to the castle courtyard to bid Beran farewell, but the last time alone was the day Lord Corin's council representative told Thien that Corin objected to Beran as heir. Thien had summoned Beran to his rooms, waved him to a chair, and, as always, started at once to speak what was on his mind.

"The representative says Corin believes you know nothing of the Westreach and may not be willing to learn." Thien fixed his intent gaze on Beran, who fought not to squirm. "What's more, he says he's not sure you're temperamentally suited to rule. He's seen you act without consideration more than once. Last week, you argued in public with Lord Danic about the Uplands—"

"He's never even been there."

"Beran." His father held up a cautionary hand. "You still lack the maturity that will temper your impulsiveness into courage, and your anger into an urge for justice. When you were eight, the stable master caught you, armed with a wooden sword and stealing a horse so you could ride after me to the Battle of Lac's Holding. The Powers only know what you thought you'd do there."

Beran had thought he would fight by his father's side. He'd thought they'd be soldiers together.

"Sometimes I think you haven't changed at all," his father went on.

That's because you don't see me at all, Beran thought. The anger that pulsed through his veins had nothing to do with justice. Or maybe it did. Justice for himself anyway, or maybe just fairness. Was something wrong with wanting that?

"For the good of Rinland, you must consider your actions before you take them. An impulsive ruler is a dangerous one."

Beran had hidden his hurt and resentment—or at least tried to—and promised to do better. What would his father think of him if he saw him here in Myla's room? Silently, Beran made his case. He'd tried talking to her first, but she'd left him no other way to learn what he needed to know.

He shoved the strange knife back under Myla's mattress, then loosened the drawstring on the bag he'd brought. The snake flicked its tongue at him. He'd brought it along as an excuse for being where he wasn't supposed to be. If anyone caught him in Myla's room, he'd say he was playing a joke and paying her back. The snake flicked its tongue at him again. He hesitated. If he left it, Myla would have no doubt who'd been in her room and taken the True mask. He could give her some time to stew, and then confront her with the mask and ask what she knew. The True were a problem his father wanted solved even if they hadn't killed Ander. He thrust the snake deep down to the foot of the bed under Myla's blankets, then dropped the covers back in place and examined the effect. The lump that was snake looked just like the lumps that had been there when he arrived. She'd have to be made of stone not to have a seizure when she shoved her feet down and felt it. He hid the mask in the bag and moved to the door.

In the corridor, he blew out his candle and was putting it back on the table when the door opposite opened and one of his grandmother's women came out. He froze for an instant before long training in manners made him say, "Fair evening, Sendra."

"Beran, is that you?" his grandmother called. Through the open door, he spotted Isadia, sitting at her dressing table wearing a night robe and holding a hairbrush. "Come in. I've been wanting to talk to you."

He edged into the room as Sendra left, closing the door behind her. The room was dominated by the big curtained marriage bed, a rune for one of the four elements carved on each post. It smelled of a familiar violet perfume. His grandmother glanced at the bag in his hand and raised an eyebrow.

"I'm playing a joke on Myla," he said weakly.

She gave an unladylike snort and pointed the hairbrush at a stool. As Beran sat, she began crackling the brush through her wine-streaked hair. "You're getting along with her and Kaven then? He seemed upset tonight."

"Something I said bothered him, though I didn't mean it the way he took it."

"Make it up with him if you can. You'd be good for one another. You need friends in the Forest, and he needs a life apart from his family."

"Is there a problem at home I should know about so I don't set him off again?" Beran belatedly remembered talk at Lady Eran's about thieves robbing Kaven's family steward. No wonder he'd been vehement about hating thieves.

"Just the troubles everyone has in life sometimes. Kaven's father is dead, but he and his mother lived with his grandfather on Sweet Stream Manor, happily, as far as I can tell. The old man doted on Kaven, and the way Kaven talks about him shows he adored him. Then last year, the grandfather died, and his Uncle Rickard came home. I gather there were debts, so they're having money problems, and the uncle asked if I'd foster him so he'd have a chance to meet people who could help him make his way in the world."

"The person he's met is Myla," Beran said, curious to see how she'd answer.

Isadia laid the hairbrush on her dressing table. "The match would be good for them, I think. We'll have to see what both their families say. Myla's father might object, I suppose. He has a very narrow idea of a daughter's value, a coin spent on a marriage for the good of Oak Ridge Manor would make up the whole of it." She frowned down at the brush and was silent a moment. Her shoulders heaved in a sigh. "I invited her to foster with me because no ne had troubled to teach her to run a household, and I thought she should have a chance to see more of the world. If she follows her father's wishes, it should be because she chooses to, not because she has no other option."

Fostering usually was meant to educate a child in some way that couldn't be done at home, and with Isadia, Myla would certainly learn to run a household. More than that, as Beran had already seen, she'd have a great deal of freedom with Isadia setting the rules. A fosterling was in the legal custody of the host. The law made the host responsible for the child's conduct and wellbeing, while a written agreement spelled out the length of the arrangement and the conditions under which the parent or host could end it. Usually a child stayed in a single place that eventually felt like home.

Beran had been fostered with various lords rather than visiting them so his father could show faith in his many hosts, Thien, too, being willing to treat his child like a coin well spent. Beran pushed the bitter thought away.

"I have a hard time picturing Myla cowed by her family," he said.

"You'd be surprised. She's learned to spread her wings quite nicely in the time she's been here, but it will take strength not to curl them up again to fit back into the space someone else carved out."

A door slammed, and Beran heard someone moving around in the room next door. Myla's room. Time to be elsewhere. He started to rise, but his grandmother startled him with a question.

"What about you, Beran? Do you need time to see what you want on your own?"

"You think I'm like Myla and Kaven, plagued by what my family expects?"

"What do you think?" she asked. "Are you less the king's son and more what you make of yourself here?"

"I'm always the king's son. That's my duty, Grandmother, not some choice I make. I can't ever honorably walk away from that." With a flash of guilt, he thought of his father's advisors endlessly repeating how important it was to Rinland that he make a good impression, how he should take care not to offend Westreachers still touchy about losing their independence by appearing to interfere in local rule. Could he square that duty with the one he had to Ander? Was he already choosing something other than his heir's role? He slid that thought away too.

His grandmother leaned toward him. "You say it's not a choice, but it is. The Heir Ceremony is a choosing that goes both ways. You can reject them as much as they can reject you." Her voice rang with passion. This wasn't some soft notion that he should enjoy his visit more. She was suggesting, arguing, that he should alter the path of his life.

Beran was speechless, unable to find words for an unthinkable act.

"Did your father tell you this manor is yours?" his grandmother asked.

"No." Beran couldn't say he was surprised. As it happened, he'd often stumbled over things his father hadn't taken the time to tell him.

"I have it for life, but your grandfather's will leaves it to you. You can live here in the Forest. We gave your mother no choice, Beran. She had to leave and live in that city. I saw what that did to her, and I've regretted my part in sending her ever since. Joining with Rinland was good for the Forest, but it was bad for Ailith. I won't have you trapped the same way."

Into Beran's head tumbled a memory of a night when he was no more than six, and a nightmare had woken him. His nanny was snoring, and rather than wake her, he went in search of his mother. In his nightclothes, he pattered barefoot along the hall to his parents' rooms. The guards outside their door looked at his tear-stained face, glanced at one another, and let him pass.

He went into his parents' sitting room, eager to reach his mother's bedroom, but a cold draft made him turn. The balcony doors were open, and his mother was outside, looking like a ghost in her white nightgown. He ventured toward her. She had her arms wrapped around her middle, and she was looking west toward the Forest. Perhaps because she was framed in the balcony doorway, his mind flashed to puppet shows.

Several times a year, puppetry troupes came to the city. Some of the puppets were unique to each group of players, but some were traditional characters with names like Lord Vengeance, Father Fury, and Lady Grief.

His mother was Lady Grief.

He cried out and ran to fling his arms around her.

She'd started and turned to catch him in a fierce embrace. "Oh, my heart," she'd said, "I wouldn't trade you for anything."

He was sixteen now, not six, and he was as certain as he could be that his mother had suffered because her life had been offered in service to Rinland. And, perhaps even more, in love to him. The walls closed in, squeezing the air out of the room.

"You put on that princely face, and I'm afraid you'll hide yourself behind it for so long that you'll forget who you are apart from your role," his grandmother said.

"No one is forcing me, Grandmother." That was true, wasn't it? "I want to serve Rinland, and I think I'd be a good ruler."

His grandmother sat back. "I have no doubt you'd be good for Rinland. I'm just not sure it would be good for you."

"It's what I want." Saying that reassured him. The idea of leaving his father's court was scarily attractive. "I should let you rest." He put a hand on the door latch. "Fair night."

"Think about what I said."

Without committing himself, he went out into the corridor. He was just closing her door behind him when a roof-raising shriek nearly blew him off his feet. Sweet Powers. The snake. He ran for the Hall only to find Carl in the doorway looking past him to the women's hallway.

"I was just talking to Grandmother," Beran said. "I think Myla saw a mouse or something. You know girls."

Carl pinned him in place with stone-hard eyes, then glanced at the bag in Beran's hand. He'd watched silently as Beran used it to hold the snake in the orchard. "I take it you're better, and that being the case, you and I will spar first thing tomorrow. If you're going to go wandering around, I want to see how well you can defend yourself." He cast one more look down the hallway, where women's voices were raised, demanding to know what had happened. Then he stepped aside.

Beran fled for the men's wing to find a hiding place for the mask other than the room he shared with Kaven. He wanted to talk to Myla about it, but with everyone watching, he'd have to keep saying he'd been in her room playing a boyish prank. He hadn't felt boyish or playful since Ander died.

Chapter 9

Myla found Carl coming out of the shed where Isadia's men-at-arms stored their gear. He wore boiled leather webbed with fine cracks and carried two wooden practice swords clamped under one elbow. Eyes directed at the dirt, he looked like his thoughts were off somewhere, plodding down paths they'd followed a hundred times before.

"Fair morning," she said.

His head snapped up, and his surprised gaze swept over and around her, probably looking for why she was in a part of the yard she had no use for. She held out the stoppered jar she'd armed herself with.

"Bruise salve," she said.

He took it with a wry smile. "You think I'll need it?"

"I think someone will."

He barked a rusty laugh, then took a tentative step toward the barracks, stopping when she failed to move out of the way.

"Carl, what do you think happened yesterday at that tomb?" Her heart fluttered. Until yesterday, she'd only heard Silvit and seen signs of his passing, but at Lady Eran's she had to believe she'd seen and even commanded Silvit himself. Carl had found her at the place where Beran lay injured. Surely if he suspected her of siccing the cat on Beran, he'd be less friendly, assuming this counted as "friendly" Carl. Of course, as a grasslander, Carl probably didn't understand what Silvit could do.

He cocked his head. "The boy says he glimpsed an animal and tripped. You know something that says different?"

"No, no. Of course not."

He continued to give her a steady look that drilled right into her head.

"I have to get back to the herb room," she said quickly. "I left something on the brazier." She trotted off, his gaze still prodding the center of her back. Silvit save her. Poor Beran.

Shoulders sagging with relief, she darted into the herb room and sank onto her stool. With a shaky hand, she pulled a book closer and looked at the page she'd left it open to. Under the drawing of the spear-leafed plant, the ink had faded to pale brown, and the letters twisted like twigs. As far as she could make out, the old northern herbalists thought chewing the leaf promoted pregnancy, but they didn't say whether the man or the woman had to chew it. Woman, she guessed. Women always took the blame for the baby that came too soon or, more likely with Forest women, the one that didn't appear when a man decided he wanted an heir.

A step in the yard made Myla look toward the open door, but whoever it was moved off. Her breathing slowed again. With Carl set to test Beran's swordwork this morning, maybe Beran had fresher worries than what had happened to him at the Steeprise tomb or what to do with the wolf mask he'd taken from Myla's room.

Last night, when her heart had stopped hammering on her ribs and she'd assured the other women the snake was just a joke, she'd locked her door and looked under her bed. The knife from the Steeprise tomb was there, but the mask was gone. The snake told her who'd been in her room. Beran had been looking for the thief's knife, of course, and instead had found Galen's True mask. He thought the True were the thieves who'd killed his guard. So now what?

A summer breeze fanned the bundles of herbs hanging from the rafters to dry. Behind her, a fire hummed in the brazier, bubbling a syrup she hoped would treat blister plague. On Myla's first morning at Green Valley, Isadia said she'd heard of Myla's skill with medicines and put her in charge of this room. Here, Myla's sense of what she could do had blossomed. The knowledge in her books was wondrous, but she'd found that no one else could use it with the same delicate strength that came naturally to her. No one else could even read it. She was chieftain in this small domain, no matter what she decided to do about Da's plans. When she worked here, sometimes night's arrival caught her by surprise. Today, though, her thoughts hopped around like rabbits in a garden.

She consulted the syrup recipe, lifted the pan off the fire, and set it among the scorch marks on the table. As she waited for it to cool, she leafed further through the book, like she'd find some recipe that would cure her worries. One drawing showed the moss that grew on the tombs. She'd seen moss in another book too, one of the first she'd made her way through at home. The writing said the moss would add to a person's strength. At least, that's what she thought it said, but when she'd drunk tea made from it, she'd collapsed on the floor of the Oak Ridge herb room, spent the next two hours in a waking nightmare, and returned to herself no stronger than before. She turned the page and found a plant she didn't know. The writing said something about fever, but when she tried to make out how to use it, her attention skittered away.

Rot Beran, anyway.

"Myla?"

She jumped and realized how addled she must have seemed when she was relieved to see Galen frowning in the doorway. He wore the shirt she'd left in the laundry, so at least he had the good sense to choose a clean one when he had the chance. A strand of his hair dangled beside his ear.

"You startled me." She inserted a funnel into the neck of a jar with a shaky hand and poured in some of the syrup. Its nutty smell curled out into the room. "Come to say how much you miss me?"

He glanced each way in the yard and stepped into the room. "Where's my ₁nask?"

She moved the funnel to the next jar, trailing a thread of syrup. "What mask?"

"You know what mask. What did you do with it?"

She clanked the pan down. "Does Da know what you're up to?"

"Who cares? He hates the roads, so if he knew, he'd think stopping them was good, heroic even." He tucked the stray hair firmly behind his ear.

She felt a flash of grudging admiration. Galen must know Da would have a fit over him making trouble Da hadn't thought up. Galen had more sap than she'd given him credit for. "I don't have your mask, so if that's all you're after, you should trot on home."

"Rot you, Myla. I know you took it. But as it happens, that's not all I'm after. Da has a task for you. What happened with Isadia's tomb? Did it open?"

"I haven't had time. Have you ever seen this plant?" She tapped the open book.

He shoved it aside. "This is important, Myla. Da wants you to get the Forest circlet."

The request—order?—was so unexpected that for a moment Myla couldn't place what Galen was talking about. Then a weed of memory sprouted. The Forest circlet was the gold crown the chieftain had always worn. Its image was carved over the hearth in Isadia's Hall. Myla had never seen it because it was buried with Isadia's husband, Arthan, a sign he was the last chieftain. After his daughter's marriage and his death, the Forest had become part of Rinland.

"You can't mean it," she said.

"Of course I mean it."

"Galen, you know as well as I do that taking anything from a tomb is irreverent. It spits at the love of the ones who left the offering. It breaks the web of life, so the Forest suffers. Silvit comes after you."

She thought of the old knife under her bed. Surely that didn't count. She'd taken it to defend herself. The tomb door had slid shut too quickly for her to put it back yesterday, and then Kaven, Beran, and Carl had been there. She'd return the knife as soon as she could.

"Da wants that circlet." Galen's face was reddening.

She snorted. "I don't believe you. If Da wanted me to rob a tomb—which I doubt—he wouldn't send you."

"You know he hasn't set foot at Green Valley since Isadia married her daughter off to King Thien. And if you'd use your massive tomb-opening brain, you'd see we need the circlet if we're going to pass you off as chieftain." He rolled his eyes. "Zale wants proof of what you can do before he'll marry you. If he doesn't agree to that, we'll get no help from him."

She knocked over one of the jars, spilling syrup across the table.

Galen's eyes widened as his own words slid into his ears and rattled around in the empty space between them. "Don't tell Da I said that about marriage. Act surprised when he tells you himself."

"But I'm not of age."

"Da can allow it."

"I won't do it. He can't make me." Her voice quivered.

"That's what I said about drowning the barn kittens." Galen's voice was even, like what he said wasn't worth getting upset about, but Myla had seen him throwing up behind the stable the day the kittens vanished.

Someone rapped on the open door. "Are you all right, Myla?" She looked up to see Beran ducking under the hanging herbs and eyeing Galen coolly. "I didn't know you had a visitor."

"This is my brother Galen," Myla forced out. How much worse could things get? Sure as spring, Beran had hunted her down to ask about the mask. Still, he wouldn't do it in front of Galen, just as Galen wouldn't go on about Da's demands in front of Beran. The Forest save her from both of them. "Galen, this is Beran of Rinland."

Galen raised an eyebrow and wrinkled his nose. "Still gracing us with your presence, Beran?" He leaned on Beran's name like saying it without a title put Galen on top.

Beran curved his mouth in a smile even Galen had to know was meant to look nasty. "I'm learning a great deal about the Westreach and its people. I hope I'll be useful when people I've met approach the king." He laced his voice with insulting politeness. He'd been trained with all the tricks to put himself in charge all right.

"I hear you're after the thieves, Beran," Galen said. "Aren't you afraid of sticking your snout where you're not wanted?"

Beran shuffled around under the herbs to face Galen full on. "I wouldn't dream of interfering, of course, but I think I might know who one of the thieves is."

"You do?" Myla's heart stretched with hope. "Who? How do you know?" If Beran rid the Forest of thieves, even Da would have to thank him and maybe leave off planning rebellion. Then he wouldn't need Zale, and he wouldn't crush Myla's heart to get him.

"I'd rather not say who it is until I can talk to Lord Corin," Beran said.

"I hope you have something more than suspicion," Galen said. "Even grassland justice must rest on more than a prince's accusation."

Beran shrugged. "As I said, I'm waiting to talk to Corin. Would you like to come into the house? I don't believe you've greeted Lady Isadia yet."

Galen looked annoyed at being reminded of his bad manners. "No need to bother Lady Isadia. I'm here because Myla borrowed something of mine, and I was hoping she'd be honest enough to give it back, but I guess not."

Hush, she urged him silently.

Beran glanced from Galen to Myla and back again. "Interesting."

He knows, Myla thought. *He's picturing Galen, not me, in a wolf mask.* To her shame, she felt a wash of relief.

Galen turned his back on Beran to face her. "Remember what Da wants, Myla."

"Believe me, it's burned into my head." She already felt herself wriggling in Da's net, trying to please him but get what she wanted too. What if she took the circlet, but said she'd wear it and be named chieftain only if Da called off the marriage with Zale? Maybe all by itself being chieftain would give her and Da enough power to negotiate some agreement about not giving away pieces of the Forest or cutting it through with roads. Maybe taking the circlet would be like taking the knife, something she could justify as self-defense.

Galen ran his finger through the syrup on the table and sniffed it. "This smells good. What is it?"

She took a quick measure of her brother. "It's not for you."

He licked his finger clean, gagged, and lunged for the water bucket. He swished the water through his mouth, sidled to the door, and spit. "You expect someone to swallow that?"

"Of course not. I expect to rub it on folks' skin if the blister plague comes again."

"You think you can cure blister plague? You're mad."

Myla laid her palm on her book. "This says I can."

"Whatever you say. Remember what I told you." Still ignoring Beran, Galen strode away. She heard him spit again just outside the herb room.

Beran leaned over the book. "'Hind the grief finely'?"

"'Grind the leaf.'"

"We have blister plague in Rin City sometimes. It's bad. You can cure it?" He sounded genuinely interested, maybe even respectful.

"I think so, assuming no one builds a road over the top of where this grows."

Beran looked ready to say more, but Kaven appeared behind him.

"Who was that?" Kaven frowned after Galen.

At the sight of him, some of the tightness in her stomach eased. She'd worried about him after he stomped off the previous night. "My brother." She damped a cloth in the bucket and wiped up the spill.

"I wish I'd been here to meet him," Kaven said.

"No, you don't," Beran said.

"He's a fool, but he's harmless." Myla looked at Beran, willing him to see sense.

"Possibly." Beran eyed her thoughtfully. "But I'd like to know what others are helping him carry out his foolishness."

Kaven glanced back and forth between them and frowned. "You looking for a dose of tonic, Beran? Something to keep you from crying for mercy in front of Carl?"

"Beran says he knows who one of the thieves is," Myla put in before the two of them could get into it again.

Kaven's eyes widened. "Who?"

"I don't want to say until I talk to Corin," Beran said.

Kaven gave him a level look. "You're bluffing."

Myla felt a moment's doubt. Was Beran bluffing? Kaven was good at seeing things like that.

Beran shrugged. "We'll see."

"Don't you have to be somewhere?" Kaven turned his back on Beran and bent over Myla's book. "What are you working on, Myla?"

Beran grimaced. "I suppose I'd better not keep Carl waiting. I want to talk to you later, Myla." He nodded to Kaven and left.

"What does he want to talk to you about?" Kaven asked.

"I don't know," she lied. "Do you know that plant, Kaven?" She pointed to the plant supposedly good against fever.

He pulled the book closer. "Maybe. There's a patch of something like it near our manor, assuming that area hasn't been cleared."

She felt a spurt of tenderness for his frown of concentration, his obvious desire to help her, to please her. Maybe she should tell him what Da wanted and ask him what he thought she should do about the circlet. After that tale he'd told her of his ancestors being burned alive, would he be willing to risk war in the Forest? She'd heard Isadia ask Kaven's advice for Green Valley Manor. If Isadia put her trust in Kaven, maybe Myla should too. On the other hand, it felt wrong to draw Kaven into Da's treason.

Apparently unconscious of her warm thoughts, Kaven straightened and pushed his hair off his forehead. "I'll take you where I think this is as soon as I have time, but for now we don't want to miss the sparring. I saw Carl this morning, and he looked annoyed." Kaven smiled at what he plainly thought was happy news.

Myla damped the fire in the brazier and went out into the yard with Kaven. In the name of all green growing things, what was she going to do?

Chapter 10

Beran rounded the corner of the house into the side yard and halted. Most of Isadia's men-at-arms, half her servants, Kaven and Myla buzzed around a cleared space with Carl at its center. Beran slid his court face on as the people on his side of the yard turned toward him and parted to let him through. Now that Beran thought about it, Kaven had known Carl planned for them to spar this morning. Carl must have spread the news because Beran hadn't told anyone. Stone the man. Apprehension twisted in his stomach.

It would be fine. He'd trained with a sword since he was seven, usually with other people watching. Whatever Carl had in mind, Beran wouldn't disgrace himself. This was an opportunity, not a danger spot. He'd prove to Carl that he could defend himself, and Carl would stop trying to block his search for Ander's killer.

Face impassive, Carl flipped one of the wooden practice swords he held and extended it to Beran, hilt first. Beran swung it to loosen his arm and get a feel for its weight and balance. Carl had chosen well. The sword felt right.

"Ready?" Carl asked.

Beran touched his sword to Carl's, then held it in the ready position. At least Beran thought he was ready, but Carl came at him so hard and fast he barely parried. Carl's sword slid off Beran's, and the next thing Beran knew, Carl poked him in the ribs. It hurt as if Beran were in his nightshirt rather than a boiled leather jerkin. Carl's face was blank. Beran narrowed his eyes. The man surely knew better than to jab that hard in training.

The watchers stamped their feet in polite approval. "Well done," said one of the men-at-arms.

Beran ignored the pain in his side and raised his sword again. This time, he slipped past Carl's guard and set his point at Carl's breastbone. There. That was the force you used when you sparred. *Take the hint, Carl.* The watchers stamped for Beran just as they had for Carl, so whatever Carl had given as the reason for this bout hadn't biased them one way or the other.

They touched weapons for an instant before Carl drove forward. Beran struggled to keep his feet as he retreated through the hastily scattering crowd. Carl's weapon swung in a blur, and Beran's sword went flying. Carl stepped back, but not before whacking Beran on the thigh with the flat of his wooden blade.

"That's the slap of reality," Carl said. "Outside of training, a disarmed man is a dead man."

Hot fury burned through Beran's chest. Carl shouldn't have hit him once he was disarmed. What's more, the precise force of the blow told Beran what Carl intended. He didn't want to break Beran, but he sure as spit wanted to bruise him.

Beran dove, scooped up his sword, and somersaulted to his feet, evading the blow Carl aimed at his backside. Without touching swords to start, he charged. The watchers laughed and stamped.

Carl backed away, brought his sword around, and smacked Beran on the other thigh. He lunged toward Beran, who scrambled back, limping and parrying as best he could. A trickle of sweat stung his right eye. For a big man, Carl was fast, and he handled a sword with nearly as much skill as the castle training master. Beran feinted and slid sideways, aiming the tip of his sword at Carl's belly, but before Beran could deliver the jab, his cursed feet tangled, and he sprawled in the dirt.

To his surprise, Carl waited for him to bounce to his feet. That apparently used up every bit of Carl's mercy because he came at Beran like a whirlwind and smacked the flat of his sword against Beran's hip.

"You think you can face down anything," Carl said.

Smack on Beran's shoulder.

"You can be hurt."

Smack on Beran's elbow.

"You can die, you young fool."

The yard faded in and out of sight. Beran's whole body throbbed with pain. He clutched his sword and raised his guard, his chest heaving for air. The watchers had fallen silent.

With a flick, Carl disarmed him and lowered his own sword.

"You're well trained." Carl's voice was unsteady. "When you've grown used to your height, your footwork should even out, and by then, you'll have the muscle to match your grit. But you don't know when you're beaten."

Beran's sword arm still trembled as if weighed down by his weapon. He stepped closer to Carl and bared his teeth. "That's where you're wrong," he said softly. "I know when I've been given a beating."

"Learn what you can from it then." Carl caught up the sword Beran had been using and stalked away. The watchers skittered aside to let him through, then began to drift off to whatever they were supposed to be doing.

Kaven and Myla came up on either side of Beran. "Carl believes in public punishment," Kaven said gleefully.

"I gave Carl a salve for bruises," Myla said before she and Kaven joined the others trickling away.

Beran dropped onto a bench at the edge of the yard and pushed his sweat-soaked hair back. So much for proving himself to Carl. He rubbed his aching thighs. Salve or no salve, he'd be black and blue for days. One of the men-at-arms patted the shoulder Carl hadn't hit. "Don't sit too long," he said. "You'll stiffen up." He went on his way.

Stone Carl anyway. Who did he think he was? Did he really need to whack Beran witless in front of the whole household? Beran would be hanged if he'd take that without speaking up. Anger dragged him to his feet and sent him limping to the vine-covered barracks Carl shared with Isadia's men-at-arms. The sound of splashing drew him around to the back. Carl had stripped to the waist and was sluicing himself down from the wash bucket. He saw Beran, but kept on with what he was doing.

"What was that about?" Beran asked.

"You ready to listen to the answer to that?"

"I asked, didn't I?"

"I'm trying to penetrate your thick skull with the news you're not immortal."

"I know that."

Carl reached for the towel and turned to Beran. An old scar snaked across the right side of his chest. Recently healed burns puckered the inside of both arms. "I hear you're saying you recognized one of the thieves."

For an instant, Beran was tempted to lie, but he was already ashamed of having misled Carl at Lady Eran's. "I need to smoke him out. I'll know him when I see him."

"You see? That's what I'm talking about." Carl spat the words. "Have you no sense of fear? No notion you can be hurt?"

"You think I don't know a killer's likely to kill again? All the more reason to find him. I can't give up. Apart from anything else, I owe Ander more than I can say. You don't have to tell me people can die. Not with Ander's body still in my head at night." And his own mother's, Beran realized, which was somehow worse because he'd never seen it. She'd been buried by the time he'd come home. He'd thought he was done with dreams of her death. "The dead can't avenge themselves. I have to do this for Ander. For my own peace."

Carl hid his face in the towel. When he lowered it, he looked away into the trees rather than at Beran. "Sometimes peace is hard to find."

"But I have to try. I'm going to do this, Carl. I'd rather do it without fighting you all the way."

Carl's mouth set. "You'd find it hard going."

Beran shrugged.

Carl sighed. "What is it you plan to do?"

"I'm going to talk to one of the robbery victims today," Beran said. "I want to know what he can tell me." Carl's undershirt lay on the ground near Beran's feet. Beran prodded it with the toe of his boot. "But here's my problem. Something I found in…Something Myla has makes me pretty sure the thieves and the True are two different problems. Does that seem possible?" Carl grunted, so Beran had no idea what he thought, but pressed on. "That leaves me with fewer clues to Ander's killer, so I have to flush the killer out somehow."

Carl swabbed water off his chest, regarding Beran with the same look the castle weapons master did when deciding what opponent to match him against. Finally, he said, "I understand why this matters to you, so I'll make you a bargain. I'll keep out of your way if you promise to do what I say."

"In matters of my safety, of course." Ander would have insisted on that too.

Carl flung the towel onto the bench. "I decide what those are."

Without answering, Beran scooped up Carl's sweaty undershirt and held it out to him. "Give me time to get cleaned up."

"I wasn't sure you were teachable. Ander may have been right about you after all." Carl took the shirt and headed into the barracks.

Beran hustled—well, hobbled—toward a side door of the house. It occurred to him belatedly that Carl hadn't offered the salve Myla mentioned, which suggested he had no intention of softening his lesson. Still, despite Beran's ripening bruises, the morning had turned out better than he'd expected when he went in search of Carl. He met his grandmother on her way out, with Kaven right behind her.

"Beran, good. I've been looking for you." She sounded as if seeing him had made the sun come up. "I want you to go with Kaven today and see the work being done on the manor's new copse."

Beran didn't know what a copse was, but he easily translated the rest of that. She wanted him to learn how the manor worked because she saw him as its lord, and she didn't care whether he achieved his father's goal of ingratiating himself with her neighbors so he could become King's Heir.

"I'd enjoy doing that, I'm sure." Beran shot a look at the smirking Kaven. "But I'd planned to visit Lord Sotar."

"That can wait," she said firmly.

So being future lord of the manor gave him no power, just responsibility. That contradiction fit Beran like a familiar, though scratchy, shirt. Still, it was impossible to refuse the task. Everywhere Beran had been, lords assigned work to fosterlings, mostly, he suspected, to keep them out of trouble.

"All right," he said. "I'll be ready momentarily."

"I'll wait in the stables," Kaven said. "I promise you this will be fun."

Yes, but for whom? "Carl will have to come," Beran said, "just in case my back needs guarding."

Kaven laughed and set off for the stables.

"I'm so glad you and Kaven patched up last night's misunderstanding," Isadia said. "He said he was willing to teach you."

Sweet Powers. Kaven hadn't been in their room when Beran got there the night before. The only time Beran had spoken to him since was in the herb room. Any patching up still needed to happen and might be painful. Beran went off to his room to inspect the bruises he already had.

Chapter 11

A copse turned out to be a bunch of trees enclosed by earthen banks topped by a hedge. They picketed their horses outside, where Kaven took two axes strapped to his saddle and led Beran and Carl through the open gate. Beran had heard the thud of axes as they approached, so he wasn't surprised to find men already cutting trees.

"Fair day, Kaven," one of the men called.

"You're making good progress," Kaven said.

"Even better, we've been blessed." The man pointed to a place just inside the gate.

Beran peered around Kaven's back to see the paw print of a huge cat. His mouth went dry. Sweet Powers. It must be the cat he'd seen at Lady Eran's tomb. Nothing else could have left a print that big.

Kaven kissed his fingertips and crouched to touch them to the print. "Lady Isadia will be glad to hear it."

Beran dragged his gaze away from the print and looked at the faces around him. Carl radiated alarm, but everyone else looked like the cake baker had dropped by. Beran slid his court face on. One thing he had learned over the years was there was no point in fighting local beliefs.

Most of the trees in the enclosure had already been reduced to stumps, which Beran supposed was a kind of progress, though if he'd had to predict how Kaven would react to timbering, he'd have expected Kaven to fling his body between the tree and the axe. That made no sense, when he thought of it. Westreachers built from wood and burned it. They must be more reasonable than most Rinlanders thought, though of course, that wasn't a high bar.

"Why is this closed off?" Beran asked.

"To keep the deer away." Kaven eyed him, and Beran knew his puzzlement must show because Kaven's face turned happy. "These trees will send up shoots," Kaven explained as if talking to a two-year-old. "We'll use them for poles, for charcoal burning, and fences, and firewood, but if we don't protect them, the deer will eat the new growth." He propped the axes against his leg, pulled gloves from his belt, and drew them on. "Shall we get to work?" He offered an axe to Beran.

Beran took it in his gloveless hand, court face clamped tight. Might as well add a few blisters to his bruises.

"Too bad there's no axe for me," Carl said. "I'll just sit over here and keep watch." He looked as happy as Kaven did. Stone them both.

Beran had chopped firewood, but he'd never cut down a tree, something that was apparently obvious because after he took three swipes with the axe, an older man hastily trotted over and gave him a lesson. When he handed the axe back to Beran, he said, "It's good to see you here, lad. We were all sorry when your mother left the Forest." The man went back to work leaving Beran with a pleasant sense of belonging. That was his last happy thought for a while though. By the time the tree was half cut, his already bruised arms, shoulders, and back were screaming, and his hands were on fire. He paused, leaning on his axe.

Kaven must have been waiting for him to halt, presumably so he could approach without Beran chopping his head off. "I forgot to give you these," Kaven mumbled and thrust a pair of gloves at Beran.

"You forgot." Beran lifted a shoulder to wipe sweat from his temple.

"Sorry, Your Princeliness. I wasn't sure you'd work hard enough to need them." Kaven slapped the gloves into Beran's chest and went back to work.

Beran caught them and pulled them on. That was the nicest thing Kaven had said to him so far.

Over the next few days, Beran split his time between visiting manors where the thieves had struck and following Kaven around Green Valley. He hoped he made an heir-like impression on the manor owners, because the visits were a loss as far as finding Ander's killer. The thieves had gone to ground since Beran started hunting them, meaning they were as aware of him as he was of them. He felt them in the shadows, watching and waiting, knowing he'd eventually have to leave whether he'd avenged Ander or not. His claim to have recognized one had produced no results, but it was the only weapon he had so he kept using it.

"You coming with me today?" Kaven asked one morning about a week later. "I'm taking Myla to look at some plants." He sat on his bed tying his boots. There were shadows under his eyes. He was a noisy sleeper, and the previous night he'd rolled around mumbling some incomprehensible plea.

"Not today. My grandmother's given me leave to visit another manor. I thought I'd go to Sweet Stream this time."

Kaven jerked upright, then swore when the lace he'd been tying tangled in a knot. "Why Sweet Stream?"

"Same reason I've been going to all the other places," Beran said. "The thieves robbed your steward. Maybe he can describe them. Can I take a message or anything else for you?"

Kaven's tone was more hostile than it had been for a while. "You could have told me in time for me to get something ready. Too late now." Kaven lowered his head and picked at the knot. "Maybe just make sure my mother's all right."

"Sure. Anything in particular?"

"No." Kaven stood and hesitated as if he'd say more, then left the room.

Beran frowned after him. Kaven was upset about something. Working side by side with him, Beran had gained respect and a certain amount of liking for his roommate. Before he let his guard down any further, it was time to do something he should have done days ago—search Kaven's things for the missing thief's knife. He'd put it off, because searching Myla's belongings had felt underhanded enough, but Kaven's were another matter altogether. He was poor and vulnerable in a way Myla was not. What's more, in the time Beran had spent fostering at various houses, he'd found that rooming with someone created a bond even when roommates didn't like one another. They saw one another in unguarded moments. They knew things each hid from everyone else. Beran felt like a worm violating the privacy Kaven had managed to keep, but the knife's disappearance nagged at him, and Kaven had been in the best position to take it.

He moved around the room, going through Kaven's things the same way he'd gone through Myla's. Pockets and boot toes, nothing. Under his bed and pillow, nothing. And last, Kaven's clothes chest, where Beran handled the folded clothes carefully. Unlike Myla, Kaven was tidy. He'd notice if Beran tossed them into tangles.

When he reached the bottom of the chest without finding the knife, he lowered the lid and for a moment, let his hands rest on it. *Good.* Whatever Kaven was worried about, it wasn't the knife. Kaven was a pain, but he was also an almost-adult trying to find his feet away from home. Beran recognized the look in half the fosterlings he'd ever lived with. For that matter, he recognized it in the face he saw in the mirror when he took a careful blade to the fuzz on his cheeks. He buckled on his sword and set off to meet Carl.

The way to Sweet Stream Manor lay along a stretch of paved road that already showed signs of hard use. The stones tilted and were cracked or even broken in places. Beran had to guess when they crossed the manor's border. Westreachers all seemed to know where one another's boundaries were—either that or they didn't care—but they'd been vague with the king's surveyors, who'd gone mad trying to map out where the roads and new manors could lie. The manor holders had all agreed their holdings were anchored to their families' tombs, but beyond that, they'd looked blank. Beran had just decided they were on Sweet Stream land when he heard men's shouts and the thud of axes. When he and Carl emerged from the tunnel of leaves, Beran reined to a halt, too startled to ride on. On the hillside sloping up from the road, every tree had been cut. Mud ran down onto the road from the gouged and eroded earth. Men worked near the top, cutting more trees. Guiding ponies, two of them dragged a trunk down the hillside toward a big wagon already half-loaded with timber. Horrified, Beran stared at them. It wouldn't take many wagons loaded like that to account for the damage to the road.

"That little girl would have something to say about this," Carl said.

"At Lady Eran's, Lord Adon said Kaven's uncle sold a lot of timber because he needed the money," Beran said. "Kaven didn't sound pleased about it either." More than once in the last few days, Beran had seen Kaven turn his face up toward leaves and birdsong with a smile of such happiness that Beran had been jealous. Poor as he was, Kaven plainly felt at home in a way Beran wasn't sure he felt anywhere anymore. The destruction of his manor would tear Kaven's heart out. Beran's horse danced as his hand tightened on the reins. The thieves had things to answer for beyond Ander's death.

Far up the hillside, a man straightened and used his hand to shade his eyes and study them. He spoke to the man next to him, who vanished into the trees.

Beran turned away, clucking to his horse. He and Carl followed the road until a lane branched off. They crossed a bridge over a mud-clogged and decidedly unsweet stream, and a short time later, rode through the sagging gate of Sweet Stream Manor. Beran handed his reins to the stable boy while eyeing the big cat stretched along the roof, a loose tile beneath its claw. According to Isadia, Sweet Stream's money troubles had surfaced only a year ago, after Kaven's grandfather died. The house looked solid enough, but all work seemed aimed at stripping the manor of its trees rather than doing the maintenance any household constantly needed.

He waited politely in the yard for someone to acknowledge his arrival. After a moment, a thin woman appeared in the doorway. "Fair day. Be welcomed and take shelter." She brushed a lock of dark hair off her forehead, and Beran had to smile at how much the gesture made her look like Kaven.

He bowed. "Fair day, lady. Beran of Rinland. Thank you for your welcome." He started toward the door with Carl at his side. "This is Carl, my…friend."

Carl smiled blandly and bowed. In any part of Rinland, including the Westreach, taking a guard into someone's house was insulting, but Carl had gone into every manor Beran had visited. Apparently, Carl meant to make up for whatever foolish trust he'd shown by letting Beran out of his sight at Lady Eran's.

The woman stepped aside and gestured them in. "I'm Teress, and I'm so glad to meet you. You're Kaven's roommate, aren't you? How is he?"

"He's well and a great help to Lady Isadia's management of her manor."

Her face brightened. "I don't see him often enough, but my brother-by-marriage says it's not safe for me to travel. Please sit while I send for ale." Teress waved Beran and Carl toward padded benches near the hearth and went out a side door.

The Hall was clean but missing the clutter of household life in a way that made Beran uneasy. No toys, no baskets of mending, no brightly dyed wool waiting to be woven or knitted. What's more, the furnishings were sliding into raggedness. The long bench cushion had been mended until there wasn't enough cloth to hold the new thread and feathers poked through a seam. Beran twisted his signet ring and tucked the signs of need into his head next to the painful picture of the ravished hillside. His father should know how at least this part of the Westreach fared under his rule. There were poor people everywhere, many much worse off than Kaven's family, but a king who was ignorant of their existence was asking for trouble.

Teress came back, followed by a servant with a tray of mugs. Carl shook his head, but Beran took a mug and stood waiting for Teress to sit so he could. Instead she held out a folded pair of blue wool stockings.

"For Kaven," she said. "Will you take them?"

"Of course." Once again, Beran felt a twinge of jealousy. He had no idea who knit his stockings. He tucked the gift into his pocket, and they all sat. He sipped the ale, schooling his face not to react to the sourness that showed the drink had been kept a day too long. "Lady Teress, I wanted to say how sorry I am that your steward was robbed. I know the king is concerned about the thieves preying on this area. Could I speak with your steward? Perhaps he can tell me something Magistrate Halid could use to find the robbers."

A step sounded in a side hallway, and a broad-shouldered, dark-haired man strode into the room. Beran recognized the man who'd watched him and Carl from the top of the barren hillside. Bits of bark clung to his wool trousers, and he smelled of sweat.

"Rickard." Teress smiled timidly. "We have company."

This was Kaven's uncle then, though his high cheekbones and blade of a nose shaped his face to look nothing like Kaven's.

Deep as a Tomb

"I saw them on the road," Rickard said. "One doesn't see too many young men with swords, so I guessed this was our boy prince." Rickard smiled and gave a shallow bow.

Not a kiss-up then. Rather the kind that liked to suggest Beran was too young to find the privy without help. Beran immediately forgave Kaven any jerk thing he'd ever done.

"Are you expecting us to attack you?" Rickard raised an eyebrow in Carl's direction. Given the Tower of Rinland on Carl's shirt and his general air of menace, his status as Beran's guard wasn't hard to guess. "Wait outside," Rickard told Carl.

"I'm sure I'd like to accommodate you, sir, but I answer only to King Thien." Carl inclined his head toward Beran. "Where he goes, I go." Beran was torn between wanting Carl to stop offending people and rejoicing that the one he offended here was Rickard.

"The prince was just asking about Delur's encounter with the thieves," Teress said in an obvious effort to smooth things. "Can we send for him?"

"I sent him out to hunt this morning after you complained we were short on meat." Still scowling, Rickard sat next to her. "Maybe I can answer your questions, Beran."

Teress's finger hovered over a bloody scratch on Rickard's hand. "What happened?"

"That fool Lanal somehow had a tree fall the wrong way. He wasn't hurt, but I barely got out of the way in time. So, Beran, can I help you?"

Beran stopped staring at what looked like a claw mark and set his mug on the table by his elbow, nudging aside a set of knucklebones. He pulled out the map he'd folded inside his jerkin and spread it in front of Rickard and Teress. "These marks show the thefts I know of. This one was your steward. How many thieves did Delur see?"

"Two, I think," Rickard said.

That was the number after Myla too. So the thief gang was small, though you didn't need many ruthless men to destroy the peace. "Did they take valuables or just money?"

"Money," Rickard said. "A lot of it. The loss hurt us."

That was what they'd taken elsewhere too, so Beran couldn't trace the thieves by finding where they'd sold jewels or other precious things. He'd have to stick with his plan to lure the thieves out after him. "I think I've recognized one of the thieves."

Next to him, Carl breathed hard enough to blow a loose feather off the bench.

"I'd heard that," Rickard said. "Where did you see him?"

"I'm not sure," Beran said. "I'm still trying to remember."

Rickard spread his arms along the top of the bench moving his scratched hand away from Teress's silent stare. She slid sideways, out from under his reach.

"Prince or no prince, you want to take care in accusing people," Rickard said.

Beran knew he was being drawn into a power struggle, but he didn't care. "I was surprised to see you've cut all the trees on that hillside. Kaven says Westreachers avoid that because it drives out animals and leaves the earth unanchored." There'd be no paw print blessing that hillside, Beran was willing to wager.

"I was lucky enough to sell a large amount of timber to Master Felur, who holds the contract to rebuild the docks in the city. Perhaps no one explained to you that the project requires a great deal of wood."

Beran gritted his teeth. He'd been at a council meeting where the dock project was discussed, but no one had mentioned where the wood would come from, and it hadn't occurred to him to ask. "The city needs the docks, but does the Forest really have to be stripped to build them?"

"My father-by-marriage never did that," Teress all but whispered.

"This is a more efficient path than my father took," Rickard said. "Weren't you listening, Teress? As Beran and I have just been discussing, Sweet Stream needs the money."

Teress wedged herself so far into her corner of the bench her elbows were forced into her lap. "I'm sure you know best."

Beran had a flash of insight about the worry he'd seen on Kaven's face. He picked up his ale, then thumped it down and rose. He needed to be on his way before he shoved the mug in Rickard's teeth. "We won't keep you from your work any longer, Lord Rickard. Thank you for your hospitality, Lady Teress."

"I hope you find the thieves," Teress said. "I want to visit Isadia. I haven't met Myla yet. Kaven says she's a real daughter of the Forest."

"Tell Kaven we hope to hear from him," Rickard said. "And tell him I'm looking after his mother." Rickard put his arm around Teress's thin shoulders. She hunched, curling herself away from his touch, and Rickard let her go. They all moved toward the door, but Rickard blocked Beran's way and let Carl go out first. He bent close to Beran's ear and nodded at Carl, who turned to watch them. "You need to control those working for you. Thien would tell you that, I'm sure, but he's not here, so you'll forgive my offer of fatherly advice to a boy left on his own."

Beran shouldered him aside and strode out the door. The idea of Rickard as his father made him ill, but even worse was the knowledge Rickard had known exactly where to stick the knife. *Thien isn't here. A boy left on his own.* Rickard had lived away from home and come back only when his own father was dying. Maybe it took a son whose company was unneeded to recognize another.

Outside, Beran gulped clean air against the ale curdling in his belly and the tension that had thrummed in that Hall. The stable boy still stood in the yard holding their horses, apparently anticipating a short visit. He offered them the reins. Beran and Carl rode out the gates, back past the treeless hillside, and off Sweet Stream Manor.

"What did you think of Rickard?" Beran asked.

Carl spat on the road.

"Me too," Beran said. "Do you think he hurts her?"

"She wasn't bruised. Not where it showed anyway."

Beran sparred with Carl almost every morning and had plenty of bruises where they didn't show, so he wasn't comforted. It must gnaw Kaven's guts to see his mother bullied as she'd been in that Hall. He slapped his reins against his thigh, then jumped at the sting. Today's trip had taught him nothing about the thieves, but he'd learned more than he wanted to know about his roommate, and hard as he wished, there was no way to unlearn it.

He wheeled his horse around. Carl followed him wordlessly as he led the way back to the manor house. He dismounted in the yard, flung his reins in Carl's direction, and strode toward the door without waiting for an invitation. He needed to confront Rickard before he thought again.

Fortunately for politeness's sake, Lady Teress met him in the doorway. She'd already tied an apron over her gown. "Beran! Did you forget something?"

"I need to talk to Rickard."

"He's gone back to work. Can I help you?"

Beran had been so intent on warning Rickard that he had to grope for an answer. "Come back with me to stay at Green Valley," he blurted.

Teress clutched the doorframe. "Leave Sweet Stream?"

"For a while. Kaven would be glad to see you, and my grandmother would welcome the company."

Her face flushed. "That's kind of you," she said so stiffly that he knew she'd read the pity in his face. "But I can't."

"Carl and I would—"

She held up a hand to stop his offer of protection. "Sweet Stream is Kaven's home and his heritage. I can't abandon it."

"But—"

"No. Thank you, but no. Tell Kaven I'm well." She backed away, closing the door in his face.

For a moment, he stared at the unyielding wood. All he could do was remount the horse whose reins Carl still held. They retraced their path.

"I thought you were trying to impress the manor lords," Carl said, "including Rickard."

Deep as a Tomb

"I'd like to *impress* my fist on Rickard's face," Beran said. They rode farther while he stewed in his own helplessness. Teress should have come with him. That set to her jaw reminded him of both Myla and his grandmother. "Westreach women are stubborn as rocks in a river," he finally snarled.

When Carl didn't answer, Beran glanced at him. Carl sat alert in his saddle, gazing straight ahead. Something metallic banged against rock—something that sounded like a pick applied to a road.

Carl leaned over and put a hand on Beran's rein. "Hush," he murmured and drew them both to a halt. He slid from his horse's back, motioning Beran to dismount too.

Beran's breath quickened. "It's the True, isn't it?"

"Probably." They led the horses into the trees, where Carl tied them to a branch. Leaves rustled overhead and crunched beneath their feet.

"We have to get closer," Beran said.

Carl looked toward the road and rubbed his hand over his hair. "I'd tell you to stay here while I make sure what's happening, but I can't leave you alone if there's more trouble than I think."

Beran's muscles trembled for action. He was making no progress catching Ander's killer, and today's visit had left him wanting to beat someone black and blue. He'd feel a lot better if he slapped a few of the True. "We can't just let this go on. I'm the king's representative here, and you can believe me when I say he wants the road wreckers stopped."

Carl thought for another moment, then sighed. "I suppose you deserve a reward."

"For what?"

Ignoring the question, Carl drew his sword and pointed at Beran's scabbard, so Beran drew his too. *Excellent! A fight.* They crept toward the noise and peered through a screen of hawthorns. Two men swung picks, neither one much older than Beran. They must not have been there long because one of them popped the first stone out just as Carl and Beran got there. A third man, maybe in his twenties, stood lookout, occasionally glancing at the diggers, but mostly scanning the road in both directions. There was no sign of horses, and none of them carried bows or swords. The older man and one of the younger ones wore wolf masks. The other young man had a cloth tied over the lower half of his face. Beran had a pretty good idea of whom it was who'd lost his wolf mask.

How could Myla be related to this fool?

"Hurry up," the older man said. "That weasel Rickard is going to send his wagon along any time now."

Pinching Beran's sleeve, Carl drew him a distance away. "I want the older one," Carl whispered. "He's the leader of this little gang anyway." He looked grimly pleased. "I'll wager Lord Corin could learn a lot just by knowing who he is and what family he's from. I suspect at least some of these pups' lords or fathers will be unhappy with them."

Beran could have told Carl which family one of the "pups" was from with no trouble at all, but for Myla's sake, he held his tongue. Besides, his brief meeting with Galen in the herb room had convinced him Myla's brother was not responsible enough to be let out on his own, so Beran didn't hold him to blame. He'd try to cut him off from Carl's wrath. The other two were fair game, though. He rocked on his feet, eager to move.

"You're about to learn an old scout's trick," Carl said. "We'll make enough noise to chase them off. We want them to split up, so don't go wild when it happens. Stay close to me. Understand?"

Beran nodded.

Carl hesitated, then shrugged. "Get more than three yards away from me, and I'll leave them and come after you."

"Just go!" He crept after Carl to a hiding place near the leader. Carl shot Beran one warning look, then raised his sword and erupted from the trees, screaming like a crazy man. Beran sprang after him shrieking and swinging his weapon. All his pent up fury roared out, making his blood rush hot through his body.

The three road wreckers spun to look. The wolf masks hid the eyes of the two wearing them, but Galen's were the size of hen's eggs. The diggers dropped their picks and bolted into the woods, the leader right behind them. Beran tore after them, still yelling. Within twenty yards, they scattered like rabbits.

Carl steered him in the direction the leader had taken. The man crashed through the woods ahead. Carl quieted his movements and stopped shouting, so Beran hushed.

"Keep shouting," Carl whispered.

Beran drew in a ragged breath and shouted some more while Carl ran silently at his side.

The leader's noisy passage fell silent. When Carl stopped and caught Beran's arm, Beran barely managed to halt his headlong rush. Carl leaned to speak in his ear. "He's gone to ground. He heard only you, so he thinks I went after the other two." He tightened his grip. "Now you're going to do exactly what I tell you and nothing else."

"I'm not staying here if that's what you're going to say."

Carl squeezed his arm hard enough to hurt. "Shut up and listen. You're going to go ahead."

Beran jerked his arm free. "What?"

"Go ahead. If you spot him, don't let on. Keep going. When you've gone three hundred paces, get out of sight and wait until I call you. Don't go after the others. Don't come back this way, even if you hear a commotion, unless ⸆ call. If he thinks the search has gone beyond him, he'll come out where I can find him."

"Once you have him, I should come back and help."

"Do that and I will make you very sorry." Carl jerked his head toward ⸯhere they'd last heard the man. "Go."

Beran gave in and started plowing through the underbrush, scanning right and left, doing his best to look like he was carrying out a thorough search. He even muttered a dramatic "Stone it. I've lost him." Once he got going, it was the most fun he'd had since he came to the Westreach. In the back of his head, he counted paces. When he hit three hundred, he looked around for a hiding place and found another inviting hawthorn thicket. He circled it, looking for a way in, and spotted broken branches that told him ⸯn animal had sought shelter here. If it could, so could Beran. He parted the branches and looked straight into the faces of the two younger road wreckers.

They'd pulled their masks down. Their gaping mouths showed below their panicked eyes. The one Beran didn't know scrambled deeper into their den, but Galen snapped his mouth shut and leaped toward Beran, one hand shoving at Beran's sword arm and the other at his chest. "Rot you! Rot you!" Galen gabbled.

Beran let himself be pushed. He didn't want to hurt Myla's brother, and even Carl wasn't after these two louts. He watched them vanish in the endless green. He hoped the noise they made didn't alert the leader. Beran wanted some result to show his father for this little excursion.

A twig snapped behind him. Before he could turn, something shoved him sideways into a bush full of sharp thorns that sliced at his neck and arm and clawed at his shoulder. A thorn stabbed his back right through his shirt. He couldn't stifle his shout of pain. Arms flailing, he fought his way free, scooped up his dropped sword, and spun to see who'd pushed him. No one was in sight. He staggered a dozen yards or so before heat flushed from his chest to his head. He swayed and blinked. As the undergrowth melted into a smear of green and brown, he thudded to his knees, sword sliding from his boneless fingers. The world swirled away into the dark.

Carl's voice summoned him. "Are you all right? Answer me, Balar!"

Beran opened his eyes. Carl's face circled overhead, like a puppet swung on a string. His voice was rising. If this Balar person didn't answer soon, Carl was going to spit fire.

The world went black again.

Chapter 12

Myla followed Kaven through the trees on the east side of Sweet Stream Manor. Somewhere nearby, water sang over rocks. The shady air glowed pale green and smelled of pine.

Kaven looked over his shoulder. "That plant's close by, but I have something else to show you first." He gestured to where a tangle of branches blocked their way.

Myla skimmed forward to see that a huge evergreen had fallen over, probably during one of the spring storms. "Too bad."

"Yes, but I thought you'd be interested in what was in the topmost branches." He led her around them, pointing here and there at the ferns and lichen that had been growing in the tree.

Myla inhaled sharply and wiggled between branches to examine a frilly plant she'd never seen before. The hairy one on the next branch was new to her too. She pried pieces loose and stored them in her bag. "These are wonderful!" She emerged from the thicket.

"You're the one who sees that best," Kaven said.

Her face grew warm under his admiring smile. Other body parts too, so she looked aside, afraid to seem she was promising too much with Da's plans hanging over her head. She swept her gaze through the treetops. "Do you suppose there are more wonders hidden up there?"

"Probably," he said. "The Forest provides."

If she could climb, she'd know. Her mouth went dry at the thought. She'd been terrified of heights since the day she found the books in the Oak Ridge attic.

Somewhere not far off, an axe bit into a tree. Smile gone, Kaven jerked his gaze toward the sound, then strode urgently in that direction. Myla trotted to keep up.

"Rot them," he murmured.

She peered around him and gasped. They stood at the top of a rise. Farther down, every tree had been cut, turning the hillside into a ruined waste. At the hill's bottom lay the king's road, a wagon loaded with tree trunks waiting at its side. Apparently not yet satisfied with the destruction they'd worked, men were cutting more trees.

"Stop it!" Myla charged past Kaven, but he grabbed her arm and pulled her back.

"Come on." He tugged her aside with him. "That plant you want is this way."

"We can't leave this!"

"We have to. My uncle owns the manor, and he's sold the trees." Face grim, Kaven towed her away from the hillside and into a dense ash grove. He pointed to a purple-leaved plant, growing low to the ground in the shade. "Is that it?"

He was trying to distract her, but she crouched to look. This was indeed the plant she hadn't recognized in the old book. She tugged on the gloves from her bag and cut some sprigs with the knife she used in the herb room. She could still hear the thud of the axes.

"Kaven, you have to stop them."

"I can't. I tried the last time I was home, and my uncle made it quite clear who was in charge." Kaven snatched up a fallen branch and threw it in the direction of the hillside.

Blinking away frustrated tears, she harvested more of the plant. Maybe she should take all her bag would hold. This plant grew in shade and was rare even then. If men with axes came here, the plant would have nowhere to live.

"Why didn't you tell me?" she choked out.

"What good would it have done? You can't stop it any more than I can."

Maybe. But Kaven wasn't the only one keeping secrets, and maybe she could stop all the destructive lumbering if she took the circlet and let Da declare her chieftain so they could bargain with Thien. She asked herself yet again if she should tell Kaven about Da's planned treason. Did she have the right to tangle Kaven in that web?

"Fair day, Kaven," a strange voice said.

Myla sprang erect. A heavy-set, dark-haired man stood only a few yards away, tapping a bow against one leg. He slid his gaze from Kaven to her, but when she tentatively smiled, he acted as if he couldn't see her doing it. "This must be Myla of Oak Ridge," the stranger said.

Kaven's face had gone still. "Myla," he said woodenly, "this is Delur, Sweet Stream's steward." He put his arm around her waist and drew her closer. Delur had done nothing threatening, but pressed against Kaven's side like this, she felt his heart galloping.

"Prince Beran is at Sweet Stream," Delur said, pleasantly enough. "Did you send him, Kaven?"

"Of course not," Kaven said.

"He's looking for the thief who killed his guard," Myla said.

Kaven's arm squeezed her to silence.

Delur frowned at her, then shifted his glare to Kaven. "At Sweet Stream?"

"Everywhere." Kaven met the man's gaze steadily. "He's decided Corin's men aren't doing enough."

"Interfering little stoner." Delur pursed his lips. "Your ma was hoping you'd visit, and I know Rickard has been watching for you."

"How is my mother?" Kaven's voice was strained.

"She's good right now. Don't know how long that will last."

"Is your mother ill, Kaven? You should have told me. Maybe I can help." Myla knew Sweet Stream Manor had money problems and had guessed

Kaven was embarrassed to take her home, which was why she hadn't met his family yet. Now she thought he might have wanted to keep her from seeing how his Uncle Rickard treated the Forest.

"Lady Teress is one of those frail ladies," Delur said. "Not really sick."

"You're Rinnish, aren't you?" Myla placed the man's accent, rougher than Beran's, but from the same neighborhood, assuming an alehouse and a castle counted as neighbors in the city.

"I am. I met Lord Rickard when he was travelling in the Vale. Came back here with him to help sort things out at his manor." Delur's teeth flashed in a smile.

Myla suddenly saw what must have happened at Sweet Stream, and her nervousness gave way under returning fury. This grasslander must have decided to ravish the Forest and cut all those trees. This outsider was to blame. He and the road that let him profit from his desecration. Da was right. King Thien and his like were working the Forest's ruin. That must be why Kaven disliked Delur.

But wait. Kaven's uncle was in charge at Sweet Stream. He'd apparently made that clear to Kaven. So maybe the blame ran wider.

"Do you hear that?" Kaven frowned toward the west.

Men's shouts, Myla realized. Growing closer. "Isn't that Beran?"

"Wait here." Kaven bolted in the direction of the sound, leaf litter swirling beneath his feet.

Myla ignored the command and ran too, her herb bag bumping on her hip. Beran's shouts stopped, but now she heard Carl's voice. She struggled after Kaven to find Carl crouching over a collapsed Beran, shaking his shoulders.

"Talk to me, Balar!" Carl cried.

"What happened?" Kaven asked.

"We were chasing some True." Carl lifted Beran to show a small, bloody-edged hole in the back of his jerkin. "They stabbed him."

Myla choked. Galen must have come looking for his mask at Isadia's because he and his lunatic friends planned to dig up a road today. The Forest help Galen if he'd stabbed Beran. Ander's death had been bad enough, but an attack on Thien's son would bring the king down on the culprit like a lightning bolt.

When Carl gathered Beran in his arms and rose, Beran's head lolled back, revealing scratches swelling on the side of his neck.

"Wait!" She put out one still-gloved hand and touched a scratch. "Kaven!" She whirled toward him. "Look for redthorn." She'd have sent Delur too, but he hadn't followed them.

"I'm taking him to Lady Isadia's. Bring his sword." Carl strode off with his burden, presumably toward where their horses waited.

Myla grabbed for the weapon, then had to grab again when the weight of it drew it through her fingers. She hurried after Kaven, who was following a trail of broken twigs and scuffed leaves. When he halted, she ran to his side and looked where he was staring. The red-twigged bush bristled with long, poison-laden thorns. A branch in the middle was crushed as if someone had fallen on it.

"The Forest save us," Myla breathed. "He has redthorn poisoning."

Three mornings later, Myla entered Beran's room and greeted Lady Isadia, who looked as if she'd again spent the night on the stool by Beran's bed. One glance at Beran weeded out the hope Myla should have known not to trust. Her hand tightened around the cup of willow bark tea. He had grown much worse overnight. He lay on his side, still as a stump, the purple shadows under his eyes the only color in his face.

When Isadia lifted his shoulders from the bed, the blanket slid to his waist, revealing his bare torso, wrapped in a bandage. It had been only three days, but the fever had already burned him thinner so his ribs showed, rippling down his side like a set of pipes. He looked like a stranger, both because of the fever damage and because he was exposed and vulnerable in a way she'd never seen before.

Isadia shook him. "Wake up, my heart."

Beran moaned, and Myla put the cup to his sagging mouth and trickled tea. He coughed and swallowed.

"Give him more," Isadia said.

Myla tried, but Beran was gone again, lost inside his own fevered head, and no amount of calling and shaking roused him. She set the cup on the table. She'd been dribbling willow bark tea into Beran for three days now, and it was keeping him alive, but only just, because it never touched the poison causing the fever, the poison that was killing him. He was weakening and harder to wake each day, so he was taking less and less even of the willow bark. She turned toward the open window, where the forest showed above the manor wall. Out there, birds sang and green life ran riot. In this room, a boy was dying.

A boy she'd finally decided she liked for his loyalty and courage in going after those who'd hurt someone he loved.

And not just any boy. The king of Rinland's only son. It didn't do to forget his role, though it made her sad to think the prince might be valued more than the boy.

While Isadia untied the bandage, Myla fetched the basin of warm water from the stand. They rolled Beran to his stomach, and Myla washed the wound on his back. The flesh around it had swelled so Myla couldn't see it, and the swelling must have been sore because Beran moaned when she touched it. After she finished, she and Isadia passed bandaging back and forth, wrapping him again.

"I don't understand it." Isadia, too, was pale, her eyes shadowed by sleeplessness. "Why would the True attack him?"

"I think it was an accident." At least, Myla hoped so. Surely Galen wouldn't have done this on purpose. "I think he just fell into the redthorn. He doesn't know enough to be careful of it." She tied the bandage off.

Isadia brushed her hand over an angry scratch on Beran's neck. "Thien intends to send him off to train with his troops next spring. I can hardly bear the thought of it."

Judging by Beran's still figure, Myla thought King Thien's plans were likely to go the way many plans did in the face of life's sad truths. A voice in her head whispered *What about your father's plans?*

"Call me if you need me," Myla said. "I'll be in the herb room."

Isadia settled onto the stool next to the bed, her hand covering her grandson's. She looked old, Myla thought for the first time, like all the things that mattered had flown into the past, so there was nothing to hope or plan for. Myla made her way out of the house and crossed the yard to the herb room, only to find Carl waiting, hunched on a stool in the green-scented room.

"How is he?" Carl rose and swayed, reeking of ale. He batted away a clump of drying boneset, dangling low enough from over head that it slapped his face.

"A little better," she lied. Carl had been drunk every time she'd seen him in the last three days.

He snorted. "Stoning forest. In the name of all the Powers, what's Thien thinking to send his boy here? What kind of father lets his son go someplace so dangerous?" He staggered out the door, still mumbling to himself.

Myla sank onto the stool, rubbing her temples. She shared Carl's doubts about Thien's care for his son. She'd seen Beran struggling to do what his father wanted, to gain his approval, maybe even his love. She knew what that felt like. Surely there was something more she could do for him. She reached for the book she'd left open to the purple plant Kaven had showed her at Sweet Stream. It called the plant feverbreak, so maybe she could use it along with, or instead of, the willow bark to fight the heat burning through Beran's body. But the book gave no hint of how to turn the plant into medicine, and without that, she was frightened to try it. Medicine and poison were sometimes top and bottom of the same leaf.

She swiveled to look out the door. From here, she saw only the yard and house on its other side, but she could hear the murmur of leaves. Carl was right that the Forest had been hard on Beran. Myla didn't blame the Forest for Ander's death, because men of no conscience were everywhere. But only the Forest had the True, and redthorn, and Silvit. The notion of Silvit worried her every time she saw the scratches on Beran's neck looking far too much like claw marks. At Lady Eran's, she'd set that fearsome force on Beran. Maybe Silvit still saw him as a threat, which meant Beran's hurt was her fault, not Galen's.

She went to the shelf by the door, shifted a row of jars, and pulled out the knife she'd taken from Lady Eran's tomb and then moved here after Beran searched her room. She slid it into her herb bag and set off for the stable. When she walked in, she found Kaven saddling his white-stockinged gelding. He paused, one hand on the pony's neck. She hadn't spoken to him alone since they'd scrambled home from Sweet Stream Manor. He'd cleared out of the room he shared with Beran, and she wasn't sure where he was sleeping.

"How's Beran?" Kaven asked.

"Not good."

"I'm sorry. I hate to admit it, but I miss working with him." He glanced at the bag on her shoulder. "You going somewhere?"

"Steeprise Manor."

"You're taking a guard, right?"

His concern was the first good thing she'd met this morning. "Can you go with me? Are you too busy?"

"Nothing that can't wait." He tightened the cinch under his pony's belly, then set off to ready her mare. Myla followed, watching with pleasure as he efficiently handled the tack. Forest ponies were notoriously bad-tempered, but every one Kaven went near seemed easy with him. "Is Eran sick again?" he asked, fitting the bit into the mare's mouth.

"I don't know. In truth, I'm not going to see her at all," she said. When Kaven raised an eyebrow, she clutched the strap of the bag hiding the knife and went on. "I accidentally took something from her tomb. I need to put it back."

He sucked in his breath, and for a moment, his hands stilled. Then he returned to his task.

"I know you're shocked," Myla said quickly. "I'm shocked at myself. Taking something from a tomb! The Forest only knows what damage I did. I didn't mean to."

Deep as a Tomb

"You don't have to convince me," Kaven said, his back to her so his voice was muffled. "I know you too well. You'd spit on a tomb robber." He led her pony out of the stall and linked his fingers to help her mount.

Chapter 13

Worried about leaving Beran untended, Myla set an urgent pace to Steeprise Manor, with Kaven a comforting presence at her side. She skirted Eran's house and dismounted at the spot where the road came closest to the tomb.

"So have you figured out what lets you open tombs?" Kaven asked, unstrapping his bow from his saddle.

"I just do what everyone is supposed to." Myla led him into the woods. "I touch the door and say that manor's prayer."

"There's nothing else? Think, Myla."

"I have thought," she said sharply. "I'm not that stupid."

"Of course you're not. Far from it." He held a lilac aside for her, shrugging as if trying to loosen his shirt. Myla couldn't help noticing it had grown too small for the muscles across his chest and arms. Not that she minded noticing. "It's just that more trees are sickening," Kaven said, "especially on the manors where the tombs are sealed. A lot of folks would be grateful if they could open them and at least leave an offering for Silvit's help."

Da wouldn't. Galen was right when he said Da much preferred that Myla be the only one who could open the tombs. Or really, he probably preferred himself or even Galen, but in a pinch, he'd take Myla. If everyone could do it, his plans would be ruined, which would free Myla from the need to marry Zale. So Kaven didn't have to urge her to think. She'd thought as much as a body could.

116

Deep as a Tomb

Ahead, the trees thinned, and Myla's skin and blood warmed at the nearness of a tomb. She took Kaven's work-callused hand, and together they walked in a hush along the mossy mound until they reached the doorway.

"I'll watch you," Kaven said. "Maybe I can see what you're doing."

She dropped his hand, put her palms on the door, and took a moment to root herself. Then she read the words around the door aloud so Kaven could hear. The door slid open at once, as if the tomb knew the touch and taste and smell of her now.

"The Forest bless us," Kaven murmured.

She stooped to wedge the door open, then stepped far enough inside that the fire lines flared. As Kaven came close behind, she felt a rush of gratitude because, like the wild thing Silvit was, like the Forest he embodied, the cat didn't always forgive people's weakness. At the foot of the steps, she saw the dust on the coffins was smeared where she'd taken the knife. She drew it from her bag and put it back where some long-ago mourner had left it. Then she turned to the altar and drew out a cat cake. *Silvit,* she thought as she put the cake on the altar, *if you're hunting Beran for my sake, you can stop.*

The scuff of Kaven's footsteps made her glance his way. He was circling the coffins, wide-eyed, open-mouthed. Of course he was. The place would make any Forest dweller's heart lift to the treetops.

"Is that gold?" He pointed to a cup she hadn't noticed on her first visit.

"I don't know. Does it matter?"

He glanced up at her, then looked aside. "Not to you." He rubbed his jaw. "I can't see how you're opening the tomb. I just can't work it out."

He sounded genuinely dismayed, and it occurred to her that he might be talking about the good she could do not just for other families, but for his own. If he could open the Sweet Stream tomb, he could claim the manor and save it from his uncle. Then he could live there, and in some future that was quietly trying to root itself in her head, maybe she could too. It would tear her heart out—and Kaven's too—to live there under Rickard's management, but where else could they go? Kaven's manor was his place in the world.

"We should go. I told Isadia I'd be in the herb room." She hurried up the steps and out the door, which slid shut behind them quickly enough to skim

117

Kaven's backside. He jumped, looking so startled that Myla laughed, and after a moment, he joined in. The day suddenly felt brighter. She'd returned the knife, and there were still things to laugh about. Grinning, she turned to go, but Kaven caught her arm.

"Wait. I've hardly seen you these last few days, and I missed you." He cleared his throat, and something about his manner made her heart quicken. "I have to tell you something. I know it won't be easy for you and me to be together, but no matter what happens, Myla, remember forever that I love you."

The breath whooshed from her body, squeezed out by joy that left no room for anything else. When Kaven bent to kiss her, she had to stop him because she had to have air or she'd fall. But the stopping didn't go on for long, and the kiss finally did. The heat and strength of him left her weak-kneed. She pressed his shoulders away.

"I love you, Kaven of Sweet Stream Manor," she said. They were the most amazing words she'd ever spoken. At the moment, even a future living at Sweet Stream under Rickard rule didn't seem too terrible. "But we do have to go."

"I know." He lowered his mouth to hers.

Silvit, she thought dizzily, *if this is because I returned that knife, you are a mighty generous giver of rewards.*

When they did ride for home, they rode too quickly for talk because they'd been gone entirely too long. Myla teetered between happiness when she thought of Kaven and worry when she thought of Beran. Kaven was quiet too, his brow puckered and his gaze straight ahead. At Lady Isadia's, he dismounted and reached for her reins.

"I'll take care of your pony. Go inside, and see how Beran is doing."

She hurried down the hallway to Beran's room. Through the half open doorway, she saw Isadia standing with her hands braced on the table by the window, looking out at the Forest. She turned at the sound of Myla's entrance, and Myla drew a sharp breath. Isadia's eyes were red and her cheeks tear-stained.

Myla dashed to Beran's bedside. He lay on his side, mouth sagging. Just as she reached him, he rasped in a breath. She collapsed on the stool. "I thought—"

"Not yet," Isadia said, "but he's worse." She came to stand next to Myla and gaze down at her grandson.

Silvit save us, Myla thought. What would King Thien do when he heard Beran was killed in an encounter with the True? She had to do something. Something for Beran, but something for her own land and people too.

Late the next morning, Myla slid from her pony in the yard of Oak Ridge Manor. She'd waited to set out until Kaven left for the work he'd meant to do the day before. On the previous night, even when they sat in the Hall with their hands clasped and their hips touching, she hadn't told him about Da's treasonous plans. Kaven had enough problems with his own family.

"I hope I won't be long," she told Allain, who'd guarded her on her way. Instead of going through the house, she circled it to get to the herb room at the back. Pigeons cooed at her from the dovecote, but the goats and geese had been herded out to forage, so at least their noise wouldn't tell Da someone was there. As she rounded the corner of the house, the person she least wanted to see was crossing from the stable to the back door. Galen stopped short at the sight of her. "What happened?" she demanded.

"What do you mean?"

"Don't fool with me, Galen. What happened with Beran?"

Galen looked around, then stepped close and lowered his voice to a whisper. "He saw me and Manther with our masks off. I panicked and shoved him, and then we ran. Did he know it was us?"

"I don't know," she said. "He fell into a redthorn bush."

"No!" For an instant he put his hands over his eyes. "Is he dead?"

"Not if I can help it," Myla said grimly. "Get out of my way." She pushed past him and went into the herb room, half expecting him to follow. After a moment, though, his footsteps pattered off. She reached for the first book on the shelf and undid its strap. She couldn't blame Galen for being afraid. She was afraid, and she wasn't the one who'd shoved the king's son into a poisoned bush. She'd set Silvit to help with the shove though, she reminded herself, or maybe even do it alone. She might have called the cat off now, but that didn't change what had already happened.

She skimmed through her books, searching for anything on the purple feverbreak plant or something else that might help against redthorn poisoning. She was all the way to the last book when she found a small picture of feverbreak. She bent over it. The words said something about making a paste.

"Your horse has been in the yard for two hours, and you haven't had the respect to come into the house?" Da stood in the doorway, head tilted back, looking down his nose, and giving off a whiff of the solution he used to kill his butterflies without marring them. She tried to remember if he'd ever come to the herb room before. Come to think of it, had he ever searched her out anywhere rather than sending for her? He stepped into the room. "I don't expect to wait when I've told you to do something, Myla. Where's the circlet?"

She rested her hand on the book. "I haven't looked for it yet."

"Why not?"

"Beran has redthorn poisoning. I've been trying to save him."

Da's lips parted, but nothing came out. He wiped his hand down his face. "Redthorn poisoning. He's a fool in the Forest. I wonder what will happen when he dies?" His eyes roamed the room, as if searching for the future. "Thien will have no natural heir, which will make all kinds of problems. Maybe he'll be distracted enough to ignore us."

"He won't ignore us. He'll want vengeance if only because he has to scare off his enemies. But Beran's not going to die if I can help it." Myla stroked the page she'd been studying, the parchment smooth beneath her fingers.

"His death is the Forest's way of cleansing itself. Don't interfere."

"I can't let him die! It'd be a betrayal of what the Forest provides." Before Da could speak, she rushed on. "I know Thien doesn't do right by the Forest, but there has to be a better way to fix that than starting a war. You don't need soldiers, so I don't need to marry Zale." Too late, she remembered she wasn't supposed to know about marrying Zale, but Da didn't seem to notice.

He charged forward, stopping only when he bumped into the table. "You'll do as I say."

Her hands tightened on the book. "I won't."

His eyes flicked down and up again. "If you don't, I'll burn every book on this manor."

For a moment, she couldn't speak. She thought of the books' knowledge lost—of children and old folks dying of things she could have healed, of mothers and fathers mourning lost babies, of hearty men cut down in their prime. She slid the book toward herself until its edge dug into her belly. "I won't let him die."

He stared at her, and she fought to keep her gaze steady. He must have seen she meant it because at last, he said, "All right. You can go ahead and play healer. But in exchange, I expect you to cooperate on the rest of it, starting with the circlet." He reached across the table and jerked the book from her grasp. "You have a fortnight to get it. I think that's more than generous. If you don't, I'll start burning books."

His eyes pinned her. She hadn't a wisp of doubt he'd do what he threatened, and all this knowledge would be gone. Galen was right that Da could force the marriage to Zale too, though he'd have trouble doing it as long as she was Isadia's fosterling.

"I'll get you the circlet." She flinched away from the betrayal of Isadia's trust, but by itself, having the circlet wouldn't do Da much good.

"And marry Zale."

"Da, please!"

"Marry Zale. Say it, Myla, or every book in here will be ashes by sunset."

Her mind raced. If she could just buy some time to think of a way around him. "If it's best for the Forest—"

"I tell you, it is."

"If it is, I'll marry Zale." She nearly strangled on the words. Oh, Silvit. What had she just promised? *Only the circlet*, she told herself fiercely, because it couldn't be best for Forest to do the rest. She reached for the book he'd taken, the one with the feverbreak picture.

He pulled it away so her fingers just grazed the page. "No. These books belong to Oak Ridge. I won't allow you to take them."

"You said I could help Beran."

"If you can do it, go ahead." He slapped the book shut and left without bidding her farewell.

She staggered to where Allain waited. His brow crinkled when he saw her face, but he said nothing, and they rode back to Isadia's, where he took the ponies and she retreated to the herb room, eager to be alone. She crossed the doorsill to find Kaven perched on the stool. He must have recognized her step because he was already smiling and setting aside the twist of wire he was using to reattach the pot handle that had come loose the day before.

His smile faded when he saw her. "What's wrong?" He rose.

Her gut filled with panic. She couldn't drag Kaven into Da's treason, and she couldn't tell him about Zale, not until she'd figured a way other than Da's to save both her books and the Forest. But she couldn't keep kissing him either, because someone would see, and word would get back to Da for sure.

"Myla?" He moved close enough for her to smell the faint scent of pine on the needles clinging to his hair. "The stable master said you rode off somewhere. Why didn't you wait for me?"

She slid away. "I've been thinking about what I said yesterday at Steeprise."

"About what?"

"About love." She looked at her shelf of books so she wouldn't have to see his face. "I shouldn't have said that. Not yet anyway." From the corner of her eye, she saw his hands fall to his sides.

"Why not?" His voice shook.

"Because I need some time."

"Time for what?"

"Time to be sure. And I can't talk about this now, Kaven. I have to take care of Beran."

For a long moment, the only sound was the music of rustling leaves and birdsong.

"Fine." Kaven bit off the word.

She spun toward him and found him striding out the door. Her vision blurred. *Stop it*, she told herself. *You did the right thing.* With shaking hands, she pushed aside the pot he'd been fixing and opened the box where she'd stored the feverbreak. On the way home, she'd tried to coax up every detail of what the book had said about using the leaves. It said boil the water, right? But should she wait until it cooled to add crushed leaves or add them at once? And it had said remove the stems, hadn't it? She'd seen the book for such a short time. She filled her head with how to use feverbreak so she could crowd out everything else Da wanted, the chance of war, the loss of Kaven.

The pageboy came to fetch her for supper, but she sent him away with an excuse. Night had crept into the yard, and she crossed through flickering torchlight to take the bowl of green paste to Beran's room. One of Isadia's women, Sendra, sat with Beran, which meant Isadia was still at supper. Good. No point in planting what were probably false hopes.

With Sendra's help, Myla unwrapped the bandage around Beran's chest and laid him on his stomach. Sendra sniffed at the piercing scent of the paste, then watched while Myla spread it gently along Beran's back and the scratches on his neck, the stuff oily beneath her fingers. She set the bowl on the table and wiped her hands on the cloth. "I'll stay," she told Sendra.

"Bless the Forest and you, Myla," Sendra said, and took her leave.

A short while later, Isadia came in, so Sendra must have told her about the paste. Isadia examined the green smear on Beran's back, then looked up at Myla, hope in her eyes. "Will it help?"

"We'll have to wait and see. You look so tired. Why don't you sleep for a while?"

Myla had meant for Isadia to go to her own room, but she lay down on Kaven's bed. "I'll just rest a bit," Isadia murmured as her eyes drifted shut.

Myla sat in the light of a single candle, listening to Isadia's deep breathing and Beran's broken gasps. Her own chest squeezed too tightly around her heart for any kind of breath. There had to be a better path for the Forest's future than the one Da had planned, but what? If she couldn't see it, then she'd traded her happiness and the Forest's peace for a chance to save her books and Beran's life. She hoped the trade was good because the thought of the price she'd pay left her empty.

Through the open window, she watched a half moon slide up over the treetops. When it was all the way up, she went to spread more paste and found a dark, sour fluid seeping from Beran's wounds. Was that good or bad? She blotted the stinking stuff away, and when she turned to reach for the paste, Isadia lifted her head.

Isadia rose and took the bowl from Myla's hand. "Let me take care of him for a while. You rest." When Myla hesitated, Isadia said, "He's my daughter's only child, Myla."

Myla gave in and retreated to the bed. Under Isadia's violet scent, the pillow smelled faintly of Kaven. The next thing she knew, pale light had thrown a leg over the windowsill. Isadia slumped by Beran's bed, asleep with her head on his pillow. Myla struggled to her feet and lurched to Beran's side. More fluid puddled in the valley of his spine. When she reached to mop it, her hand brushed his skin. Sweat filmed his back, his shoulders, what she could see of his face. The sheet was soaked in it. And he was cool to the touch.

Isadia stirred and sat up. "How is he?"

"Better." Slowly, Myla smiled. "The Forest provides. I think he's going to be all right."

But what about me? said a voice in her head. *Am I going to be all right? Is the Forest?*

Chapter 14

Beran rolled onto his back, pleased his wound barely hurt when he edged onto it. He stared at his bedroom ceiling. At least the view was different. Maybe he wouldn't go mad from boredom for at least another hour. He tapped his signet ring against the wall, rapping out a song whose words repeated endlessly. Stuck in bed, how was he going to find Ander's killer? How was he going to impress Westreach manor owners? How was he going to avoid hurting the next person who walked freely out of his room, leaving him behind?

The shutter crashed against the wall, and Myla climbed in through the window.

Ah. Much better. "There's a door, you know," Beran said.

"Now that you're not unconscious any more, some people think I shouldn't be alone in here with you, especially with the door shut."

Beran could believe that. His grandmother allowed Myla to do more or less as she liked, but even Isadia might draw the line at that closed door. And Kaven would wait just long enough for Beran to get up before punching him flat again.

"How are you?" Myla dragged the stool next to the bed. She smelled of rosemary and sun-warmed skin.

"Fine. I'd be even better if I got up. Exercise is very healing, they say."

"Your grandmother will decide when you get out of that bed, and the poor, deluded woman thinks you're precious and fragile, so I wouldn't count on it happening soon." Myla leaned forward, the way his father's chief advisor did when he was getting down to business. "Beran, could you get your father to stop buying so many Forest trees?"

The question was so ridiculous he laughed. "Of course not. He needs the wood."

"But if too many trees are cut, plants will disappear too, including the one I used on you. If you told him that, wouldn't he change his mind?"

Beran was pretty sure he knew the answer, and he didn't want to share it with Myla. "Look. I know this matters to you especially because of what Rickard is doing at Sweet Stream—"

"It would matter anyway. Can't you at least get him to say manor holders shouldn't abuse the land?"

"He won't do that. He leaves Corin to rule because of how touchy you Westreachers are about him interfering." When she opened her mouth, he kept talking. "Tell me about the True."

That stopped her. "What do you mean?"

"I mean I know how I was hurt, and I bet you do too. I saw a pair of them without their masks, one being your brother. They ran, and I thought they were gone, but someone shoved me into that bush, so they must have circled around behind me."

Some of the tension in her shoulders eased. "They got away? Then it wasn't Galen who pushed you."

"Someone did."

"He'd never come back once he ran."

Beran chewed on that. Myla knew her brother better than he did, and even to Beran, it sounded plausible that Galen would keep running.

"Beran," Myla said hesitantly, "the scratches on your neck make me wonder if Silvit pushed you."

"Why would he do that?" Sweet Powers. He was talking like he believed in the great cat. But he'd seen the paw print in the copse. Maybe he did believe a little.

Myla squirmed on the stool. "Maybe Silvit thought you were threatening Forest folks. Someone could have sicced him on you, accidentally maybe."

"Oh right." He didn't believe that much.

She let it go, almost as if relieved. "What are you going to do?"

Did he want to accuse Galen of shoving him? To his regret, he felt unexpectedly sorry for the hapless fool. "I'd be willing to be merciful if Galen convinced his friends to leave the roads alone."

"He might be stubborn about the roads. Also, I don't know how much influence he has on the other True."

The door banged open, and Kaven strode into the room.

Beran silently cursed the interruption. He was so close to nabbing these Westreach equivalents of street vandals, so close to doing at least one thing that would please his father.

Kaven looked from him to Myla and back again. "What are you doing in here with him?"

Cheeks flushing red, Myla stood. "I'm checking on how he feels."

She was wearing trousers again today. Good for climbing through windows, Beran supposed, and good for showing how round her backside was.

Kaven picked up the jacket he wore in the evenings when the house grew cool, and as he shrugged into it, he shot Beran a dagger-tipped look. "I can tell you how he feels."

Beran hastily redirected his eyes to the ceiling.

"None of this is your business, Kaven," Myla said.

Beran snapped his gaze toward them, taking in her rigid spine and Kaven's glare. Kaven and Myla were quarreling? No wonder Kaven had been grouchy when he moved back into their room. Beran had tried to sympathize because of what he'd seen of Kaven's mother, but his shallow pool of patience was nearly dry.

"Is he the reason you backed away?" Kaven jerked his head in Beran's direction.

"Of course not."

Beran found Myla's tone a little insulting, but insult beat having Kaven strangle him in his sleep. Kaven opened and closed his oversized hands. Beran couldn't help feeling sorry for him. Girls wreaked havoc not just with your body, but also with your head and your heart.

"Fair evening." Isadia stood in the doorway, regarding the tense pair in the middle of the room.

The air quivered with what Beran felt had to be suspicious fosterling silence. Kaven mumbled a response and slipped past Isadia.

"Myla, dear, you shouldn't be in here." Isadia came all the way into the room.

"Sorry," Myla said. "I wanted to see how Beran was doing." Beran half expected her to leave the way she'd come, but instead she went out the door.

"How do you feel, Beran?" His grandmother seated herself on the stool.

"I'm fine. I should get up."

"Are you hungry?" She was almost as good as his father at ignoring what Beran said. It was irritating, but for some reason not nearly as enraging.

"Starving," he admitted. He'd emerged from his fiery nightmare with what felt like a permanent hollow in his middle.

"Your supper will be here soon." She smiled. "We may have to hold a Thread Feast if we want to satisfy you though. We can ask the neighbors to bring food."

"What's a Thread Feast?"

"A Forest custom. Neighbors meet after one of them has suffered a misfortune. They bring small gifts and celebrate the thread that holds them together so they help one another survive."

Beran blinked and saw opportunity dancing behind his grandmother's back. In his present shape, he couldn't go around ferreting out information about the thieves, but if everyone came to Green Valley Manor, he barely had to leave his bed to get what he wanted.

"A Thread Feast is an excellent idea. My father wants me to meet manor owners, and being bedridden has left me with less than a month to finish doing that."

His grandmother tapped a finger against her knee. "That's true. It would be good for you to meet them all and good for them to see you here as future lord of this manor."

Beran marked the rare moment when his grandmother and father agreed. More or less. Not the part about ruling this manor, of course. Which was fine because what mattered most was that he and the neighbors could talk about the robberies and maybe find a pattern to them. They could agree on a way to keep watch for the thieves. Maybe they could even lay a trap that at last would close around the stoner who had murdered Ander. Best not to talk about that too much to his grandmother, though. If she thought he was doing something dangerous, she might decide the feast was a bad idea.

His grandmother rose to take her leave. "I'll send out the invitations at once."

He grabbed her hand. "Seriously, Grandmother, if I'm not allowed up, I'm afraid I'll do something we'll all regret."

"What you mean is that you'll get up anyway. Don't bother denying it." She freed herself from his grip and studied him while he tried to look vigorous. "You can get up tomorrow."

"Thank you," he said fervently.

She patted his hand. "You frightened me. Losing you would be more than I could bear."

After the door shut behind her, he lay for a while planning what he would say at the feast. The lords' stubborn independence would make it difficult ') steer them all the same way, but he'd seen his father accomplish the same sort of thing at council meetings. He'd have to be subtle, though, because they'd resent any interference in their right to enforce local laws. If any hint he was doing that got back to Lord Corin, it would hurt Beran's chances of being named King's Heir, and his father would be frantic over the future of ninland, and maybe even the future of his son. Not that Beran was bitter.

Of course, if he wasn't named King's Heir, he could always come back to Green Valley. Isadia's people seemed to like him, and they talked fondly of his mother. He could stay here and be useful.

He pushed temptation aside. If he managed the Thread Feast well, he'd be a long way toward catching Ander's killer.

The next morning, Kaven slammed around the room, grumbling about how much work the Thread Feast was causing. Beran tottered repeatedly out of his way, but managed to pick up that guests from any distance would spend the night so they didn't have to make the long ride home after dark. The amount of work Kaven described happening in Isadia's brew house also suggested guests might fall off their horses and break their necks if they tried to ride without a long sleep first.

By the time the door shut behind Kaven, Beran had got as far as pulling up his trousers. He was still buttoning his shirt when he shuffled into the Hall. The front door stood open to the blue morning. It had rained in the night, and the trees beyond the wall shimmered with drops like diamonds. Beran's heart lifted. He would go out into the woods, he decided, then had to laugh at how much he sounded like a Westreacher.

Since he was far too puny to take another beating just then, he made his slow way around to the barracks to fetch Carl. One of Isadia's men-at-arms was just coming out. When he saw Beran, he glanced back inside and closed the door.

"Carl's asleep," he said. "Best let him be."

"Is he sick?"

"He's better."

"What's wrong with him?"

The man opened and closed his mouth. "He took it hard when you were hurt, Beran." He must have seen that Beran was still puzzled because he added gently, "He's been drinking. He's stopped now, but he needs a little while to get back on his feet."

Deep as a Tomb

Beran felt unutterably selfish not to have asked about Carl sooner. "Tell him I wish him well," he said. The man nodded, and Beran wandered to the front gate and looked out in time to glimpse Myla striding along a path into the trees, her herb bag over her shoulder. He'd go after her, he decided. Carl or no Carl, he simply couldn't stay inside the manor walls for a moment more. Myla was far enough ahead that he lost sight of her, but even if he didn't catch up, he was enjoying the morning riot of birds and cool air washing over his skin.

Ahead, the trees thinned, letting sunlight through to glow on startlingly green grass. No wait. Not grass. Moss, like what he'd seen covering the tomb at Lady Eran's. He walked into a clearing and into the presence of what had to be Green Valley Manor's tomb. The sight of it filled his head, making everything else feel small. He drifted along it, and when he rounded the north side, the door loomed into sight, and across from it, on a fallen log just inside the tree line, sat Myla. There must have been a gap in the leaves overhead, because a shaft of sun made a halo of light around her. She looked like a wood sprite.

A wood sprite who was crying.

Beran flinched and glanced at the path behind him. Maybe he could just slip away. He sighed. No. Myla had cared for him when he was deathly ill. He owed her. What's more, they were friends in the way he'd experienced with other fosterlings who backed one another up because they were all young, uncertain, and living among strangers.

She wiped her cheeks as he approached and dropped down next to her on the log. He should probably ask what was wrong between her and Kaven. Girls liked to talk about that kind of stuff. But the castle weapons master had been very clear on how stupid it was to enter a battle without scouting the situation first. Also, having watched Kaven and Myla together for weeks now, he had no doubt they'd make up, and when they did, experience had taught Beran that anyone who'd interfered would be in trouble with both of them. So he sat in silence and kept her company, appreciating the chance to rest.

Finally, Myla nodded toward the tomb. "It's horrible that your mother's not in there."

He shifted. He'd dreamed of his mother's death again the previous night. "She's in the castle graveyard at home."

"Your father's home," she said in a voice bitter as willow bark. "That's what happens to women. They're married off and become part of some man's plans for power. No one cared that your mother loved someone else."

"My mother loved my father." The sharpness in his own voice startled him.

Her eyebrows shot up. "She loved Lord Corin. Everyone's heard of their romance."

If she'd punched him in the stomach, he'd have been less breathless. "Everyone has heard wrong. Their marriage was political, but they fell in love."

Was that true? He searched for memories of his parents together and saw them in the snowy castle courtyard. His mother had whacked his father in the back of the head with a snowball, and his laughing father had scooped her into his arms and threatened to hurl her into a snow bank. A small Beran had galloped around them, so full of happiness that he couldn't stop shrieking.

Surely they'd loved one another. It was suddenly vital to him to believe that. He thought of the tiny red birds embroidered around the neck of Ander's cloak. Would the woman he married love him enough to sew him something whimsical and lovely so he'd think of her every time he wore it?

He wrenched his thoughts back to what Myla had said. "Corin loved my mother," he said slowly. "No wonder he's hostile to my father." Thien must have known about the romance, but withheld word of it, leaving Beran to grope for reasons Corin didn't trust him, when all the time Corin was reacting to his father, not Beran. Beran felt a familiar stab of fury at the way his father expected him to carry out plans without being told anything.

He picked up a twig and stabbed the dirt, disturbing a clump of heart-shaped red flowers. He plucked two and inhaled their honey-sweet scent. "What are these?"

"Remembrance," Myla said, picking one. "They grow near tombs. In the old days, folks used them as burial offerings, something from the Forest that was better than any jewel." She rose, tucking the flower into her belt. "Shall we see if you can take me into the tomb? I've been wanting to honor your grandfather. The last chieftain," she added in a murmur.

"Take you in?" Beran stood. "What makes you think I can open it?"

"If your mother's blood runs true in you, you can. Let's try you out as a possible ruler of Forest land." With a firm step, she walked into the clearing and approached the door.

After a moment, Beran followed. If he could open Green Valley's tomb, maybe his grandmother was right and he was meant to abandon his father's under-explained plans and rule this manor instead. The thought burned through his brain that it would serve his father right.

"Rest your hands on the door," Myla said.

He slid the flowers he still held between the buttons of his shirt, wiped sweaty palms on his thighs, and obeyed.

"Can you read the runes?"

Time had worn the marks so thin Beran wouldn't have seen them if Myla hadn't pointed them out. He squinted and leaned close. "May we live in harmony with the Forest."

The door quivered and slid sideways, revealing a dark passage. He stood with his hands still raised, not quite believing they weren't still pressed against stone.

"You're Forest enough to do that anyway, which is more than my father can say," Myla said. "Go in."

When he edged into the entryway, thin lines of fire rolled down each wall. He gaped at them as Myla wedged stones under the door, then followed her down the curving steps, their footfalls and his excited breathing echoing off the walls. The first chamber held four coffins, blanketed in dust, and an altar beneath a picture of Silvit.

Myla fished a small green cake from her bag and laid it on the altar. "Lord Arthan should be this way." She gestured to a doorway on the right, through which Beran saw descending stairs.

"Should be?"

"I asked Sendra." Myla's voice was subdued. "She went to the funeral of course, and she was afraid of being lost, so she studied the twists and turns." She steered him through more doorways, until at the top of a third stairwell, they entered an empty room with no other door.

"I thought tombs opened rooms as they were needed," Beran said. "Who's this room for?"

"My guess would be your mother." Myla sounded close to tears. "It was cruel of her father to make her leave." She was more upset than Beran had realized. "Let me try again," she said.

He followed her back down the stairs and through a different door. This time, they found a room with a single coffin. On one end rested a heap of statues, plates, and cups, all of them silver or gold and many studded with red or green or blue jewels. On the coffin's other end, a circle gleamed gold in the light from the walls. Beran recognized it from the carving above the main fireplace in Isadia's Hall: the chieftain's circlet, symbol of the ruler of the Forest.

He reached, drew his hand back, reached again. With careful fingers, he picked up the circlet. Myla tensed at his elbow. The circlet was heavy for its size, but gold was like that, a beautiful burden on a ruler's head. According to Beran's father, his grandfather had seen trouble coming when he and Isadia had had no son. He'd seen the power of Rinland growing and decided the Forest would be better off joined with its neighbor rather than fighting it. Myla talked about the web of life and how everyone was stronger together than apart. Arthan, the Forest's last chieftain, had extended that wisdom beyond his own borders and married his daughter to Rinland's young King Thien. Arthan must have been incredibly sure of his influence over his people to do that. Beran grimaced. How did an ordinary man ever get to be that sure of himself?

To the sound of Myla letting out a long breath, Beran put the circlet back where it belonged, nudging it into the dust-free ring on the coffin top. He bent closer. What was that tiny circle inside the larger one? He prodded the little thing, shedding dust from a plain, gold ring.

"Isadia's wedding ring," Myla said.

Beran pictured his grandmother's bare hands. His grandparents' marriage had surely been political too. A lump in his throat dissolved. "She loved him."

"She did. You can tell by how she talks about him." Myla's brows drew down. "You say your mother came to love your father? And he felt the loss of her?"

Beran rested a hand on the coffin, the stone cold against his fingers. "I wasn't there when it happened. She'd been failing, growing weaker by the day. I was thirteen, but I knew she was dying." He cleared his throat. "I was supposed to go to my father's council meetings as part of learning to rule. They were tedious beyond my ability to describe." He aimed a tentative smile Myla's way, but her gaze was on the circlet. "The day before I was to leave for two months fostering in the Basket, I skipped the meeting and went to see my mother. She could barely lift her head from her pillow, and I decided I wouldn't go. Then my father came into her room, and as you can imagine, he was angry about my missing the meeting. He didn't take it well when I told him I wanted to stay home."

Beran paused, remembering the tightening of his father's mouth and the sharp jerk of the head he'd given to send Beran into the sitting room. His father had followed, closing the bedroom door.

"You don't have the right to indulge your feelings, Beran," his father had said. "You have a duty to Rinland." When Beran had continued to study the intricate pattern on the wool carpet, his father had placed warm hands on either side of Beran's head and tilted it so Beran had to meet his hawklike gaze. "I know this is hard." Unexpectedly, his father's face had softened. "But I have to send you, and you have to go."

For the first time, Beran wondered what it had cost his father to do what was right for Rinland and send him away. Had Thien been forced to wrap another layer of ice around his own court heart? His father had certainly become more remote after Beran's mother's death.

He became aware Myla had turned away from the circlet and was looking at him, waiting for him to go on. She gripped the strap of her herb bag so tightly her knuckles gleamed white.

"I'd been in the Basket about a week," he said, "when I overheard two maids saying there'd been a message the queen was dying, and at that moment, more than anything, I wanted to see her alive one more time. I knew even Ander wouldn't let me go, so I ran away."

"Of course you did!" Myla said. "What did your father expect?"

She sounded as if she truly understood the pain Beran's father had forced on him. "As soon as I was missed, people were out looking for me, but it was Ander who found me and took me back. Two days later, word came my mother was dead." He looked off into the darkness. "I've never been able to decide which I regretted more—failing to serve Rinland by running away or failing to fight hard enough to stay home in the first place."

"He had no right to ask you to go." Myla's voice shook. "A father shouldn't ask a child to walk away from love."

Beran lifted his hand and let it thud back onto the dusty coffin. "There'd been flooding in that part of the Basket. Crops destroyed. They wanted more help than the king could give, and sending me was supposed to show he took their troubles to heart and was doing the best he could. He sent his son to eat as they ate and live as they lived."

"What about your troubles?" Myla's indignation echoed off the stone walls.

She seemed desperate to understand, so he struggled to find an answer. "His decisions couldn't be based on what I needed." As he spoke the words, their truth slammed into him like an arrow.

"And what about your mother's needs?"

"They couldn't be based on what she needed, either." The more he answered, the stronger his own recognition of the truth grew. "People with power have a responsibility to others that comes first. We can't give in to our feelings. Sometimes we can't even have them."

"Rot," Myla said. "You think you don't have those feelings, but you do. I understand what you mean. Someone with power—any kind of power—can't think just of their own happiness, but a powerful person with no feelings would be a monster. Only…it's hard sometimes to know if it's right to act on a feeling."

Beran recognized the truth in that too. He looked at Isadia's wedding ring, a sign of love resting inside a symbol of power. Was it possible to do his duty to Rinland without smothering the part of himself he hid away behind a court face and a court heart? With shaking fingers, he reached into his shirt and drew out two fragrant red flowers. He laid one on his grandfather's coffin. "For my mother," he whispered, "your daughter, who was loved where you sent her, I swear." He hesitated, then laid the second flower. "For Ander."

He stepped back from the coffin. "Shall we try to find our way out?" he asked lightly. He moved toward the door, with Myla following slowly.

Halfway down a stairwell, Myla stopped, took another step, and turned. "I forgot to leave the flower for Lord Arthan. Wait here." She bolted back to the tomb.

Beran waited, tapping his toe. A growl rumbled down the stairs, and he spun to look up.

Myla clattered back down the steps, clutching the strap of her herb bag.

"What was that?" His eyes went to a long tear in her sleeve. "You're bleeding."

"I cut myself on a sharp stone," she said, brushing past him. "It's nothing. Let's go."

He blinked after her. Nothing? To Beran, the wound in her arm looked a lot like the one on his own from outside Lady Eran's tomb. He followed her back to the living world, glancing over his shoulder as if the mythical cat might lurk below them.

Chapter 15

Beran dumped another bucket of steaming water into the tub and settled onto the bench against the brew house. Rubbing the itchy remains of his wound against the rough wall, he thought some more about how to get the manor holders to cooperate in finding Ander's killer. Forest dwellers claimed to believe they were better off joined than separated, so maybe he could use that. But in his visits, he'd seen that though Westreach lords wanted the thieves gone, they resented anyone telling them what to do, be it Beran's father, Lord Corin, or their own neighbors. People didn't always act on what they claimed to believe.

And of course, he still had done nothing about the True and had no idea who had pushed him into the poisonous bush.

He sat up when Myla came out of the house, lugging a platter big enough to hold a sheep. She flung the platter into the tub, splashing hot water on Beran's thighs. "Ow!" He scooted back on the bench. "It's important I produce an heir some day, you know." With a snort, she turned to go. "Wait," he said.

She shoved a strand of hair off her sweaty forehead, leaving a streak of dirt. "What?"

"Have you sent word to your brother yet? Can he call off the True?" If Beran could at least stop the damage to the roads, he'd accomplish something his father wanted, and he could put the True out of his mind and concentrate on the thieves.

"I've had no chance." Myla's normally lively manner had gone flat. Her quarrel with Kaven had pinched up her insides and made her into a sad and silent girl Beran didn't know. "I need a little time to think about how to argue before I see him or my father." She trudged back toward the house, but stopped when a man in unfamiliar livery met her at the door. He handed her a folded parchment and waited while she slid her finger under the seal and read.

Beran watched her, absently pushing up his sleeves and fishing the platter out of the water. Footsteps scuffed close, and he looked away from Myla to see Kaven had wandered from cleaning out the stable loft to make a place for guests' servants to sleep. He, too, watched the house doorway, though when Beran glanced that way, Myla and the messenger had both vanished. Kaven shifted his stony gaze to Beran.

"What's the matter with you?" Beran asked.

"I've been asking myself that same question. Maybe it's just hard for a manor brat to compete with someone who can use a sword."

"You think Myla's gone off you because she's on to me? No."

Kaven opened and closed his fists. "You think you're going to impress her more when everyone comes to celebrate your recovery at the feast."

Beran sighed. "Kaven, I'm just doing what my father expects me to do. You must know what family expectations are like."

Kaven's face went pale. He stomped back toward the stables. Beran ignored him.

"What's got up his nose?"

Carl had approached more silently than a big man should be able to manage, an ability that was likely to complicate Beran's life. This was the first time he'd seen his guard since he was hurt. Carl's eyes were shadowed, but he was clean shaven and steady on his feet. "He's quarreling with Myla, so misery is eating his brains."

Carl flicked a finger at the edge of the platter, making it chime. "Is this what king's sons do?"

"You must not have run into my grandmother today. She's like a general organizing a campaign, and the rest of us are foot soldiers. I do what I'm told."

"Makes a nice change," Carl said, but without sting in his voice. "How do you feel?"

"Much better."

Carl shifted his weight. "Did you see the scum who pushed you? Would you recognize him?"

Beran met his narrow gaze. "No." *You owe me, Myla.*

"Stone it. I never should have left you alone." Carl rubbed his left arm where the burn scar lay under his sleeve. "You need to start training again. Get your gear, and meet me where we were before."

"Uh, are you fired up about losing the True leader? Because if you're planning the same kind of 'training' we did the first time, I'll pass."

"Don't be a baby. I said you need to train, and that's all I mean. Get your gear. I'll fix it with your grandmother."

Myla came out of the house clutching a fistful of mugs.

"Unless you'd rather wash dishes," Carl said.

Beran laughed, waved at Myla, and took another route into the house.

The day the guests were to arrive dawned cloudy and cool, and Beran worriedbad weather might keep people away. He spent the morning helping Myla clean the extra trestles and table boards Isadia's men hauled down from the rafters. Kaven passed through the Hall twice with baskets of last year's apples for the cook, though the Hall was a very indirect way to get from the fruit cellar to the kitchen. He walked through slowly, hefting the heavy baskets as if to warm his biceps, and glaring at Beran. Myla kept her eyes lowered.

"What did the poor fool do?" Beran finally couldn't resist asking.

She threw down the rag she was using and ran out of the room.

He finished the chore by himself, vowing not to let curiosity overcome self-preservation again. When he was done, he brushed spider webbing off his hands and went out into the back yard to see whether the clouds to the north had cleared. They loomed, dark and angry, like Kaven's face when he stood up from behind the huge bowl of apples he was peeling and chopping.

He took a step toward Beran. "She was crying. What did you do?"

Mindful of the kitchen knife in Kaven's hand, Beran backed away. "Nothing."

The trembling of Kaven's muscles was Beran's only warning. Kaven flung the knife away and leaped, driving his shoulder into Beran's knees. Beran hit the ground flat, driving all the air out of his lungs. He kicked and drove his fist at Kaven's face, but Kaven jerked his head aside, so Beran's knuckles just grazed his skull. Kaven punched him in the ribs.

A voice Beran didn't know shouted, "Here you two! Stop it!"

Beran shoved at Kaven's shoulders. They rolled over and over, until Beran managed to pin him. Beran drew back his fist, but someone caught his elbow, wrapped an arm around his chest, and yanked him to his feet. A second man in a black and green uniform dragged Kaven erect too.

"What's going on here?" a third man said.

He stood to one side, dressed in a cream-colored silk shirt under a silver-embroidered, green jerkin. His dark hair and beard showed only a few threads of purplish red, so Beran guessed him to be about his father's age, and like Beran's father, he radiated authority. He peered intently into Beran's face, some complex emotion Beran couldn't read flitting across his mouth and eyes. He let out a long breath. "You look like your mother." He nodded to the men, his apparently, and they released Beran and Kaven. The stranger spoke to Kaven. "Would this by any chance be a fight over a girl?"

Kaven brushed his hair out of his eyes. "Yes, my lord." His face flamed red.

"Let me guess," the stranger said. "She was your girl until the king's son came along."

Kaven's mouth fell open, lending him a pleasingly soft-headed look. "Yes, my lord."

The stranger gave Beran an unfriendly smile. "You may look like your mother, but you're Thien's true son." He slapped his riding gloves once against his thigh. "You should both be ashamed of yourselves for fighting in Lady Isadia's yard." He strode away into the house. His men followed.

Frowning, Kaven rubbed his sweaty cheek on his lifted shoulder, then snatched up the bowl of chopped apples and stalked off toward the kitchen.

Beran ran his hands over his face. He'd never met the man, but he knew with sick certainty who he was. Corin, the lord who thought Beran's father didn't understand the Westreach, the man who threatened to oppose Beran being named King's Heir, the man who'd loved Beran's mother, the man who was already supposed to be hunting the thieves. If Beran even hinted that the thieves weren't being pursued doggedly or cleverly enough, Corin's prejudices would be hardened into stone. And yet, Beran had to try. Someone had killed Ander and preyed on the people of the Forest. How could anyone let that go on if there was a hope of stopping it? Especially how could anyone in power let it go on? These were Corin's people, Thien's people, and whether Beran was King's Heir or lord of Green Valley Manor, his people too.

Thunder cracked. The wind picked up and sent leaves and dust swirling across the yard. Fat raindrops splatted into the dirt and stung Beran's face as he ran for the side door closest to his room. It was time to put on his Beran-of-Rinland clothes and greet his guests. Time to act like the ruler he hoped to be.

A short while later, Beran paused at the entry to the Hall, running his finger around the inside of his high, embroidered collar. The center of the room was crowded with long tables and benches, though no one sat there yet. Lord Corin stood near the open front door talking to Isadia. Framed in the doorway, rain pounded the yard to mud. Corin's two men-at-arms lounged near the hearth, carefully acting like guests rather than guards. Myla was pouring them mugs of ale. Her face was blotchy, and Beran was willing to bet she couldn't have repeated anything the men said to her. She moved along to Carl, who refused the ale, but bent and spoke quietly to her, evoking a faint smile that Beran found himself echoing. Good for Carl.

He drew a deep breath and skirted the tables to join his grandmother, who took his arm. "Lord Corin is here," she said brightly. She held up a fine leather belt pouch embossed with green and black wavy lines, the sigil of Black River Manor. A gift, Beran realized an instant too late. She'd said the guests would bring them.

"We met in the yard." To Corin, he said, "Be welcomed and take shelter, sir. Thank you for the pouch."

Corin swept a look from Beran's polished shoes, to his formal clothes, to his carefully brushed hair. "That was you, was it?"

"It was, as is this." Beran kept his tone polite, but edged. Lord Corin resented Beran's father, true. Beran shouldn't have been brawling, true—though Kaven jumped him, not the other way around. But no matter what Corin thought of him, he owed him courtesy for the sake of his father and grandmother.

"Beran has been learning how to manage Green Valley's woods." Isadia leaned on Beran's arm as if she were already relying on him.

"And what have you learned?" Corin asked.

The most truthful answer was that Beran no longer believed that if he'd seen one tree, he'd seen them all, but he could hardly say that. "A forest is a connected web," he finally managed, using Myla's words.

In the yard, a blob emerged from the curtain of rain and turned into a pony cart, the ponies' hooves splattering mud in great circles. A cloaked man dismounted stiffly. As he raised his arms to help a similarly cloaked woman, his hood fell back, and Beran glimpsed Lord Naeth's bright, yellow hair. One of Isadia's men sloshed up to take their cart. Another came running with an armful of straw to spread over the mud.

The woman Naeth escorted into the house was as ancient as he, though the years that had dried him into a stick had turned her into a wrinkly dumpling. Lord Corin greeted them, then strolled toward the hearth to collect a mug of ale. Naeth introduced the woman as his wife. She handed Beran a jar of honey, which he placed next to the ball of yarn and chimes on the small table Isadia had used to stow the pouch from Corin.

"I'm so glad you came despite the weather." Isadia looked around. "Kaven," she called, "would you please take these wet cloaks?"

Kaven came into their room as Beran left it, bumping Beran's shoulder despite having plenty of room. He wore a well-made scarlet linen shirt Beran had seen when he searched Kaven's clothes chest, but his wrists showed at the sleeve ends, and a hand's span of new blue stocking was visible beneath his trouser legs. He didn't look at Beran as he came to fetch the cloaks.

"I heard you recognized one of the thieves, Beran," Naeth said, making Isadia turn sharply toward him. From the corner of Beran's eye, he saw Corin's head swivel their way. Stone it. So much for not looking like he was interfering. "When are you going after him?"

"I don't know his name or where he lives. One of the things I'd like to do today is ask Corin's and Halid's guidance on getting rid of the thieves. I'd like that from all of you so I can pass it along to the king."

To Beran's relief, Naeth nodded. "Smart boy." With his wife on his arm, he creaked off toward the hearth, where Corin now took a mug of ale from Myla.

For the moment, Beran was alone with his grandmother. She looked ready to ask questions, but Beran spoke first. "You didn't tell me Lord Corin was coming."

"I wasn't sure he would. As you know, he and your father have an unfortunate history."

As Beran knew. Right.

"But you asked me to invite influential people, and you can't get more influential than Corin," she said.

No, he couldn't imagine a more important influence on his future than Corin. Too bad that, judging by his words in the yard, the man had already decided Beran was as unwelcome as his father.

Lady Eran and Lord Adon arrived, having apparently met on the road. Eran looked stronger than the last time Beran had seen her. Once she'd greeted Isadia and Beran, she toddled off to tell Myla how well her medicines were working. Magistrate Halid came next, and then a string of familiar manor holders bearing small gifts. Finally, a lone pony trotted up to the door, and Kaven's Uncle Rickard dismounted and strode through the doorway, his cloak soaked and his hair slicked back as if he'd just climbed out of a swimming hole. He stamped mud off his feet and slapped at the layer of it around the bottom of his cloak. Beran's gut curdled at the sight of the man.

"Be welcomed and take shelter," Isadia said.

Kaven appeared, and his uncle dropped his sopping cloak onto Kaven's arms. Kaven slid it off his sleeves and into his hands, but not before it had left a dark blotch on his best shirt.

"It's good to see you, Kaven," Rickard said. "We haven't heard from you in a while."

Kaven tightened his big hands around the cloak, squeezing rainwater into the mud Rickard had knocked onto the floor. "You didn't bring my mother?"

"She had work to do. So did I for that matter, but when the king's son calls, how can one refuse?"

Beran decided he'd like it better if Rickard were a kiss-up.

"Mother's probably happier at home," Kaven said in a tone Beran couldn't read.

"I expect she is," Rickard said.

Adon strolled up with a mug of ale for himself and one he offered to Rickard. "Good to see you again," Adon boomed. "Hard to believe we live cheek by jowl now, but haven't met since that seedy inn in the Vale." Adon winked at Beran. "We were snowed in for a week with nothing to do but trade stories and toss knuckle bones." He rearranged his face to suggest sorrow. "As I recall, Rickard, you hadn't heard your father was dying."

"I never had a chance to thank you for giving me that news, sad though it was," Rickard said. "Without it, I wouldn't have known to come home and say good-bye." He took Kaven's elbow. "Excuse us. I need to speak to my nephew." With nods to Isadia and Beran, he propelled Kaven to a corner. Kaven dropped the cloak in a heap on the floor and kicked it under the drying rack.

"Beran, there may be one or two more coming, but you go and get things started," Isadia said.

Beran didn't want to snoop on Kaven, and he didn't want to go near Rickard, but he'd stowed his map in the corner where Rickard had Kaven penned. Beran walked slowly toward them, stopping a short distance away.

"What do you mean, you can't?" Rickard's back was rigid. "Sweet Stream Manor needs you."

Kaven's gaze caught on Beran. When Rickard jerked around to see what he was looking at, Kaven slipped out of the corner and hurried away. For a long moment, Rickard's eyes met Beran's. Then, smiling stiffly, he bowed and started past.

Beran blocked his path. "I enjoyed talking to Lady Teress at Sweet Stream."

Rickard scanned Beran's face. "Did you? She's usually quiet."

"Quiet or no, I liked meeting her. She's one of the king's people. Her wellbeing is my concern."

Rickard half lowered his eyelids. He knew exactly what Beran was saying, or rather not saying. "I'm sure she'd thank you for your interest." He stepped around Beran and joined the crowd near the fire.

Beran hoped he hadn't just made things worse for Teress or Kaven. He retrieved his rolled-up map from the corner, then took up a place in front of the low-burning hearth, where, for the moment, he set the map aside. He picked up the small hammer on the gift table, tapped the chimes, and waited for the echoing tone—and talk—to die down before he spoke the words his grandmother had taught him. "In the Forest, each depends on all." He took the ball of green yarn from the table and passed it to Lady Eran, keeping the end in his hand. She handed the coil to Naeth, still gripping a stretch of it. When it had made the full circuit of the silent room, and everyone held onto it, Beran passed his end to Eran and they rolled it up again, finally returning it to Beran, who set it on the table and struck the chimes a second time, feeling unexpectedly peaceful.

"Neighbors, friends, be welcomed to Green Valley Manor." He gestured toward the downpour framed in the open doorway. "Be welcomed, and on a day like this, take shelter you sorely need." They laughed politely. "I'm grateful you've all gathered to help me celebrate the end of my illness because I want to continue getting acquainted, of course, but also because I want to talk with you about making the Forest safer. Since I came here, I've seen how much stronger folks are working together. We should work together now." He unrolled his map, anchored its top on the mantel with a pair of heavy candlesticks, and used one hand to keep the bottom from curling up.

Lord Corin leaned a hip against the back of a bench, arms crossed, gaze turning from Beran to the guests and back again. Corin would fit in well at the king's court. Beran couldn't read his face at all. Isadia was grimacing, but looked resigned to letting Beran soldier on.

"These marks show where the thieves have struck," Beran said.

"Are you still worrying about the thieves?" Flushing, Magistrate Halid shot a quick look at Lord Corin. "I told you I was hunting them down."

"You say that, but what have you done?" Lady Eran asked sharply. Beran suppressed a groan as the peaceful moment vanished. "I told you Myla of Oak Ridge was attacked on my manor, and you've done nothing, not that I've heard of anyway. And of course one of them killed Beran's guard."

"Luckily for us, Beran is going to get help from the king. Maybe he can get Thien to send soldiers." Adon bowed in Beran's direction.

All eyes turned the same way. "Surely not," someone's appalled voice said.

"Is that so, Beran?" Corin said.

"If there's something the king has a right to know, I'll tell him," Beran said hastily, "though I doubt he'd send soldiers. The king is far away, and we're all here with an immediate problem. Look at the marks. They show the thieves have attacked in a limited territory. That suggests they live within ten miles of here. You may even know them."

Someone gasped. "They have all been close," someone else murmured. "When it's all put together like that, you see it." For a moment, the faces in front of Beran looked ready to believe. Beran's heart quickened. If they'd work with him, the thieves would have no chance.

"We know them, all right." Rickard's voice grated over the low-voiced talk around him. "We all know who the local lawbreakers are. It's obvious the True have been playing at rebel and gotten out of hand."

"I told you so," Adon said.

"You're wrong!" The exclamation came from a round-faced lord named Elthor, one of those Beran had visited. He had a son who was maybe eighteen, Beran recalled, studying Elthor's reddening face. Elthor licked his lips. "The True are a bit wild, the way Forest boys get when they're turning into men, but they're not thieves, and they're not killers."

"No, they're not," another man said firmly. He, too, had a son the right age to be True. "You ought to know that, Rickard. You raised so much havoc at that age your father told you to clear out until you'd grown some sense."

"That's so," Rickard acknowledged, "so I know how easy it would be to slip over the edge into serious trouble. I tell you, that's what's happened with the True."

Halid frowned at Beran. "You've accused the True from the start. I told you that was a mistake."

"Surely none of us, young or old, would lower ourselves to steal from one another," Naeth's wife said. "If nothing else," she added more practically, "the risk of being seen and recognized would be too great."

"That area fans out from the road," Magistrate Halid said. "It has to be outsiders coming down it. They think they're safe because they're strangers."

Relief spread through the crowd, thick and sweet as honey. Then face after face dissolved into a scowl aimed straight at Beran. The only exception was Corin, whose impassivity had given way to a look of half-amused exasperation.

"You can try to pin this on us, boy," Naeth said, "but we know ourselves better than that."

"I don't believe it's the True," Beran said, fighting to keep his voice calm, "but I do think the thieves live in this area."

Someone took hold of his arm, and he caught a quick whiff of violets. "Excuse us." His grandmother smiled at the guests. "I need my grandson." She tugged him aside, the map snapping into a tight roll when Beran let it go.

"I'm right, Grandmother. You know I am."

"You may be," she said, "but Rickard scared them talking about the True. It's natural for parents to protect their young." She flinched as if at a sudden pain, but she went on. "I need you to look for Myla. She's gone, and she's been so upset that someone should make sure she's all right."

Beran thought she was less worried about Myla than she was about his alienating the people she wanted him to live among permanently. She was protecting her young like a mother bear, making up for the protection she thought she'd failed to give her daughter, and also for the protection she believed Beran's father was failing to give him.

"Grandmother, this is too important for me to give up on."

She shoved him toward the door. "Go. I'll soothe them, and you can try again later." He hesitated. "I really am worried about Myla," she said.

Maybe a temporary retreat was in order. He should show the manor holders he'd listened to them, calm their fears for their sons, and try again. "I'll find her. Don't worry." He set off toward the solar to see if Myla might have hidden there, too unhappy to face the chattering guests.

Chapter 16

Myla rubbed salve into the claw mark on her arm. The scratch was taking forever to heal. Her mouth went dry just thinking about what had happened in the Green Valley tomb, but at the moment, the throbbing pain in this scratch was the least of her punishments. She rolled her sleeve down and buttoned the cuff. She'd been unsurprised when the Oak Ridge messenger turned up. She'd expected Da to demand a meeting today because the fortnight he'd allowed was up. He'd be here any moment, and she still hadn't decided what to do.

I have to bargain, she thought. *I'll give it to him, but only if he doesn't make me marry Zale.* Or was that too selfish? Would it be better for the Forest if she did what Da wanted? If she helped him seize rule, he could stop Thien from giving away land to people like Adon. He could stop the roads that carried timber and so made it worthwhile to ravage a hillside the way Kaven's uncle had done. Or could he? Thien wouldn't surrender part of his kingdom without a fight, and war would be disastrous even if the Forest won in the end. She'd been over and over these arguments and still hadn't lit on one side or the other. Her life was a tree splitting into two forks. What should the Myla tree look like?

She sank onto the stool just as a figure blocked the gray light from the doorway. Bringing the scent of wet wool and mud, Da strode over the threshold, with Galen close behind him, trying to crowd into the herb room out of the rain.

"Do you have it?" Da asked.

"Fair day to you, too, Da."

"I don't have time for your impertinence. Zale is waiting. Do you have the circlet?"

"Yes." She hunched her shoulders. *Mouse*, Kaven whispered in her head.

Da held out his hand and snapped his fingers.

"Da, listen. Maybe we can bargain with King Thien about how he rules the Forest. We don't have to fight."

"Don't be stupid," Da said. "Where is it?"

"Rot you, Myla," Galen said. "We need to be out of here before B...anyone sees us. It's here, isn't it? You wouldn't leave it anywhere else." He ran his gaze around the room. Myla kept her head turned away, but she couldn't help a quick look from the corner of her eyes. Galen pounced on the herb bag, yanked the buckle free, and pulled out the circlet. "There you are, Da," he crowed and handed it over.

Da held it up in both hands. "So you really could open the chieftain's tomb," he marveled.

For an instant, Myla wavered. Some part of her had hungered for that tone in Da's voice since she was a little girl. *Here, Da, I hemmed this kerchief for you. Da, I read this myself. It's willow bark tea, Da. I made it.*

But she wasn't a little girl any more.

"I didn't open the chieftain's tomb," she said. "Beran did."

Da lowered the circlet. "You couldn't do it?"

"I didn't try. This is Isadia's manor, and she says that, when she dies, it will be Beran's. I have no right to open that tomb." She looked past Da at Galen. She likely had as much chance of finding violets in the snow as she did of changing what Da meant to do, but Galen was a different kind of weed. "Isadia wants Beran to live here, and I think he may consider it. He's warming to the Forest even though he had a run-in with the True."

Galen's face froze.

"He says he'll forgive them if they stop destroying the roads."

"Forgive them." Da snorted. "As if he has any right to deliver judgment."

Galen licked his lips. "The True don't need the prince's mercy if Da has the circlet." He nodded sharply, convinced by his own argument.

Da set the circlet and the leather bag he carried on the table, nudging the book aside. "Is that book one you found at Oak Ridge?" he asked as he loosened the bag's drawstring. She nodded. "Here's what you're going to do now, Myla. You're returning to that feast Isadia is giving for her grasslander grandson, and you're telling everyone that you can open any tomb in the Forest. It's time to show our neighbors that you're something special." Behind Da's back, Galen rolled his eyes. "Also, tell them I've arranged the match with Zale."

"Da, think about the harm war would do!"

"Silvit save a man from having fools for children." Da upended the bag to spill ashes and bits of charred parchment on the table.

She opened her mouth to ask what it was, then jerked back at the lightning flash of insight that came from years of living under this man's thumb. Her heart sped up. "You said I had a fortnight. You said you wouldn't burn any books if I did what you said."

"And did you do what I said? By your own words, you didn't even try to open Isadia's tomb. This is one book, Myla, meant to teach a lesson. If you do as I say now, the rest will survive." He closed the book on the table and stuffed it into the ashy bag. "Get the others, Galen. Wait. Put this back where she had it." He handed Galen the circlet. Galen shoved it out of sight, then moved along the shelf of books, putting as many as would fit into Myla's bag.

"Da, I need those," Myla said. "What's in them makes a difference to whether people live or die."

"The books are Oak Ridge's." Da added more books to the bag he still held. "You shouldn't have taken them."

"I assure you, sir," came a cool voice, "they're safe here."

The book Galen held thudded to the floor. They all jerked toward the doorway, where Beran stood, shaking out a wet cloak. He looked steadily at Galen, who backed against the shelves, hugging Myla's herb bag. Myla half expected it to glow with what it held. She felt a terrible temptation to snatch the bag and hand it to Beran.

"I believe I've met your brother twice now, Myla," Beran said, pleasantly. Galen flinched. "Is this your father?"

"Lord Talun of Oak Ridge Manor," Myla managed. "Da, this is Beran of Rinland."

Stiff with outrage, Da barely nodded. "The books belong to Oak Ridge."

Beran strolled across the room to where Galen cowered and stooped to pick up the book he'd dropped. "Myla makes good use of these. She's been telling me about how they draw on plants that grow only in the Forest. Perhaps you heard that after I was pushed into a redthorn bush, she saved my life with knowledge she gained from one of them." He offered the book to Galen, who took it with a shaking hand.

"I was telling them how you're willing to forget the True if they stop destroying roads," she said.

"Anyone who stopped them would be a hero," Beran said, eyeing Galen closely. "Lord Corin or even the king might issue a proclamation of praise."

Galen licked his lips. "Really?"

"Good fortune reasoning with those louts," Da said. "Get the rest of those, Galen. Myla, do what I told you."

Galen shouldered the bag's strap and snatched up a jumbled armful of books. He and Da moved toward the doorway.

"For Silvit's sake, Galen, at least put your cloak over those books," Myla said.

Galen slammed the stack onto a now empty shelf, then wrapped wet wool over them before sliding them off into his arms again.

At the last instant, Da looked over his shoulder at Beran. "You should go home, boy. The Forest is not for the likes of you." He flipped his hood over his head and plunged through the curtain of rain, Galen at his heels.

Myla braced her hands on the table and stared into the horror of what Da had ordered her to do.

Beran twisted his signet ring and studied the empty space where her father had been, his mouth working slightly. He shifted his gaze to frown at the ashes on the table. "They came in the rain just to get the books?"

"They happened to be nearby." She had to stop Da from destroying her books or starting a war, but surely that didn't mean she had to name him traitor. Her family was her manor, her past, her future, her safety, her pack. Betraying it was unthinkable.

"Do you think Galen understood what I want?" Beran asked.

"He understood. That doesn't mean he has enough sense to do it."

"I probably should hope he doesn't. Otherwise I'll have to wangle him a proclamation of praise." Beran shook himself, shedding whatever worried him. "We should go in, Myla. My grandmother is fretting about you." He took her cloak from its hook and draped it over her shoulders.

Go in? She groped frantically for a way out of the trap Da had laid for her. With Kaven right there, how could she say she was marrying Zale? And yet, if she didn't, what would Da do? She looked again at the mess on the table, and something snapped inside her. Something turned from one branch and flowed up another. She would do what she could to keep more of the Forest from winding up like that hill at Sweet Stream Manor, but she'd be blighted before she helped Da start a war. Betraying him to Corin or Beran would break her heart, so she'd do something else if she could only think of what. And before she did anything, she had to save her books. Save her books, keep Da from starting a war. Those were the two most important things. Her love for Kaven mattered, but not in the same way.

Beran took her elbow, and together, they ran through the yard and into the back hallway where he let her go. Without his support, she swayed. "Are you all right?" he asked. She planted her feet more firmly and nodded. He hung her cloak beside his own.

"Your collar is unbuttoned," she said. He grimaced and refastened his high collar, then opened his hand for her to go ahead of him. "Wait," she said. "Beran, please, can't you talk to your father about the way the Forest is being destroyed at Sweet Stream?"

"He won't want to interfere."

"There must be something you can do. Would you want Green Valley trees cut that way?"

"My grandmother would never do that."

"But the Forest is all one thing."

He blew out his breath. "Myla, I really can't."

"You mean you won't. Just when I was starting to think better of you." She stalked into the Hall.

Isadia smiled from where she stood talking to Lady Eran and Lord Corin. With shaky steps, Myla joined them.

"Eran was just telling me how much better she feels," Isadia said.

"The Forest provides," Myla said, trying not to picture the heap of ashes on the table in her herb room.

"If we have the wisdom to see it." Corin's gaze shifted to the hearth, where Beran had joined several people studying his map. He was talking earnestly, and they seemed to be listening. Corin bowed and drifted in their direction.

Halfway across the room, she spotted Kaven, his face bleak with the misery she'd put there. She should tell him what was happening. She took a tiny step toward him before his Uncle Rickard caught his arm and spoke fiercely into his ear. Kaven pulled free and started her way.

"Soon, Kaven," Rickard called after him. "No more than a week. Send word."

Before Kaven reached her, Myla became aware that people were turning toward the door. A tanned, muscled man in his mid-forties dripped on the doorsill. He flung back his hood. Myla's heart stopped.

Zale.

Beckoning to Beran, Isadia crossed the Hall to greet him. "Be welcomed and take shelter, Lord Zale. You're so late, I thought you might not be coming. This is my grandson, Beran."

"I'm glad to meet you, sir," Beran said. "I've been hoping the manor holders will be able to guide me in making the Forest safer for us."

"Us?" Zale asked. "You're King Thien's son, I believe."

"He's the future lord of Green Valley Manor," Isadia said sharply.

"Or perhaps he'll go home." Zale scanned the room until his gaze settled on Myla. "But of course I came," he said loudly. "I intend to take every chance I can to see my betrothed."

The room crashed into silence. Heads turned as Zale crossed to where Myla stood with Eran, but the only face Myla saw clearly was Kaven's as it drained of all color. Rickard spoke in Kaven's ear again, and Kaven arrived at her side. "Myla?"

"I don't believe I know this boy." From far away, Zale's voice cut into the private space between her and Kaven. "Is he a friend, Myla?"

Myla forced down the acid in her throat. She'd rot before she married Zale, but she couldn't reject him in front of all these people. Word would fly like an arrow to Da, and her books would be lost. People would die who could have lived. She had to buy time. She looked beseechingly at Kaven, willing him to see what lay behind her words. "This is Kaven of Sweet Stream Manor, Lord Rickard's nephew."

Zale scanned Kaven's wet shirt and the trousers that stopped above his ankle bones. "That would be Rickard the gambler?"

Kaven's gaze never wavered from her face. "Myla?" he repeated. He raised his hand as if to touch her cheek.

Zale put his arm around Myla's shoulders and pulled her away. She shuddered at the touch, her body trying to escape without her willing it. Zale inhaled all Kaven's fury and despair and spoke with the assurance of a man used to ruling a manor. "Come near my future wife, and I'll kill you."

"There'll be no threats in my Hall," Isadia said sharply.

Ignoring Zale, Kaven met Myla's gaze for one more moment, then turned away.

"Kaven?" She tried to catch at his sleeve, but Zale's grip pinned her arm as Kaven strode out of the room, his back muscles rigid under his too-tight shirt.

"You're betrothed, Myla?" Isadia asked. "That's true?" Beran came to his grandmother's side, looking as shocked as everyone else did.

"I'm a lucky man," Zale said. "Did you know this girl can open any tomb in the Forest? Isn't that right, Lady Eran?"

"She opened the Steeprise tomb," Lady Eran said, "and left offerings for Silvit and my man."

"I don't know that I can open all tombs." Myla heard the tremor in her voice, and she couldn't tear her eyes away from where Kaven had disappeared. "I opened Lady Eran's and Lord Zale's, and I'd be happy to try others if folks want me to." *And I won't claim those manors*, she told herself, *no matter what Da wants.*

The room burst with surprised exclamations. "Leave an offering for Silvit." "Cure the blight in my woods." "Bless me with a baby!"

Isadia smiled thinly at Zale. "I need to speak to my fosterling."

"There can be no secrets between me and my betrothed," Zale said.

"This is women's business," Isadia said. Zale wrinkled his nose, his face registering disgust. Isadia lowered her gaze to his arm gripping Myla.

"Lord Zale," Beran said, "would you be kind enough to look at a map and give me your insight about the robberies?"

"Assuming you're not blind, you don't need much insight," Zale said. "The thieves are grasslanders coming along the king's road."

"Could you show me?" Beran said.

The instant Zale loosened his hold, Myla slipped out from under it. Isadia shepherded her to a quiet corner, sending Beran a grateful look over her shoulder. Face blank, Beran led Zale toward the hearth.

"Myla, what's this about?" Behind Isadia, the Hall buzzed with the word *tomb.*

"I'm sorry I didn't tell you sooner. My father's been talking about this betrothal, but it wasn't set until today."

"Do you want to marry Zale? I can stop it or at least slow it down, you know. As long as you're fostering with me, I'm responsible for you by law. Lord Talun shouldn't have arranged a marriage without at least talking to me. I'd have told him you're too young to marry anyone right now. You're just learning what you can do. You should have some life of your own before you become a wife, a mother, a manor's mistress. Those are good roles, but only if you're ready to fit them to you, not squeeze yourself to fit into them."

Myla looked away, desperate to keep Isadia from seeing how the thought of marrying Zale sickened her. "Please don't say anything to Da. He'd just make me come home."

"But you want to marry Zale?"

"I...I'm not sure what to do." True enough. She'd made up her mind she wouldn't claim the chieftain role and, Silvit save her, she wouldn't marry Zale, but she had no idea how to free herself and her books. Everything was going wrong at once. She needed time to think.

Zale's raised voice came from near the hearth. "Rickard, you've let your own family turn to such trash only a fool would listen to a word you say." Myla looked over Isadia's shoulder in time to see Rickard flick his wrist and toss his ale into Zale's face. It flowed over Zale's moustache and down the front of his purple shirt. Rickard flung his mug to bounce on the floor, snatched his wet, muddy cloak from the floor, and stormed out of the Hall. As the room lapsed into silence, Beran scraped a hand over his face, then glanced at Lord Corin, who, for once, seemed to have lost his cool detachment.

Isadia stalked to face Zale and spoke loudly enough to be heard throughout the Hall. "Lord Zale, I won't have you insulting my guests."

Zale dripped ale and looked astonished. "Then I won't trouble you any longer." He flung himself to where he'd dropped his cloak, snatched it up, and stalked out, slamming the door behind him. The knot in Myla's stomach loosened. She silently vowed she'd fight like a wild animal before she let Zale touch her again.

Tall and grim-faced, Isadia turned to her guests. "Please sit. Our feast is ready."

In the general bustle of gossiping voices and shuffling feet, Myla fled to the privacy of her room.

Chapter 17

Beran stood in the house doorway, looking out at the night. All two-and four-footed guests were finally bedded down. With a sigh of relief, he unfastened his collar and scratched his neck. Behind him, servants cleaned up the remains of the feast. Outside, the storm had blown away, and stars dusted the sky. He stepped out into the cool night air and wandered toward the corner of the house, mud sucking at his shoes. He had no intention of going to his room until he was sure Kaven was asleep. The feast had been bad enough for Beran. For Kaven, it had been a disaster.

The kitchen was quiet at last. The garden lay in blackness, its sharp smell of thyme and rosemary damped down by the rain. Beran paused at the postern gate. An owl hooted, and leaves rustled as it swooped from its perch after some small night creature. He pictured the woods outside the gate leveled the way the Sweet Stream hillside had been, and his muscles tightened, poised to fight off some unknown enemy. Isadia would never permit it, he reminded himself, and when the manor came to him, he wouldn't either. Still, he'd learned enough working with Kaven to know Myla was right about how damage done in one place would affect other places too. His father said more or less the same about governing Rinland, though of course he dealt with different kinds of damage.

Beran tapped his ring on the top of the gate. From the jumble of thoughts in his head slipped the image of Myla's father delivering his departing words. *You should go home, boy.* Other manor holders had shown skepticism over Beran's or his father's right to rule the Forest, but only Talun and Zale had been recklessly rude as if it didn't matter what Beran thought of them. Myla's father especially made the hair rise on the back of Beran's neck. What had he been telling Beran? Why had he been there at all? Surely not just to retrieve some books.

The revelation that Myla could open tombs had certainly stirred up the manor holders. They'd talked of nothing else as they ate, and Lord Corin had spent the whole meal listening to them. He'd been measuring their mood, Beran judged. He'd seen his father do much the same thing. Opening a tomb mattered more than Beran had realized since it was apparently linked to keeping the Forest and its people healthy. He squirreled the news away with other bits of information he'd pass along when—if?—he went home. He wondered if one of them would be that Ander had died in a struggle over treasure. When he had met Myla, she'd probably been carrying Lady Eran's tomb offering, and the thieves had attacked her for it. Beran couldn't say he was surprised. Most battles were over treasure. But it seemed unbearably sad that a good man's life was wasted over something so cold.

He turned from the gate and strolled toward the barracks, where light still showed through one window. Someone was sitting on the bench along the barracks wall, quietly waiting for Beran to pass. The person moved, and Beran recognized the broad shoulders and went to sit next to Carl, who pulled a bundle closer to make room.

"Lord Zale certainly knows how to seize a crowd's attention," Beran said. "I don't believe anyone gave a second thought to the thieves after he stormed through."

"You didn't do so badly," Carl said. "They were bending your way until Rickard accused the True. Keep pushing. You'll shake something loose eventually."

Astonishment flashed in Beran's chest, giving way to pleasure at the unlikely Carl-granted praise. "The manor holders won't like it," Beran said.

Shifting as if too annoyed to sit still, Carl spoke in a more familiar tone. "You're going to rule some day, here or in Rin, so act like it. Stop turning yourself inside out over what other people might think."

Deep as a Tomb

Beran tried to see Carl's face in the glow from the window, but the light was behind Carl and turned him into a shadow. "For the council to name me heir, what people think of me matters. I don't just want people's approval. I need it."

"You need your own approval first. Not that you should do any fool thing that comes into your head, mind you, but I've had to listen to you worry about your father and the manor holders and Corin, and I'm tired of it. What do you think a ruler, even a future one, should do?"

"Serve," Beran said promptly. He'd been thinking about this since he had talked to Myla in the tomb. "A ruler serves the realm and the realm's people."

"Then do that. But don't fool yourself over what you can make happen. I've watched you for a while now, and it strikes me that you're confusing 'serve' with 'save.' You think if you try hard enough, you can stop death, undo it even. Believe me when I tell you no matter what you do, Ander will still be dead."

"I know that."

Carl gave a short laugh and slumped back against the barracks wall. "Of course you do. At your age, you know everything. Who am I talking to?" This last was said so softly that Beran wasn't sure he'd heard it right. Carl sat up again and spoke more normally. "Your father's not here and you are, which means there's no one but you to decide whom to serve and how. So stop whining, make up your mind, and do it."

"I'm not whining. I'm just…growling at the world."

"Then stop growling."

Beran had been sleeping badly since Ander died. What's more, he'd been ill near to death. So he knew he hadn't always been thinking clearly. Now he felt as if icy air was blowing in through his ears and swirling around in his head, sharpening everything. He drummed his fingers on the bundle between him and Carl, a small pack, the kind Beran had had when he was seven or eight. It even had a B embossed on the flap, though no Tower of Rinland above it.

"Whose is this?" Beran asked.

Carl shot to his feet and snatched the pack. "Leave that alone."

Beran was so startled his tongue rattled off a question before he had time to wonder if it was wise. "Who's this B person?"

"He was a young fool. Like you." Carl strode away into the dark, taking the pack with him. The door to the barracks slammed shut.

In Beran's account book, slamming a door counted as growling.

The side doors were already locked, so Beran had to go back inside through the Hall. Half a dozen guests were stretched out on pallets near the hearths, so he moved quietly across and tiptoed to his room. In the dark, the lump of covers that was Kaven didn't move. Beran felt his way toward his own bed and sat down to pull off his shoes. The first one slipped from his hand to bang into the floor, and when he looked up, he saw the glitter of an open eye. "Sorry," he murmured, knowing the word was inadequate for the territory it had to cover that went far beyond waking Kaven up. On top of Kaven's fears for his mother, he had Zale threatening to kill him if he went near Myla, and his uncle pushing him to do something for Sweet Stream Manor that Kaven didn't evidently want to do.

Kaven rolled over to face the wall, and Beran was bending to untie the other shoe when his muffled voice came: "Sorry I jumped you."

"It's all right. I've been dying to slug you for a while."

"Happy to oblige. Try it again, and I'll kick your rear."

Smiling to himself, Beran shed his clothes and crawled under the covers. As it nearly always did when he wasn't busy, his mind went straight to Ander. He thought about the day Ander died and all the little things that had happened just like they always did, neither of them knowing they were the last things. What would Ander say Beran should do now? Carl seemed to believe Beran should do what he liked. No, not what he liked. What he thought was right even if the manor holders or Corin or his father thought otherwise. So the question would be, what did Beran think was right?

Isadia sent a serving man to roust Beran out of bed at dawn so he could join her in bidding the guests a bleary-eyed farewell. They were eager to be on their way, probably to spread gossip to the neighbors who hadn't attended. When Beran finally had a chance to sit and eat his porridge, he found Lord Corin still at the table, drinking mint tea. Beran hesitated, but he was hungry, so he plunked down on the bench next to Corin and started shoveling it in.

"You know, Beran, I told your father people would resent him giving manors away, but he disregarded my objections. Folks will come around about the roads once they get used to them and see how much easier it is to import grain and sell their timber and furs, but they'll never accept handing out pieces of the Forest."

Beran stopped his spoon halfway to his mouth. Carl had been right the previous night. It was time to become a man who judged his own truth and lived by it. If Lord Corin thought him unfit to be King's Heir, so be it. "You were right, of course, but the king needs the timber. He needs ways to reward those who serve him, and he also needs enough people in the border areas to make them securely part of Rinland."

"Does that justify the trouble he creates for me in trying to rule?" Corin asked.

"A king needs to serve the good of the whole country."

Corin rubbed his chin, his gaze not on Beran, but on his men-at-arms carrying saddle packs across the Hall and out into the yard. "Lady Isadia tells me you might decide to stay at Green Valley Manor."

"No." As soon as the word slipped out, Beran knew it was the answer that had been inside him all along. "I'll be sorry to leave the Forest. It's beautiful in a way that took me a while to see, but I have duties elsewhere."

"As heir, you mean." Corin's tone was flat.

"Or not. Either way, I owe service to Rinland, and I can't just walk away. I won't just walk away. I love Rinland." It occurred to him that Rinland was likely to be the love of his life, jealous of any other. Beran drew a deep breath. "I made a copy of my map and gave it to one of your men. I hope it will be useful in catching the thieves."

Turning to Beran, Corin raised one eyebrow. "Are you suggesting I haven't done enough to hunt them?"

"Far from it, sir. I'm saying it's a difficult task, and we all can do more to help you if we share what we know and act as one."

Corin drummed his fingers on the table. "Naeth said you recognized one of the thieves."

Beran suppressed a flinch. "I didn't really. I was just trying to lure them out of hiding, but no one rose to the bait."

"By 'bait,' you mean you. You took a risk putting that about," Corin said. "One might almost think you acted on your Forest blood." One of his men signaled from the doorway, and Corin stood. "Don't get up," he said when Beran made to rise. "Isadia will see me off."

"By chance, does your ride home take you past Sweet Stream Manor?"

"No. Why?" Corin pulled gloves from his belt.

"You should go around that way and see for yourself. Also, one more thing. What do you know about Lord Talun?" Beran silently apologized to Myla for bringing trouble down on her family, but Corin had a right to know if Talun was dangerous.

"He keeps to himself," Corin said slowly. "He resents me and your father equally, but I'd have judged him too weak to do anything about it."

"Weak men can do harm," Beran said, thinking of trouble he'd seen his father forced to squash.

Wearing a half smile, Corin scanned Beran's face. Beran darted his tongue at the corners of his mouth, searching for stray bits of porridge or milk. "Thank you for the warning. I'll see you in Rin next month." He raised a hand and was gone.

Corin would see him, all right. In what role, was the question. What had gotten into him? He'd told Myla he couldn't interfere, and then done it anyway. Too late to take it back now. He finished his second bowl of porridge, then went to the stables to check on his horse and ask the stable master to exercise it again today. He was rounding the stable doorway when he heard Kaven.

"Why didn't you tell me?" His voice was tight.

Beran backed a step away.

"I didn't want to involve you," Myla said, "and now, I don't know what to do."

"There must be something."

Beran retreated. He'd see to his horse later.

The next day, Beran was trudging back from a training session with Carl when a man rode into the yard, and he recognized the messenger he'd seen giving Myla a note. The messenger spoke with one of Isadia's men, who escorted him into the house. Beran followed them into the Hall and along the corridor to the solar, where he knew his grandmother and her women were weaving because he'd heard the clack of the looms through the window earlier. From the doorway, he saw that even Myla had settled to the housewifely task today. When she saw the messenger, she half rose, ready to speak, but he ignored her and handed Isadia a letter.

Isadia slid her thumbnail under the seal. As she read, her shoulders drooped. She looked up at Myla. "Your father's ending the fostering arrangement, dear. He wants you home tomorrow."

Myla sank back onto her seat at the loom, her lips silently shaping *tomorrow.*

In the hallway outside the solar, Beran slumped against the wall and watched the messenger being led away to eat and rest. Absentmindedly, he plucked at his leather jerkin, trying to pull the sweat-soaked shirt underneath it away from his skin. That morning, Beran had spoken to his grandmother about Kaven's mother, and Isadia had shocked him by hesitating to "interfere." But Beran had already interfered when he'd spoken to Corin, so why not do it for Kaven and Myla?

When Myla came out of the solar and started toward her room, her head was down, so Beran had to grab her arm to get her attention. "Let go." Her voice shook.

"Wait." He hurried her into the Hall and then into a corner with his back to the room and his body shielding her from the view of the servant laying a fire. "Do you want to marry Zale?" She tried to slip away, but he put his arm out to block her escape. "Do you?"

"Of course not," she snapped with something of the normal Myla sting. "You saw him. It's what else to do that's the problem. This is more tangled than you know, Beran."

"Tell your father you won't do it. Be honest with him and Zale too. If you marry Zale, let that be your choice and no one else's. Even he deserves that the woman who marries him be willing."

She laughed unhappily. "You met my father. How likely do you think he is to listen to me? I wish I could bind myself to Kaven," she went on, as if to herself. "That would put an end to all my father's plans."

"What does that mean, bind yourself?"

"It's a promise of marriage that can't be broken."

"So why don't you do that?"

"I'm not of age. The pledge wouldn't be valid unless Da consented."

"You're my grandmother's fosterling. She'd consent, I'll bet anything. She's not big on forcing anyone's daughter to marry someone they don't love."

"Weren't you listening? My father revoked the fostering agreement."

"Can Lord Corin do anything or maybe even my father? Isn't there anyone else? Another relative?"

She'd been shaking her head, but abruptly, she stopped. Eyes narrowed, she looked away from him, then pushed against his restraining arm. "I have to talk to Kaven." When Beran moved out of her way, she hurried toward the door, but stopped long enough to say, "Thank you, Beran. You've been more help than you know." She flashed out the door, leaving Beran pleased, but puzzled.

A little later, he saw Myla and Kaven in the yard, with their heads together, talking. Beran couldn't guess what she told him, but Kaven looked a little less dead after that and even whistled as he rode out to whatever his task for the day was.

Deep as a Tomb

Beran went to bed dreading the morning and Myla's departure. He didn't know how long he'd been asleep when the bang of the shutter woke him to see Kaven climbing out the window. Beran didn't begrudge him and Myla their last private time together, so he closed his eyes, ready to sleep. They shot open again. Kaven had bumped the shutter because he was wearing a pack. Where was he going that he needed a pack?

Beran scrambled into his clothes, then climbed onto the table and slid over the windowsill into the vegetable garden. Before he did anything rash, he needed to be sure what was happening. The white stones of the path glowed in the moonlight. Bent low, he ran along the back of the house until he reached the women's wing where he paused to count windows. The one he thought was Myla's stood open. He squirmed along until he crouched below it, then edged up to see. The moonlight fell over his shoulder and across the rumpled covers of Myla's bed. No Myla. And no Kaven and Myla. Thank the Powers. Beran wanted to find them, but that would have been awkward.

Stone it. What were she and Kaven thinking?

That they'd be honest and do what they think is right, sang an unforgiving voice in Beran's head.

He hadn't meant they should run away together. Did he say they should do that? No, he did not. He'd told Myla to let her father know what she felt. This was not his fault.

But you're the one here, the voice said. *And anyway, what does it matter whose fault it is. What are you going to do about it?*

He shifted from foot to foot. He could wake up his grandmother and tell her what had happened so she could send her men after them. But if he did that, the whole household would know, and there would be no way this could be kept quiet. Gossip would fly all over the Westreach as everyone told one or two others supposedly sworn to secrecy. Lord Talun and Lord Zale would hunt Kaven down and kill him. Beran wasn't sure what they'd do to Myla, probably marry her to Zale anyway if he'd have her. What a happy wedding that would be. And the quarrel between Myla's family and Kaven's would rupture the peace of the Forest. No, Beran wouldn't wake anyone up, not yet anyway.

167

What then? He gnawed on the inside of his cheek, then crept across the yard to the stable and slipped in the side door. The stable boy slept in a small room overhead, so he catfooted down the row of stalls. Sleepy ponies lifted their heads. His horse blew its lips in a noisy greeting. He darted a few steps farther, saw that Myla's and Kaven's ponies were still in their boxes, and spun to flee back outside. As he pulled the door shut behind him, a sleep-blurred voice said, "Is someone there?"

Heart pounding, he ducked behind the watering trough and waited. No one came out. No raised voice summoned help. After a while, he slid out of hiding. He'd have to go after them himself. If he found them and got them back before morning, no one need ever know what they'd done. Without horses, they couldn't be far away yet, and given the guard out front, they had left by the postern gate. The garden and yard were still empty. Before that could change, he hurried across them and out the gate.

Chapter 18

Myla sloshed through the icy stream and onto the path on the other side, where she braced herself on Kaven's shoulder to put her stockings and boots back on. Kaven clasped her hand, his warm palm pressing against hers. They trotted along the path as fast as they could in the dark, until it petered out at a deadfall of old trees. Someone let out a relieved breath, and the man she'd met near Sweet Stream Manor stepped out of hiding. Myla groped for the name. Delur, that was it. Sweet Stream's steward.

"You got away clean?" Delur asked.

"I think so." Kaven's voice was tight. "Where are the ponies?"

"I decided we'd be better off without them."

"It will take us at least three days if we have to walk," Myla said.

"A pony is a great, neighing beacon, and your folks will be after us. I don't fancy a knife in my back. And you don't want them getting hold of Kaven, do you?"

"Silvit save us." Silently, Myla vowed to be glad Delur was there. She'd been wary the first time she met him, but he'd be useful at fighting off Zale or Da.

Delur picked up the pack at his feet and shrugged into it. "Let's go. Rickard is meeting us as soon as he gets rid of anyone looking for you at Sweet Stream."

"You know we're going to Oak Ridge Manor first, right?" Myla said.

"What? Are you st—" He stopped himself. "We can't do that, sweetheart. Your folks are there."

Glad to have Delur was one thing. Letting him pick her path was another. She was done with letting anyone do that. "Oak Ridge first. My father will never know we've been."

"We can't," Delur repeated, looking to Kaven for help.

"We do what she says," Kaven said.

Something large stumbled in the dark, smashing a bush. All three of them jerked toward the sound, Delur's knife flashing into his hand.

"Fair night," a heart-shriveling voice called, and Beran walked into the moon-washed clearing. His smile disappeared in a flinch when Delur lunged and put a blade to the side of his neck.

"Stop that!" Myla cried. With a glance at her, Delur eased back a little, and she swallowed her heart down out of her throat. *He's protecting us*, she reminded herself. If Zale had walked into the clearing, she'd have welcomed Delur's fierceness. "What are you doing here?" she asked Beran. Rot his royal head. It would serve him right if she let Delur cut him. Just a nick.

"Who's he?" Delur plucked Beran's knife from its sheath and slid it into his belt. "How did he find us?"

Myla drew breath to answer, but Beran spoke first. "I'm Balar. I'm fostering with Lady Isadia. I followed him." He tipped his head carefully toward Kaven, away from the point of Delur's knife.

Myla snapped her mouth shut on Beran's name.

"Did anyone else see Kaven or Myla go?" Delur asked.

"No," Beran said, sending Myla a look that was probably supposed to mean something, though she didn't care what. "They could go back, and no one would be the wiser."

"Put the knife away, Delur," Kaven said. "He's just another rich manor holder's brat. Probably figured he'd get an eyeful if he followed me and Myla. He's harmless."

Myla let her breath trickle through her teeth. Kaven had apparently decided to back up Beran's story, and she trusted him enough to follow his lead even if she didn't understand why.

Slowly, Delur pulled his knife away, and Beran's tense stance eased. "Delur? Sweet Stream's steward?" Beran said. "Kaven's family is helping you two run off?"

"Yes, though we're not 'running off,' as you so charmingly put it," Myla said.

"What would you call it then?" Beran said. "You won't be missed until dawn. You should go back."

"What business is this of yours?" Delur said.

An excellent question. "You were the one who told me to be honest, *Balar*," Myla said.

"I didn't mean you should run away, and you know it."

Myla didn't bother explaining further. "We're not going back."

"Your people will kill Kaven over this," Beran said.

"Shut up." In a blur, Delur's hand shot out, grabbed a startled Beran's collar, and twisted, tightening the cloth around Beran's throat. Beran gripped Delur's wrist and tried to force it loose.

"Let go!" Kaven shouted. "Rot you, Delur. Let go!"

Delur let go, dropping Beran to his hands and knees.

Myla rushed to his side and laid a hand on his heaving back. "What was that for? Have you lost your mind?" She shot a desperate look at Kaven. Surely he wouldn't have put their fate in the hands of someone dangerous.

"You will not hurt him." Kaven's voice shook. "You work for my family, which means you work for me, and I order you not to hurt him."

Delur laughed, but when Kaven stiffened, he said, "You're in charge, Kaven."

Myla fervently hoped so. Her knees trembled. *We need him*, she reminded herself.

Grabbing Beran under one arm, Delur hauled him to his feet. "You wanted to be here. Fine. You can come with us." Beran shook his hand off, glaring hard enough to make Delur take a step back before he leaned in again. "And don't get clever about delaying us. We've a long way to go." Delur nodded to Myla to lead the way.

She trotted to where she knew the path lay. *Rot Delur and Beran both.* She'd thought she was taking charge, but things threatened to slip out of her control already. Delur fell back to the rear of the group, and Myla was profoundly grateful to have Kaven and Beran between them. She forced herself to concentrate on what lay ahead. In the dark, she had to pick her way with slow care, fighting a hot urge to go faster. Beran was right that they had only till dawn before Isadia sent searchers out after them. Through every break in the canopy, she checked the wheel of the stars. The trip seemed to take a month, but at last, she led them to a grove where they'd be hidden but someone in a tree would have a clear view of Oak Ridge's house and yard. Kaven immediately shed his pack and started up a maple, climbing as sure-footedly as a squirrel. Distractedly, she watched the muscles in his legs until he vanished in the branches and she could tear her gaze away.

"Now what?" Delur shifted from foot to foot. "Is this going to take long?"

"It will take what time it takes," Myla said.

"Sweetheart—" Delur started.

"Don't call me that," Myla said, "and stop arguing, because I'm not going on until this is done." She was talking to herself as much as to Delur. Now they were here, her heart sped up, trying to pump away her trickles of fear. Delur's worry wasn't helping her any.

"You could go back," Beran said.

Delur rounded on him. "One more word, and I'll take my fists to you."

"Kaven told you not to hurt him." She was pretty sure Delur was angry because she'd insisted on this side trip, and Beran was a more acceptable target. It must have been the first time in his life Beran had been in that position because he was making trouble like he had the right, like the prince he'd not admitted to being. "Hush up, Balar. This is important."

Beran glanced at her, then looked away, frowning.

Kaven clambered down, jumping the last two yards to land lightly as a cat. "There's more men guarding the yard than you thought there'd be."

"Who are they?" Myla had been sure there'd be only the usual guard at the front gate.

"I couldn't tell for sure, but I think they're Zale's."

Her breath caught, her body recognizing the meaning before it climbed up into her head. Of course Zale and his men were there. Da expected her home tomorrow. Today, really, since midnight had come and gone. He intended her to marry Zale within an hour after she walked through the door. Fear and revulsion twisted her stomach.

"You still want to do this?" Kaven asked.

"Do what?" Delur demanded.

"I have to." Swallowing what little spit was in her mouth, Myla turned to Delur. "I'm going into Oak Ridge's yard. I'll try not to be long."

"Don't be a fool!" Delur cried. "Kaven, if you don't stop her, I will."

Myla twitched with the urge to kick the man.

"I'm going with her," Kaven said. "Don't worry. We'll both be back." Kaven and Delur exchanged a long look before Delur threw up his hands.

"You'd better take care then," he told Kaven. "Zale would slit you open and sit down to breakfast with his appetite sharpened." He shoved Beran toward the tree Kaven had climbed. "You sit down and keep quiet if you know what's good for you." Face a mask, Beran slid to sit against the trunk.

"Maybe you should stay here, Kaven," Myla said. "I can go alone."

"No," Kaven said, and she was ashamed of how grateful she was. He hustled her out of the clearing and into the surrounding greenery.

"I don't like him," she murmured.

"I don't either, but I promise no one will hurt you. I swear I love you, Myla."

Despite her fear, she smiled, though she was sure he couldn't see. "I know."

"How did you plan to get into the yard?"

"The postern gate. Was it guarded?"

173

"I couldn't see."

"Let's try it." She pushed through the undergrowth until she spotted a path she'd wandered almost every day since she could first toddle. Her throat loosened. At last, she knew where she was and where she was going. She hurried along the path, Kaven's reassuring presence at her back. From under their feet, the scent of crushed leaf litter rose like dusty perfume. They slowed when they came out into the orchard, which, like Green Valley's, lay just outside the postern gate. The manor's stone wall loomed, pierced by a solid wood gate. Beyond it, on the house roof, Silvit lay bathed in moonlight. The sight stopped her, the way her own dithering had done for days. *Please, Silvit*, she prayed silently. *I know I took the circlet, so I don't deserve your help. But the Forest's wisdom is in those books, your wisdom. Help me do this, not for me, but for all those your medicines could heal.*

Stupid, Da's voice whispered in her ear.

Into her head flashed a question she'd asked in the Steeprise tomb. Was she predator or prey?

Kaven touched her shoulder. "Myla?"

She drew a deep breath. "Let's go."

The orchard's open spaces would make it easier for a guard to spot them, but Myla knew this place like she knew her own bed. She crept through the rows of apple-laden trees, listening hard and hearing nothing but the sighing of the tree tops and the call of a hunting owl. She beckoned Kaven on. A man coughed, and from beyond the gate came the creak of leather armor. Kaven hissed a soft warning, but she'd already frozen. She slithered back into the shadows and retreated with Kaven to the orchard's edge.

"Where else could we get in?" Kaven whispered.

She gnawed her lower lip before forcing herself to answer. "There's a low spot in the wall behind the laundry." Her stomach churned. If she and Kaven went over that wall, the "low" spot wouldn't be nearly low enough. She hadn't climbed higher than the top of a stool since the day she found her books in the attic.

"We can go back to Delur," Kaven said. "You don't have to do this."

"I do. It's this way."

She skirted the yard, keeping a distance between them and the wall. When she judged they'd reached the laundry, she slipped closer. Last winter, ice had shifted the wall's top stones here, and half a dozen had fallen off. She'd seen the break, behind the laundry where clothes were hung to dry. Myla thought the younger laundress had a sweetheart who used the gap as a way in. At any rate, no one had reported it to Da or the steward, and they never came back here. She eyed the spot, breathing hard. The wall came to her shoulders. Her head whirled.

"Can you do it?" Kaven asked.

"I have to." Even to herself, she sounded close to tears. Her feet seemed rooted where she stood.

"Myla, we have to hurry."

"I know." She shuffled close enough to pat the wall's rough stones, like it was some scary animal she could coax into being less threatening. She reached up to put her palms on the top of the gap.

"I can help," Kaven said. "I will unless you tell me you don't want me to."

She swallowed, mouth too dry to speak. Kaven seized her around the waist and heaved her up onto the wall. "No!" she cried, too late. His hand was on her backside, boosting her over. For an instant, she fell and then, to her surprise, she was crouched on her feet in the yard.

Kaven landed next to her. "Are you all right?" His voice was low, and she remembered the extra guards. In their pen not far away, geese had awakened.

"I'm…I'm good."

Kaven gave a soft laugh. "Of course you are. Where now?"

"This way." They ran to the corner of the laundry. Someone had forgotten the sheets on the line, and they couldn't see far, but then they'd be harder to spot too.

Steps trotted their way. "Who's there?" a man called. He swatted a sheet aside and stared toward the goose pen. At the sound of his threatening voice, the geese squawked louder. Myla took Kaven's hand, and they slid silently into deep shadow around the building's corner.

"Shut up," the guard snarled.

Every goose in the pen honked like a fox was slinking through their fence.

Someone laughed, and a second voice spoke. "Afraid of being pecked to death, Arnil?"

Arnil wished blight on several parts of the second guard's body. Pulling Kaven after her, Myla moved toward the front of the laundry and peeked around the corner into the yard. A man was just passing out of sight along the side of the house. Heart pounding, she sped to the door of the herb room. The latch rattled under her shaking hand. She shoved the door open, and she and Kaven fell into the room. She closed the door silently behind them and leaned against it, breathing hard.

She waited for her eyes to adjust to the dim light, inhaling the familiar scents of herbs and books and Kaven. Gradually the room emerged. On the table lay a heap of books with her herb bag flung down on top of them. The books Da had taken from Green Valley had been dumped from the bag like so much kindling. A page had come loose and lay crumpled on the floor. Fury drove out every other feeling. Rot Da and Galen both.

She seized the bag and started tucking books into it. "Get as many as you can," she told Kaven. "We'll need two trips."

"I see why you said we couldn't just take them with us." Kaven scooped up an armload.

Her bag was full. She gathered as many more books as she could in her arms. "Ready?"

"Where to?"

"The kitchen first. Da never goes there. He wouldn't know if we moved the hearth from one wall to another."

She had to put some of the books down to have a free hand. No matter. She'd make as many trips as she had to. She cracked the door ajar and peered out. Through the narrow opening, she could see in only one direction, and the thunder of her heart drowned out any hope of hearing footsteps. She inched the door wider and crept out. When she saw no one, she dashed to the kitchen and shouldered the door open. Kaven closed it behind them without a sound, despite the load of books in his arms.

Deep as a Tomb

The room glowed with the banked fire. Skirting the big table, she went to crouch by the right side of the hearth, where she put down the books and used her fingertips to pry out the second stone from the wall. A dark hollow lay behind.

"What's this?" Kaven whispered.

Despite her tight nerves, she smiled. "I used to play in here sometimes, and when I found this, Cook let me claim it to hide things." Memory opened like a flower. It was snowing, so she couldn't go out in the woods, but the kitchen was warm and safe. Cook oohed and aahed over her find and called her clever.

She felt around to be sure the space was clear. The books were going to take up a lot of room. Her fingertips brushed something soft and dry, and she pulled out a cloth doll.

Kaven gave a quiet laugh. "Yours?" He reached over her shoulder to touch the place where the doll's left arm should have been. Instead, clumsy stitches sealed the gap where it had been ripped off. "You were a healer even then."

"Her name is Rose." Myla smiled apologetically at the shabby thing. Had she really abandoned Rose here? Well, there were worse places at Oak Ridge than the fragrant kitchen. "I put her here to keep warm while she got better. And to keep her away from Galen, of course," she added.

"He being the one who removed her arm."

"He being the one." She stood and looked around. "Fit as many books as you can in there." She crossed to the shelves of dishes, moved a few around, and laid Rose down in an ugly, seldom used bowl.

When Kaven had filled the space and put the stone back, they snuck through the yard to the vegetable garden and into the gardening shed. She opened the chest in the dark corner at the shed's rear. As long as Myla could remember, Old Brach had tossed broken tools in here, pledging to mend them come winter, but the pile never shrank. When she and Kaven had hauled out all the junk and piled it on the dirt floor, she carefully stacked the books from her bag and then added the last of those Kaven carried. She spread a torn canvas over them and, with Kaven's help, replaced the tools.

177

She shouldered her empty bag as Kaven closed the chest, then opened the door a sliver, only to snick it shut again when she heard footsteps. Kaven pressed close behind her as she waited. His breath stirred her hair, and his scent addled her brain. He bent to speak in her ear.

"You are amazing, but then, I knew that the first time I laid eyes on you at Isadia's."

She smiled at the cracked wooden door. She would save her books. She would pledge herself to Kaven, and someday when she was ready to run a manor, she would marry him. She would never again creep like a mouse in her own home.

When the footsteps faded, she led Kaven back to the herb room where they gathered the rest of the books. There was a little room left in her bag, so she took the time to speed around the room and fill a fat pouch with medicines they might need on their trip. Then she scanned the room, making sure they'd missed nothing. Her eye caught on the loose page under the table. She smoothed it out and slid it between two books. She added the medicines, then went to where Kaven waited at the door.

"All these should fit in the laundry," she said.

"Another place your father never goes?" Kaven said, amusement in his voice. "I think when I get back to Sweet Stream, I'll have to poke around where all the women's work is done. The Forest only knows what I'll find."

In the laundry, she showed him the cupboard where her winter clothes were stored. She was piling books behind her fur-lined boots when a man spoke on the outer side of the wall.

"Our relief better get here soon. I'm pinching myself to stay awake."

"Give me a swallow from that flask of yours," a second voice said.

Myla stopped moving, nearly stopped breathing. It was the two guards who'd come running when the geese squawked.

There was a thud, like one of them was leaning against the laundry wall, kicking his heel about a foot in front of her nose.

"There'll be wine at the wedding," the first one said. His foot kept up its rhythmic tattoo.

Silently, she pulled the last book out of her bag, untangling it from the medicine pouch. She set it down like a feather and covered the pile with her heaviest cloak. Kaven noiselessly closed the cupboard door.

The man kept kicking.

She felt Kaven looking at her and knew what question would be on his face. The men were between them and the gap in the wall. How were she and Kaven getting out of Oak Ridge?

She thought furiously. The guards needed to be running around worrying about something that wasn't her and Kaven. Beckoning Kaven after her, she tiptoed to the laundry doorway and peeked out. No one in sight.

"Be ready to go out the front gate." Hunched over, she crept through the yard to the goose pen. As soon as she drew near, the geese began to mutter, but softly yet. After all, they knew her, as much as geese ever knew anything. She drew a steadying breath, unlatched their gate, and flung it wide. Ignoring Kaven's stifled exclamation, she dashed into the pen. Now the geese were waking up and making noise. She ran around the pen, flapping her arms and shooing them out into the yard.

"What's that?" a man called.

She tore out of the pen, seized Kaven's hand, and fled through a flock of frightened geese to the deep shadows along the wall. Heavy steps and shouting men headed for the goose pen. She stopped near the dovecote, straining to see what was happening at the front gate. The guard there turned toward the noise. He took two steps, then stopped.

Go, go, she urged him silently. *They need your help.*

A goose waddled into sight, honking and flapping its clipped wings.

"Catch that, you fool!" a man shouted.

The guard dove for the goose, which hopped out of reach, more afraid than ever. The guard chased after it.

Kaven grabbed her hand, seeing the same chance she did. Staying in the shadows as long as they could, they ran for the gate, tore through it, and were into the trees before Myla had time to start shaking.

Hidden in the woods, they stopped. She listened for cries of alarm, but heard only the geese, frustrated men, and her and Kaven's panting.

"Silvit save me, you're fearless," Kaven murmured.

"I'm getting there."

She could see the manor between the trees. For a moment she stood still, looking at the place where she'd been a little girl, where she'd learned to use medicines, dreamed by the Hall fire on an autumn night, played, been lonely, always felt small. *Goodbye, Da,* she thought. She turned, took Kaven's hand, and ran. She didn't look back.

Chapter 19

Beran leaned against the maple. Chill night air slid into the front of his shirt and down its neck. He wrapped his arms around himself and considered getting up to pace like Delur. Even if he weren't cold, movement would ease his tense muscles. Every time he looked at Delur, an alarm drum throbbed in his head. This man was not the sort to risk himself for Kaven and Myla out of warm-hearted kindness. What was his game?

"They've been gone a long time," Beran probed. "You sure Kaven means to come back?"

Delur snorted. "He's not settling down as Lord Talun's guest, I can tell you that much. He'll be back. He needs me."

"Needs you for what?" Beran asked. "Where are they going?" When Delur had greeted him with a knife to the neck, he'd hidden his identity, unsure whether his rank would make Delur back down or slit his throat. Even Ander had sometimes concealed who Beran was when a situation looked chancy. But being Balar had proven unexpectedly useful. Balar was willing to be nosy in very unprincelike ways. Balar didn't care if anyone approved of him.

"Shut up," Delur said.

Unfortunately, being Balar didn't help him get answers.

In Beran's head, those unanswered questions galloped around in circles. At the feast, Kaven's Uncle Rickard had pushed him toward Myla and muttered that he should do something quickly. Maybe running away with Myla was what Rickard meant. But why? On the two occasions Beran had seen Rickard, Kaven's happiness had not been high on Rickard's list of worries.

"If they're caught, what are you going to tell Rickard?" Beran asked.

"Stone Rickard," Delur said. "He owes me, and if Kaven fouls up, he better find some other way to pay me."

"Rickard owes you money?" Beran asked.

"I told you to shut up."

Beran turned his signet ring around and around. Sweet Stream was short of coin, so maybe Rickard hadn't paid his men. Under normal circumstances, when Myla married, she'd have a substantial dowry, but Kaven and Myla couldn't marry, so helping the two of them run off wouldn't solve Rickard's problems. The alarm drum beat louder. Kaven had said his grandfather had left no debts. What had happened to Sweet Stream's money?

"I hear the thieves robbed you, Delur," he said. "How much did they get?"

Delur crossed to him in two steps and backhanded him where he sat. Beran's head thunked against the tree truck. Little lights danced in his vision, and he tasted blood.

"I said shut up." Delur leaned over Beran, breathing hard, daring him to fight back.

Beran's muscles quivered. Being Balar apparently went only so deep. It took almost more restraint than he had to look away, as if intimidated, and swallow his instinctive "How dare you?" His outrage surprised him. He apparently had a stronger sense of royal entitlement than he'd realized. He kept his eyes averted until Delur resumed pacing, then cautiously wiggled his right hand into his belt pouch and slipped off his ring. Balar had to rely on his own wits, training, and strength, and hope they were enough.

Once more, he let his thoughts gallop free. Whatever was going on here, Kaven and especially Myla were in more danger than they seemed to know. Not that they'd listen to him if he told them. They were both typical Forest wooden heads, and he feared they were about to be mugged in a dark alley of their own making. Beran couldn't leave them now even if Delur let him. They were his friends as Beran. They were his people as prince. Either way,

182

he owed them. He needed to bide his time and learn as much as he could before he acted. His mouth twisted. His father would have been proud of his patience. Maybe.

Leaves rustled, and Kaven and Myla trotted into sight, holding hands and looking pleased with themselves. Beran lifted his gaze to the dark treetops. Wooden heads.

"You took your time," Delur said. "I hope whatever you were doing was worth it."

"It was," Myla said. "Let's go." She reshouldered her pack and struck off on another path heading north.

Feeling like he'd been tied up and cut loose, Beran sprang to his feet.

Delur pointed at him. "Keep up, or I'll have your hide."

Beran ignored him. In charge of his own life, Balar was a hard man to intimidate. With Delur's hot breath on his neck, he followed Kaven and Myla. The path emerged onto a rutted dirt lane, still soft with the recent rain. Unlike the rest of them, Beran carried no pack, but by the time dawn grayed the sky, even he felt the effects of a strained, sleepless night. When Myla stumbled, Kaven caught her elbow and looked over his shoulder.

"We need to rest for a while, Delur."

Delur eyed the lane, where their feet had left the only marks Beran saw. "Not long," Delur said. "Not if you want to live." He looked ahead again. "Let's see if those rocks will hide us." A short distance farther, they walked between two boulders into an open area sheltered by huge rocks. "Not long," Delur repeated, and then wandered off to check the rocky passages. After a moment's hesitation and a quick glance at Beran and Myla, Kaven followed him. Beran hoped he meant to get the man under control and had the means to do it, because the drum still pounded danger in his head.

Myla dropped her pack with a thud, took a folded blanket, and spread it on a pile of leaves blown against the foot of a rock. "You can share with Kaven and me."

Beran flopped down next to Myla to wait for Kaven and a chance to ask them both what the plan was. He lay looking up at a patch of blue outline by treetops. "Don't you miss the sky?"

"What do you mean? It's right there."

"But look at how small it is. In Rin, it stretches from horizon to horizon."

Myla spoke slowly. "You sound as if you love Rin."

"I do, though I only notice it when I'm away. I've sometimes thought life would be easier if I didn't care where I was."

"I can't imagine having to leave the Forest all the time. I hadn't thought until recently about how loving a place can leave you as vulnerable as loving a person."

Beran had a quick vision of Lord Corin's face saying, "You look like your mother."

"Love's dangerous in general," he said soberly. "It's likely to leave you wanting things you can't have."

"I mean to have Kaven and the Forest too," Myla said.

Kaven strode back into the clearing. Glaring at Beran, he got his own blanket and brought it over. Beran motioned for him to place it on his other side so he could talk to them both. Kaven gave him a you-are-a-blister-on-my-backside look, but lay down so Beran was in the middle. Beran felt like a governess keeping watch. He suspected that was one of the things Kaven was mad about.

"You took care of Delur?" Beran asked quietly.

"I hope so." Kaven spoke with equal softness.

"How well do you know him?" Beran asked.

"As well as I care to. He and another man were friends with my uncle in Rinland and they came back to Sweet Stream when he did."

Beran considered that information before speaking cautiously. "Delur says your uncle owes him money."

Kaven was silent a moment before saying, "They gamble sometimes. My uncle doesn't know when to quit."

"Delur seems to hope this trip will let your uncle pay him off," Beran said.

"Delur hopes for a lot of things," Kaven said.

"Stop fretting," Myla said. "We know what we're doing."

That seemed unlikely. "We can still salvage the situation," Beran murmured. "Kaven can tell Delur we're going back, and when we get to my grandmother's, we say we knew Myla was going home, and we wanted to spend our last night together in the woods. But we got lost, and that's why we were gone overnight."

"It's too late for that, and you know it." Kaven sounded almost despairing.

For a long moment, Beran clung to hope that Kaven was wrong. Then, with a sigh, he let that notion slip away. If Kaven showed up where Myla's family could find him, he was a dead man. Beran covered his face with his hands, searching in the dark for a way out and finding only the grazed spot Delur's knuckles had left on his cheekbone. "So what's this plan you have?"

Myla spoke softly, but the words burst out, pushed by her excitement. "We're going to Jorn's tomb." She must have read the lack of understanding on Beran's face, because she clarified. "The first chieftain's tomb in the north. Both Kaven's family and mine descend from him, so the ones buried there are our ancestors as much as my father and Kaven's uncle are. If they approve, that's all Kaven and I need to pledge ourselves to one another in a way Da can't undo. We can't marry until we're of age, but we'll be bound. After that, there'll be no point to Da coming after us any more."

Beran opened and closed his mouth in his best fish imitation. "How can they approve? They're dead."

"Sometimes you really are just a grassland outsider." Her disgust was plain. She changed the subject as if tired of correcting his ignorance. "Why did you give Delur Carl's son's name?"

"What?" The image of a child's pack flitted into his head, a pack marked with a B. His breath caught. "Carl called me Balar once by accident."

She faced him so she could continue speaking softly. "Did he tell you the story of how Balar died?"

Beran cringed. "No."

"It happened just last winter. Balar was an apprentice city Watchman, stationed in a bad area. What did he call it? The Shambles maybe?"

"Yes, that's what they call Rin's slums."

"A house caught fire, and the Watch was responsible for putting it out, but Carl says there aren't many fountains in that part of town."

Carl was right. Beran had sat in meetings of his father's council where the lack of water in the Shambles was talked about with no action ever taken.

"A little girl was trapped in an upstairs bedroom," Myla said. "Balar went in after her, and the roof collapsed. That was when Carl arrived. He'd heard the alarm and knew his boy was on duty. He went mad when they told him Balar was inside. He burned his arms before they got hold of him and dragged him away."

The Powers help him. Beran had seen the scars. He felt sick. He'd been away all winter, fostering in the Vale with a lord who had suggested his six-year-old daughter as a possible match for Beran. He'd never heard about this fire. By the time he'd come home, no one even thought it important enough to still be talking about.

"It's such a shame," Myla said. "Carl's wife died when this boy was born. Losing him nearly killed Carl, and it did turn him into a drunk for a while. I gather the guard captain was very patient."

"How do you know all this?" Beran asked.

"Carl was in bad shape after you were hurt, so I went to see if I could help him. He told me then." She bit her lip, then added, "I think he might have been too drunk to guard his tongue."

"Carl believes in protecting his family." Kaven's wistful voice made Beran jump. He'd been so absorbed in Myla's story that he'd forgotten Kaven was there.

Delur loomed over them. "Sleep while you can."

Kaven got up and skirted around Delur to settle on Myla's other side. He flung his blanket over them both. Myla tried to tug hers out from under them, clearly meaning to give it to Beran, but he waved it off. The day washed warm over his skin.

He closed his eyes, felt sun on the lids, and heard Delur move away. He wished Myla hadn't told him about Carl. He knew who'd be coming after them today, frantic at the loss of someone he was protecting. If Beran did what his father would expect and called the searchers to him, Myla and

Deep as a Tomb

Kaven would be parted from Delur, at least temporarily, but Myla's family would lie in wait for as long as it took to kill Kaven. On the other hand, Myla seemed sure that if they went on, she and Kaven could make some sort of binding Forest pledge. Beran could think of no other way out. It didn't matter what his father would expect. Beran was here, not his father. He was the one who knew all the details, so the decision was his. If he wanted to save Kaven and Myla from their own impulsive actions, he'd have to evade Carl no matter how cruel it felt.

"Get up," Delur said. "We need to move, and I have an idea."

The sun told Beran it was mid-morning. He peeled his tongue from the gummy roof of his mouth. Myla was sitting up next to him, combing her hair. Kaven, too, was awake, though he looked groggy and hadn't gotten beyond lifting his head to look at Delur.

Delur groped through his saddlebag and pulled out a packet wrapped in waxed cloth. He opened it, took one of the hard-boiled eggs, and sent the rest from hand to hand so they all could help themselves. Beran's stomach burbled happily at the sight. He peeled an egg, then gratefully accepted a lukewarm drink when Myla offered her water skin.

He expected Delur to make an effort to clean up the campsite so no one following would know they'd been there. Instead he had them gather their belongings and sent them back and forth out of the gap to the lane and onto a faint path on the other side, leaving obvious tracks. Then he led them along a passage poking farther back into the rocks. He stopped facing a sloping stone wall.

"Climb it," he told them, grinning at his own cleverness. "The rocks will hide our tracks." He went back along the passage and vanished.

Beran shielded his eyes against the sun. He'd learned to climb when he fostered in the Uplands, and apart from a shaky-looking stretch of rock on the left, the climb looked easy. Next to him, Myla swallowed hard enough that Beran heard her. Her face had gone pale. So there was something she feared after all.

"You want me to go first?" Kaven asked Myla, voice anxious.

"No, I want this over with. Besides, I'm fearless, remember?" Myla reached for a handhold and set her foot on an outcropping. Her knee was shaking, but she pulled herself up and moved to the next foothold.

Kaven hovered on the ground beneath her. "That's the way," he said. "You're doing fine."

Beran envied the obvious bond between them. Not that he'd ever imagined tying himself to Myla, mostly because he'd seen from their first meeting that she regarded Kaven as if he'd invented spring, but also because she was too unsuited to court life for his father to ever approve. She was too Forest. Of course, Thien had married Beran's Forest mother, but the nature of their relationship was a mystery Beran had set aside as unsolvable for now.

Myla inched her way up. Each time she searched for the next place to move, Beran glimpsed her face. Her jaw was rigid with terror. She might not be fearless, Beran thought, but she was brave.

Delur ran into sight, clutching a leafy branch he'd evidently gone to fetch. "Someone's coming. Get up there now." He spun to face the campsite and back toward them, sweeping the branch over their tracks.

Myla turned her head to look at him. Big mistake. The look down sent her lurching against the rock face, and her left foot slipped. Kaven hurled himself onto the sloping rock and scrambled upward, his frantic ascent closing the space in an eyeblink to put him right below her. His mouth was moving, but he spoke softly enough that Beran couldn't hear what he said. Myla never made a sound. Instead, she pressed her cheek against the rock, closed her eyes, and dragged herself up so both feet were once again supported.

"Hurry." Delur shoved Beran hard, though Myla still hadn't reached the top.

Before he could stop himself, Beran snapped, "Don't touch me." He started up the rocks. Pebbles and dirt rained down on him, disturbed by Myla and Kaven. He squinted up. Myla's face was streaked with tears, but she was close enough to the top that Kaven boosted her to safety and followed right behind. Beran had climbed when he fostered in the Uplands, and he was at the top before Delur had time to wipe the snarl off his face. He looked back down at Delur dragging himself up the wall of rock. For an instant, he pictured driving the heel of his boot into Delur's face, and something must have shown in his look because Delur's eyes widened. Beran felt a flush of shame. The man was a weasel, but Beran sadly concluded he had no right to hurt him that badly. The moment passed. Delur heaved himself over the edge.

They were on a stretch of rocky ground that sloped down for maybe two hundred yards to end in more woods. Myla huddled a few yards back from the edge with Kaven's arms around her.

Rolling onto his stomach, Delur peered down over their campsite, then pointed at Myla and Kaven. "Lie down. I don't want anyone spotting you against the sky." He shrugged out of his pack and pushed it away from the lip of the drop.

Ignoring Delur's glare, Beran lay down next to him, as Kaven belly-crawled up on Delur's other side. A hand grabbed Beran's ankle, making him jump. He looked over his shoulder to see that farther back from the edge, Myla was stretched out to grip one of his ankles and one of Kaven's. He had time to share a smile with Kaven over Delur's head before a horse neighed, and four men rode along the lane and into the campsite. Beran recognized three of Isadia's men-at-arms, along with the messenger who'd come from Myla's family to take her home. Isadia's guard captain spoke one word, and they dismounted and fanned out to search the area.

Beran's fingers opened and closed, clawing his nails over rock. He'd decided Myla and Kaven couldn't go safely home, and it was his responsibility to help them find another way out of their troubles. Still it was hard to side with Delur against what his father, his grandmother, Lord Corin, and anyone with a thimbleful of sense would expect.

Something pricked the side of his neck. Delur pressed his knife tip a whisker deeper. "Make a sound, and you're dead," he whispered.

Beran held very, very still.

Three of the searchers paced around the campsite, while one inspected all the tracks in the gap between the rocks. "They've gone into the woods on the other side," he called.

"That's right," Delur murmured. "Follow us."

The messenger walked part way into the passage below where Beran lay.

"Stone it." Delur's hand twitched.

Beran put one finger on the hilt of the knife and eased it a hair's breadth away. From the corner of his eye, he glimpsed Kaven grip Delur's other wrist. Delur gave a muffled curse and withdrew the knife farther.

The messenger scanned the ground, then returned to the campsite, having never looked up. Beran tried to squelch his indignation at the man's carelessness and be grateful instead, but Ander would have made Beran repeat the search and do it right a half dozen times if he'd been that lazy. The men mounted their horses and rode off, following the trail Delur had laid.

Delur pulled his knife away and started to rise.

"Wait." Beran caught his arm.

Delur frowned at him.

"My…A guard is missing."

Delur's eyes narrowed as he took in what Beran meant. He grunted back onto his stomach.

Out of the woods came Carl, ready to spot them if they'd somehow hidden in the campsite and were now trustingly emerging. Like the others, he dismounted and drew his sword. He turned slowly, then circled the camp's edges, scanning not only the tracks, but every possible hiding place. Then finally, he lifted his gaze and ran it along the ridge where Beran lay.

Beran tried to flatten himself parchment thin. Grit dug into his bruised cheek. He didn't even breathe for fear Carl would see the rise and fall of his back. It was better not to see Carl anyway. Guilt pulsed through Beran's body with every beat of his heart.

After what seemed a week, he heard Carl ride away. He lifted his head just enough to see Carl going in the same direction as the others. The Powers only knew why Carl thought Beran had run off with Kaven and Myla. He was probably too busy planning how to make Beran suffer to care.

Beran let out a soft sigh. There'd be no changing his mind now. He'd tied himself to helping Myla and Kaven bind themselves to one another, and then to escaping whatever threat Delur might pose.

They stayed put for a few more moments before Delur rose, signaling the rest of them could too.

"Let's go." Myla started down the slope behind them.

"Wait." Delur rubbed his stubbly jaw. "We're not supposed to have Big Mouth here with us. Rickard won't be happy if we show up with him in tow." His knife was still in his hand. He turned it and eyed the blade thoughtfully.

Beran shifted his weight to the balls of his feet. Let Delur try to come after him without the element of surprise. Not for nothing had he trained since he was seven. He'd have the man's knife out of his hand and break his wrist.

Kaven scrambled back up the slope to stand between Beran and Delur. "Let him be, Delur. He's harmless." A growl rose in Beran's throat. Over his shoulder, Kaven shot him a pointed look. "Delur is helping us." He turned back. "We agreed my uncle still needs my cooperation, right?"

Delur studied him. "Your ma is hoping for it too. Did I tell you how worried she is?"

Kaven's back stiffened at the threat even Beran heard. He glanced toward where Myla waited, watching and listening with a faintly puzzled air. "There's no need to do anything now. Once Myla and I are pledged, no one will be able to undo it, and we can just let him go."

Lips pursed, Delur tapped the flat of his knife against his trouser seam.

"I mean it, Delur," Kaven said sharply.

Delur thrust his knife back into its sheath and bared his teeth in what was probably meant as a smile. "As long as he makes no trouble, there's no reason to fret."

The ghost of Delur's knife point still prickling under his left ear, Beran drew a deep breath. Never having had a guard, Balar supported and depended on his allies, even if he could kick Delur's rear.

Delur led them through and around undergrowth until they found a game path heading north again. Beran's thoughts tugged endlessly at what he'd seen and heard, and slowly, like a child's puzzle, the pieces fit together: an old, treasure-filled tomb, a girl who could open it, a ruthless man who wanted money. Myla obviously didn't know Delur, but Kaven did, and he was ordinarily no fool. How could he be witless enough to trust the man?

Love and desire, Beran guessed. He'd seen them turn both men and boys useless before. Girls and women, too, for all he knew. He hadn't lived close enough to them to tell.

Eventually, they found another old dirt track, one Delur and Myla had evidently been looking for. Delur pressed on throughout the afternoon. The sun was filtering through the treetops when they came to a clearing around a cabin that looked to have erupted from the forest floor like a rotten tooth. The thatch had blackened in some spots and sprouted plants in others. One of the shutters hung from a single leather hinge. Inside, a table and two stools sat in one corner, with a narrow bed opposite. The place smelled of mice and damp.

"Found it." Smiling, Delur eased his pack off. "We beat Rickard here after all. Go close the shutters, Kaven." He opened his pack, pulled out flint and tinder, and kindled several candles. He dripped wax on the table and stood the candles upright in it.

Kaven went out. The room dimmed as he closed the good shutter and tried to wrestle the broken one over the window. Someone hailed him, and Beran recognized Rickard's voice. He braced himself. His time being Balar was about to come to an abrupt finish. Maybe his instinct to hide himself had taken him far enough to make a difference in Kaven and Myla's fate. Other than that, what Rickard's presence would add to the power struggle here, Beran couldn't predict.

Chapter 20

Beran leaned one hip casually against the table, drawing on years of watching his father to arrange himself like a man whom fear couldn't touch.

"Help him, Lanal," Rickard called to a person who'd evidently come with him. Then the cabin door opened, and Rickard strode in. Ignoring Delur's greeting, he scanned the room and broke into a smile when he saw Myla. "Good—" he began. His gaze went past her to Beran, and the smile vanished. He spun to face Delur. "What's he doing here?"

So no warm welcome from Rickard. Beran glanced at Myla, who took a step closer to him.

"Balar?" Delur said. "He came after them, and we couldn't let him go off and warn her folks."

"Balar? Is that what you think he's called? You fool!"

Delur's jaw tightened. "Watch who you're calling a fool."

"I'll call you worse than that. Do you know who he is?"

"Silvit save us!" quivered a voice from the doorway. A wide-eyed, skinny man stood there with Kaven crowding into the room behind him. The fear-frozen man—Lanal, presumably—looked vaguely familiar. Beran groped through the scattered bits in his head, and suddenly the world rearranged itself.

The room narrowed to a tunnel between him and Lanal. Like metal shavings to a lodestone, Beran felt pulled along it, fists opening and closing. His heart pounded. His blood roared in his ears. "You're the thief who attacked Myla. You killed Ander."

He flung himself at Lanal, slamming him back against the door frame with his forearm across Lanal's throat. With the other hand, Beran snatched the man's knife from his belt. Lanal gripped Beran's wrist in both hands and struggled to hold him off. Beran strained to tear loose and stab him.

Men's voices shouted. Someone grabbed Beran's shoulders, but he shook the clutching hands off. Lanal rolled off the door frame, and the two of them spilled to the filthy cabin floor. Beran drove the knife closer. The fear on Lanal's face sent glee spurting through him.

"Not me," Lanal cried. "Delur."

Someone grabbed a handful of Beran's hair. Someone else wrapped an arm around his neck. Then he was on his feet, held between Delur and Rickard, Delur twisting his wrist until the pain stabbed strong enough to shatter it and he had to drop the knife. Delur caught it and tossed it to Lanal. Rickard stepped between Beran and Lanal, who scrambled backward, brandishing his blade.

"Delur killed him," Lanal panted. "Not me. It wasn't me."

"Shut up, stupid," Delur growled.

In his mind's eye, Beran saw again the place where Ander died. The wounded Lanal cowering in his hiding place, Ander approaching him, someone coming from behind, slipping the leather thong down around Ander's neck and twisting, the way Beran's wrist had just been twisted. In a breath, he ran his thoughts over what he'd seen of Delur. He'd known the man only a night and a day, but he knew with stone certainty that Delur was capable of murder. As if he felt the heat of Beran's gaze, Delur turned his head to meet it. Fear flickered in his eyes.

"I should have kicked you off that cliff when I had the chance," Beran said. "But it doesn't matter because you're going to be dead anyway."

"What are you saying?" Myla sounded dazed. If Beran's notion of things had changed, hers must have been falling around her ears.

"It was an accident," Rickard said hastily, looking from her to Beran and back. "Delur was just defending himself against the guard's sword. I told them no one was to be hurt."

Beran laughed in his face. "Ander's sword was still in its scabbard when I found him."

Rickard frowned. Beran could almost see the thoughts churning behind his eyes. "Is that true, Delur?"

"Of course not," Delur said. "And you were the one who shoved His Mouthiness here into that killer bush."

"I told you I didn't." Rickard and Delur glared at one another.

Beran watched Lanal's knife, waving in a weak threat, and maybe in reach, once Delur let him go. The knife came into focus. A thin line of blue ran around the base of the hilt. The last time Beran had seen that knife, it had been on the table in his room at Isadia's house.

"How did you get that back?" Beran asked.

Lanal glanced over Beran's shoulder.

Beran looked behind him. Kaven stood pressed against the wall, his face gray with misery.

"You gave them back the knife." Beran choked on the words. "You knew they killed Ander, and you said nothing. You're filth, Kaven." He flung himself against the hands holding him.

Myla's voice was faint as if she could barely muster breath to speak. "I've wondered how the thieves happened to be by Eran's burial mound. Galen said they must have been after Beran, but that wasn't so, was it, Kaven? You told them I was going to open it."

"I'm sorry," Kaven said. "I'm so sorry. But I love you, Myla. You have to believe it."

She turned toward the door and went silently out into the night. For a moment, no one moved.

"Go after her, Kaven," Rickard snapped, and Kaven pulled himself off the wall.

Beran shouted at him as he crossed to the door. "Stone you and your so-called love, Kaven. She trusted you. *I* trusted you." Kaven vanished.

Rickard yanked the arm he held up behind Beran's back and twisted, forcing Beran to his knees. "Lanal, come here and help Delur hold him, while I get a rope." Lanal edged around them and closed his hand around Beran's bicep. "Got him?" Rickard released his hold.

Beran heaved all his weight against Delur's grip on his other arm, and when Delur yanked him backward, he used the momentum to kick hard and drive the heel of his boot into Lanal's face. There was a satisfying crunch, and Lanal howled.

Delur threw Beran to the floor, straddled him, and crashed his fist into the side of Beran's head. Beran tried to roll away, but Delur held him and punched him in the face hard enough that darkness flickered in and out of Beran's sight.

"Hold him!" Rickard cried over the sound of Lanal's continued wails. Then he and Delur were looping rope around Beran's wrists and tying them behind him. His back scraped over the rough wooden floor as he struggled against being pulled to the bed and tied to the frame. Rickard bent over him, and he kicked until Delur landed on his legs while Rickard tied them together at the ankles.

"You think I'm going to let you get away with killing Ander?" Beran's chest heaved. "You're a dead man. You can't tie me up forever."

"One of us is dead, but it's not me." Delur drew his knife.

Rickard grabbed Delur's wrist. "Stop it. You want Thien on our tails until we die?"

"Thien's never heard of us."

"He will unless you mean to kill Kaven and Myla too. If we don't hurt him, they'll all cooperate rather than stir up more trouble."

Looking away from Rickard, Delur spat, then sheathed the knife. He curled his lip at Beran. "You ever killed anyone? Rickard, I'll give you five to two odds he hasn't."

"It doesn't matter." Beran tilted his head back so he could look down his bleeding nose. "Any good ruler would execute you. A realm's people need to trust a ruler to defend them by battle and by law."

Delur snorted. "I don't see a ruler, just you."

"Just me," Beran agreed.

Rickard shoved to his feet, dabbing at a scrape near his mouth that Beran had no memory of inflicting. "Don't pretend you're looking for royal justice. This is personal. It's revenge."

"You'll find that in my case, personal and royal are pretty much the same thing."

"If they are," Rickard said, "Rinland is in trouble."

Beran said nothing, only lifting a shoulder to blot the blood dripping down his face. Rickard might be right in some cases, but not in this one. Ander's murderer deserved to be punished.

"Lanal," Rickard said, making the whining man jump. "Divide the new supplies we brought between the packs, except for Myla's. Leave hers light. And Delur, you fill the water skins while I see how Kaven's doing." At the door, he paused. "Leave him alone, Delur. I mean it."

Delur grunted, and Rickard left. "Leave my pack light too, Lanal," Delur said, "and stop that noise." Lanal clamped his mouth shut and dumped supplies on the table to sort into piles. Delur looked down at Beran. "Stone you and your royal, personal revenge. You think you're better than me? You think I'm a killer? I've been in the army. No one kills like a king does. He just keeps his own hands clean."

Beran ignored him, watching Lanal who was indeed making two small piles of goods rather than just the one for Myla.

"Cross me, and Rickard won't be able to stop what happens." Delur went to gather water skins.

Beran had spent enough time watching courtiers to recognize when one was testing his father's rule and knew Delur was about fed up with Rickard's. He squirreled that fact away for possible future use and began twisting his wrists against the ropes binding them.

Chapter 21

Myla shut the cabin door behind her and walked steadily away into the trees. She was blind in the dark, but that seemed right. She couldn't be any blinder than she'd been.

The cabin door opened, spilling candle light. "Myla?" Kaven called. "Myla, where are you?"

Where indeed?

She shoved through the underbrush, pushed through clawing twigs, until she caught her toe on a root and sprawled headlong into the leaf litter. She couldn't have moved if she wanted to. Her body felt pressed beneath a lead weight. *I'm dead*, she thought. *I'm dead through and through.* Proving that she wasn't, but only wished it, pain swelled in her chest and broke from her mouth in wild sobs. Around her spread the Forest, which wasn't providing at all.

Kaven dropped to his knees beside her. "Are you hurt?"

The question was too ridiculous to answer. She hurt to the tips of her fingers and toes, to the ends of her hair.

Tentatively, he laid a warm hand on her back. "Myla?"

Silvit save her, his touch still comforted her. She curved her spine away from his palm and, after a moment, he withdrew it. She spoke through her torn throat. "Was there any truth at all in what you said to me?"

"I love you. It's the truest feeling I've ever known."

She turned her face toward him. He sat with his arms wrapped around his drawn-up knees. In the dark, his face was a pale blur, but she heard his unhappiness. "Then how could you?"

Arms still locked around his knees, he rocked back and forth. "They threatened my mother."

"Your uncle did?" She levered herself halfway up, lifted by her horror.

"Rickard owed Delur a lot of money even before they came to Sweet Stream—gambling debts—and Delur kept on him about paying. Rickard won't say so, but he's scared of Delur. That's why he sold so many trees." Kaven paused, drew a long breath, and rushed on. "It's why he sent me to Lady Isadia's once you were there. I was supposed to court you for your dowry. I tried not to let Isadia give me anything, tried to help her, so I wouldn't feel so much like a…thief. But courting you turned out to be easy because I fell in love with you. Then once Rickard found out you could open tombs, he saw another way to pay Delur off."

Supposed to court her. Shame at her own gullibility made her sit up and scoot away from him. "He 'found out.' You mean you told him."

"I'm so sorry, Myla. The thing is I wanted Delur gone. He shoved my mother hard enough to knock her down. She was so scared she told me about it the next time I was home. But my uncle kept losing money to him, and I knew Delur would never leave if he thought there'd be more coin in staying. I thought if he had tomb goods, he'd have to go back to Rinland to sell them."

"So you sicced Delur and Lanal on me instead," she said.

"No! They were supposed to watch and see how you opened the tomb, rob it if you left the door open. But Lanal's not very bright. He panicked when you saw him. I'd never put you in danger."

"You did put me in danger! And when they killed Beran's guard, you said nothing."

He lifted his hands helplessly. "It's my family, Myla. Your father and brother are planning treason. Have you told Beran?"

She bit her lip and listened to the night breeze stirring the leaves overhead. Somewhere not far off, a frog croaked lies to his froggy lover. "I don't know what to do," she said, more to herself than Kaven. "I believed you completely. I'm as stupid as Da always says."

"You're not! By Silvit, I swear I'll never forgive that man for what he told you about yourself. Sometimes I think you'll never get over it."

"None of us gets over what our families do to us," she said wearily. "Not completely. Sure as sunrise, not you or me or Beran."

"Pledge with me anyway," he said. "Why not? We love one another, or at least, I still love you."

"You deceived me. And we can only bind ourselves in Jorn's tomb. If we take Delur there, he'll rob it."

"Jorn is long dead. He doesn't need what's in that tomb."

"It's a tomb!"

A twig snapped, and Rickard stepped into sight. "It's time to come inside," he said cheerily.

A shiver slithered down Myla's spine. What had she been thinking? These men weren't going to let her just walk away. She climbed to her feet, shook Kaven's hand off her arm, and strode back toward the cabin. He rushed ahead to open the door for her. When she stopped short rather than brush by him, his face twisted in pain, but he pressed backward so she wouldn't have to touch him. Rickard herded both of them in and shut the door.

Delur and Lanal turned toward them. Lanal's nose was bleeding and starting to swell. His eye was blackening as well. Breathing hard, Beran sat on the floor, tied hand and foot, and roped to the bed frame like some sort of wild animal. Bread and cheese were laid out on the table.

"Everything all right?" Rickard asked.

"He's still alive," Delur said grimly.

Myla walked straight to the bed, skirted Beran, and flung herself down with her back to the room. The mattress exhaled the odor of moldy straw.

Male feet shuffled uncomfortably. "Leave her," Rickard said. "She'll feel better in the morning." She heard puffs of breath, and the candles went out.

She would never feel better again. She closed her eyes, covered her ears with her forearms, took shallow breaths, and pretended the world was honest and kind. She filled her head with pictures of herbs, her books, a mound covered in green moss. All of it felt far away. Her mind escaped into sleep.

Something shook the bed, jolting her awake to see a rough wood wall looming inches from her nose. Her heart jumped, and then memory flooded back, and it slowed, evidently dismissing the idea of danger. Fool heart.

"Will she still open it?" a man whispered, Rickard she thought.

"I don't know," Kaven said.

Myla knotted her hands in the blanket someone had laid over her during the night. She'd stay here. Why not? What reason did she have to move?

"She can be made to open it," Delur said.

"Breathe hard in her direction, and I'll kill you," Kaven said. Steps drew near the bed. "Myla?"

For a moment, she lay still, denying she'd heard him, denying he was there at all. Then she rolled over to see Kaven's big hand holding out bread and cheese.

"We're getting ready to go," Kaven said. "You should eat." She met his gaze, and he looked away. When she didn't reach for the food, he set it awkwardly on the edge of the bed. His hand hung by it for an instant, unsure it was done. Behind him, the other men were loading their packs with whatever they'd taken out for the night. All except Beran, of course, who was still tied to the end of the bed.

"Proud of yourself, Kaven?" Beran asked. "Happy now that Myla's in the hands of a murderer?"

Kaven cringed and walked away. Despite herself, Myla flinched at his hurt.

"Leave be that murderer talk," Delur snapped. "I had to defend myself."

The bed shuddered again as Beran jerked his bound wrists against it. "You're a thief and a liar, Delur."

Delur flushed scarlet and took a step their way, but stopped when Myla surprised herself by gathering the bread and cheese and sliding off the bed to sit next to Beran. They were in this together, she thought bitterly, two fools who'd believed they could choose their own paths. She waited for Delur to turn away before saying, "Your face is already bruised. It might be smarter to stop flapping your tongue." She broke off a handful of bread and fed it to Beran, then ate a mouthful herself.

He shrugged and spoke softly. "You need to get away. Watch for your chance and go."

She fed him a chunk of cheese. "What about you and Kaven?"

Beran had been watching Delur like a hound stalking a pheasant, but now he flicked a disbelieving glance her way. "You can't seriously still be worried about him. He sheltered the man who killed Ander. Rickard might really have believed Delur killed in self-defense, but Kaven was there. He saw Ander's sword in its scabbard. He knew."

She dragged her front teeth over her lower lip. "They threatened his mother."

Beran gave a scornful pop of his mouth. "He lied to you."

"You'll want a girl to care for you some day, but I bet you'll keep all kinds of princely secrets from her."

"I hope I never put her in the hands of someone like Delur."

She ate the last of the bread. "If it was for the good of Rinland?"

He scowled, then tugged at his bonds. She could see that the rope on his wrist was already dark with blood.

"Why are you defending him?"

She let her head drop back against the stinking mattress. "I don't know. I guess like you said, love is dangerous."

"Are you going to untie me?" Beran called in Rickard's direction.

Rickard shoved the leftover food on the table into his pack. "Untie him so he can travel, Lanal."

"Not me." Lanal rubbed his swollen nose and winced. His left eye had blackened and closed in the night.

Beran smiled wolfishly. "Come on. I won't kick you again."

Deep as a Tomb

Rickard nodded at Delur who wiped his mouth on his sleeve and came toward them. As he approached, Myla dusted her hands of crumbs and rose to fetch her water skin. It was heavy, so someone had refilled it for her. She drank and went toward the bed to offer it to Beran.

Delur still crouched, working at the knots in the rope binding Beran's wrists. "Keep talking," Delur was murmuring as she came close enough to hear. "Give me an excuse. We don't need you."

They needed her to open Jorn's tomb, of course. And they needed Kaven to court her, to keep her sweet, or so they thought. But Delur was right. They needed Beran for nothing.

"Delur, are you threatening Beran?" she said loudly. "You must want to draw every soldier in the king's army down around your ears."

"I told you there'd be none of that, Delur," Rickard said. "After we get to Jorn's tomb, we'll leave him somewhere he'll be found once we've cleared out. King Thien won't care about Forest tomb treasure if he has his son back."

He sounded to Myla as if he were trying to convince himself as much as Delur. She tipped water into Beran's mouth.

"Let Beran and Myla go now," Kaven said. "I'll go with you."

Myla's heart pinged like the stupid thing it was.

"Did you finally do what I asked and learn how to open the tombs?" Rickard asked. "What good are you by yourself?"

"Then give up on this," Kaven said. "It's gone too far wrong. Just take your men and go."

"He's what's gone wrong," Delur said, finally loosening the last knot. The rope drooped around the leg of the bed, but it was still tied to Beran's right wrist, and Delur yanked it so Beran sprawled onto his side, splashing water from the skin Myla still held in front of Beran's face. A deep-red welt circled Beran's free wrist. Delur retied Beran's hands in front of him. Keeping hold of the rope's end, he glanced at Myla. "Can you untie his feet?"

Beran laughed nastily. "Worried about a boot in the nose, Delur? Smart."

Myla worked at the ropes around Beran's ankles. The knot was tight. Either Beran had been struggling against it, or whoever had tied him wanted to be sure he stayed tied. Most likely both. The instant she got the rope loose, Delur grabbed Beran's arm and hauled him to his feet.

Rickard motioned them toward the door. Lanal had already gone out, and Kaven came a careful distance behind Myla, carrying her pack with his. She slid the strap of her herb bag over her shoulder. Outside, birds still sang their dawn song. Dew gleamed on the long grass in the yard, dampening her trouser legs. The morning smelled of Forest earth and growing things, as if nothing had happened to change her world, as if what she felt had no connection to anything else in the green world.

"You think they'll be happy robbing just one tomb, Kaven?" Beran asked. "You think they'll just let Myla go after she opens it?"

"Let him be, Beran," Myla said wearily. "You can't change anything." She watched as Kaven pushed his hair off his forehead in a gesture she'd always loved. He drifted toward the trees, his hands opening and closing as he studied the underbrush.

"Are you going to just accept what Rickard owes you and go home, Delur?" Beran said.

Delur jerked Beran's arm hard enough he nearly fell. "Shut up," Delur said.

Lanal and Rickard turned toward them, so only Myla saw Kaven snatch up a long stick.

"Run, Myla!" Kaven cried. He spun, sweeping the stick to catch Rickard behind the knees. His uncle grunted and crashed to the ground.

Beran dove, butting his head into Delur's belly. They both went down, but Myla had eyes only for Lanal slipping up behind Kaven, wielding his knife. She scooped up a rock and flung it with all the strength in her arm. It bounced off Lanal's head, and he crumpled like a sheet unpinned from the clothesline.

"No!" Rickard cried.

For an instant, Myla thought he was talking to her, but he was looking at Delur, who had his knees planted on Beran's chest and his knife in hand. He drew his arm back.

Myla lunged and grabbed his elbow. "If you do, I'll never open another tomb. Never. You hear me?"

Delur quivered under her grip. Then she felt him relax.

"If I stop, will you promise to open this one? This Jarn's?"

"Jorn's." She closed her eyes, and what came to mind was the chieftain's circlet she'd taken from the Green Valley tomb. She was already a tomb thief, but rather than shame, her body tightened in fierce anger. *Do what you must, Silvit*, she thought. *I'll do what I must to save Kaven and Beran.* Not because they deserved it, but because she wasn't ready to be a person who abandoned the ones with whom she had shared part of her life. She opened her eyes, and the first thing she saw was Kaven, the stick still in his hands, watching her.

"Why didn't you run?" he asked, sounding exasperated.

She couldn't bear looking at him. She glanced down at Delur, still gripping the knife. From the ground, Beran regarded her with wide eyes.

"Promise not to hurt Beran or Kaven, and I'll promise to open Jorn's tomb."

Delur sheathed his blade and rose, yanking Beran to his feet. "Sweetheart, you have a bargain."

A gust of wind fluttered the tree tops as if the Forest were talking to itself. What it said, she could no longer guess.

Chapter 22

Two days later, dusk was thickening when Rickard pointed to where a fall of brighter air suggested a clearing not far off the path. "We'll camp there." They waded through pricker bushes, burs flinging themselves onto Myla's ankles and driving tiny spikes through her trouser legs.

"There's no water." Still wearing his pack, Delur glared at Rickard. "We should have stopped where I said."

"Grasslander," Rickard scoffed. He jerked his thumb to the east. "The ground slants that way. There'll be water. Go look for it, Lanal." Lanal waited until Delur nodded, then collected all the water skins and set off.

Myla fought the urge to interfere as Delur dragged Beran to a spindly ash, ⌐oked the extra rope from his belt, and looped it around Beran's waist. ¬ied repeatedly to get near Beran as they walked, but Delur had always her, often following up with a cuff to Beran. Now she stood still, ⸱ ⸱ran. For the merest breadth of time, he hesitated before twisting ⸱ound hands toward Delur's knife, but Delur ducked behind the ⸱ rope, and the knife lurched out of reach. As Delur stalked ⸱ d down the tree and sat. "How does it feel to be dead, Delur?" answered with a rude gesture.

⸱ved around, performing the same chores they'd done ⸱ et up camp. Thinking about what she'd just seen, Myla ⸱ and dead leaves to make beds, her own as far as she ⸱ of the men. Lanal passed out dried meat, and Myla ⸱hing again as Lanal approached Beran, his cautious gaze on Beran's feet. When Beran grinned at him, he flung meat into Beran's lap from three feet away and strode away to safety. Beran's grin faded as he looked down at his filthy hands. Unlike the rest of them, he'd had no chance to wash, even after Delur had hauled him away to relieve himself. He scrubbed his palms on his trousers before picking up the meat.

Myla had heard Galen bluster enough to be faintly skeptical of the threats Beran kept spouting. She didn't doubt he had enough Forest in him to kill if he were in the kind of rage she'd seen in the cabin, but she thought executing someone in cold blood might be beyond him. She wasn't sure what she thought about that. A leader who couldn't act to protect his followers wouldn't last long in the Forest. She fished a jar from her pack, rose, and started toward Beran.

"Stop," Delur said. "Keep away from him."

Reluctantly, Myla turned toward Rickard, hoping he'd be willing—and able—to overrule Delur. She'd kept her gaze elsewhere because Kaven sat near his uncle, looking so unhappy that Myla couldn't help feeling sorry for him. To her bitter dismay, she'd let love root itself so deeply inside her that she couldn't seem to dig it all out. She held up the jar. "I can see from here that his wrists are bleeding."

"He'll live," Rickard said.

Delur laughed, making Myla's gut lurch.

Kaven stood. "I'll do it." He came toward her, hand out, but she kept hold of the jar. His fingers curled, then stretched again. "Please, Myla. You can trust me with this at least."

Blinking against the urge to cry, she gave him the jar and retreated to her bed.

"No, Kaven," Delur said.

As if Delur hadn't spoken, Kaven crossed to the tree where Beran was tied. A yard away, he halted, his back to everyone else. "Salve for your wrists?"

Myla could see Beran starting to shake his head, but Kaven must have said something more because he grimaced, and said, "Why not?"

Kaven crouched to examine Beran's wrists. "I'm going to have to loosen these ropes," he called to where Rickard, Delur, and Lanal sat near the fire.

"I'll tighten them afterwards." As he tugged at the rope, he turned enough that Myla could see him talking with uncharacteristic speed. The rope gaped around bloody bracelets just above Beran's wrist bones. Frowning, Kaven bent over them, picking out something fine, probably strands of rope fiber. He scooped a fingerful of salve from the jar and spread it gently. Beran flinched, and then said something Myla couldn't hear. Kaven answered, still concentrating on Beran's wrists.

Delur glanced their way."Can you build up the fire, Delur?" Myla said hastily. "I'm cold."

Delur was still frowning at Kaven and Beran, but then Beran spoke up. "You have nerve coming near me, Kaven." Delur turned back to the fire and added another stick.

The boys looked like they were arguing, until Kaven stood. "Your Princeliness, you're a fool," he said loudly enough that the men all turned to look. Delur rose and ambled toward them.

"It's not that I don't trust you, Kaven." Delur grabbed Beran's arm and lifted it so he could test the ropes. He bared his teeth at Kaven. "It's just that I don't trust you." He tugged the rope tight enough to make Beran gasp. Satisfied, Delur returned to the fire. Kaven stomped to his pack, then went back to fling his blanket at Beran before approaching Myla to lay the salve jar in her hand, his nails barely brushing her palm.

"You can share my blanket, Kaven," she said stiffly. *Stupid*, she jeered at herself. His lips parted, but he said nothing, just came toward her with slow steps, and then hovered as if expecting her to take back her invitation. "It's all right," she said. Cautiously, he lay down next to her. She flung her blanket over them both, then slid away to its edge.

"Move closer, Kaven." Lanal laughed.

"Hush," Rickard snapped.

"What were you and Beran talking about?" Myla whispered.

"I told him to run in the night if I could manage to leave his ropes loose. I think Delur is going to kill him as soon as you open Jorn's tomb. Assuming you're going to."

"He seems too set on going after Delur to run." She ignored the question of the tomb.

"He said he couldn't leave us because Delur will never let us go once he decides the tombs are an endless source of treasure." Kaven stirred, making the bedding shift beneath her. "Not that letting us go would do much good with Zale and your father after us. Maybe I can get close enough to Beran tomorrow to cut him free."

"Delur promised that if I opened the tomb he wouldn't hurt you and Beran."

Kaven gave a short laugh. "One of the things I love about you, Myla, is your optimism."

She turned her back on him and pulled the blanket up to her ears. Love was indeed dangerous, she decided, dangerous and complicated and powerful. Loving someone was like being part of the Forest. It could cure your pain or kill you, if you didn't come at it right. She felt Kaven's warmth along her spine, an inch away, but not touching.

The next afternoon, the sun was brushing the western branches when they reached a stand of huge, old trees. Some tug of power made Myla look right. "It's this way," she said simply, then struck off the path between trunks so thick it would take the arms of four men together to span them. Her feet whispered through layers of leaves. Sweetness flooded her mouth, coming from nowhere she could see other than the air itself. Her heart soared. For this moment, at least, she felt back in harmony with the Forest. The men rushed after her, as she couldn't help moving faster and faster. The great trees parted, and they emerged into a clearing around a glowing, green mound surrounding a stone doorway. They halted, and for an awe-weighted moment, no one spoke.

"Sweet Powers!" Delur's cry broke the air. "This is it!" He dropped his pack and emptied it, dumping dirty clothes, dried food, his blanket, all his belongings, to make room for treasure. His stained stuff near the tomb jarred like garbage flung before a shrine. "Open it," he ordered Myla, reshouldering the pack.

"Cut Beran loose," Myla said.

"Open it first."

She shot a desperate look at Kaven, who moved between Beran and Delur, hand on his knife hilt. Beran's arms strained as if he were frantically twisting his wrists. Open the tomb or not? Her heart thudded against her ribs. Both boys' lives depended on her making the right choice. *Help me know what to do, Silvit,* she thought. *Lend me your wisdom.* She took off her pack to remove a two-handled cup and the small knife she used to cut herbs. Facing the tomb, she closed her eyes and stood still.

"Stop dawdling and open it," Delur said.

"Shut up," Kaven said. "She's praying."

The hard note in Kaven voice told her if she defied Delur and he tried to hurt her, Kaven would die to stop him. She opened her eyes, walked to one side of the tomb's doorway, and carefully shaved off a patch of moss, which she put in the cup. She would trust to the Forest to provide some chance for her, Beran, and Kaven to form a fosterlings' pack that would save them all.

"What's that stuff for?" Delur asked.

"We need it for the Asking." Myla put the cup in her herb bag and slipped the strap over her head. Slowly, she moved toward the door. "You'll let Beran go as soon as it's open?"

"I said I would." Delur still stood a yard from Beran and Kaven. "Wait at the door for me once it's open."

"No, Delur," Rickard interrupted, surprising Myla. "You and Lanal stay here while the boys and Myla and I go in. I'll give you what you're owed when we come out."

Myla's breath caught. Alone with Rickard, she and the boys could take him down and then figure out what to do.

"Stone that." Delur's face went purple. "We'll help ourselves."

"You fouled up by bringing the blighted prince of Rinland along," Rickard said, "and now any fool can see you're stupid enough to kill him and have the king on our tracks till the day we die. I'll pay what I owe you, but not a coin more. You take what I give and go back to Rinland. Both of you."

"You know we can't do that." Delur left the boys to stalk toward Rickard.

"We're wanted," Lanal squeaked. "The king will take off our hands for thieving."

"Lanal, will you shut up!" Delur said.

Rickard turned his back on Delur. "You're not going in."

The shoulder of Kaven's yellow shirt blocked Myla's view of Beran, whose hands flew apart as Kaven's knife slid back into its sheath. She didn't even have time to rejoice before a cry and a gurgle made her spin to see Delur standing over Rickard, who lay face down with Delur's knife in his back. The knife handle quivered, the only thing in the clearing that moved. She stopped breathing, then sucked in air as Rickard would never do again. She couldn't look away, couldn't move.

"Keep Beran away from me, Lanal!" Delur said. "Open the door, Myla."

The urgency in his voice made her look up at last. Delur had an arm wrapped around Kaven's chest and Kaven's own blade pointed at his neck. He was turning to keep Kaven between himself and Beran, while Lanal hovered just out of Beran's reach.

"Open it," Delur barked.

She moved as slowly as she dared toward the tomb door, never looking away from Kaven's rigid body.

"I thought this might be where you were going, Myla," a familiar voice said, and her father and Lord Zale entered the tomb clearing, both staring at Rickard's body. Her knees sagged in relief.

"That's Delur holding Kaven, Da!" she cried. "He killed Rickard and Beran's guard too. Seize him! Only be careful of Kaven."

Da looked shocked, then drew himself up and said, "Not our affair. We're here to rescue you, Myla. Come."

Zale flicked his gaze warily from Delur to Lanal, who had turned from Beran toward the two newcomers.

"You can't mean to leave Kaven and Beran here with him," Myla said.

Da shrugged, and said again, "Not our affair."

Some long tether on Myla's heart snapped, and she edged closer to Beran and the still-captive Kaven. Da's presence changed nothing. More than him, the boys were her pack here, though at the moment, Beran was walking purposefully away from her.

"Where did you get that?" Beran took another step toward Da, who raised a hand to touch the chieftain's circlet on his head. Beran spun to face Myla. "You took it that day in the Green Valley tomb. You had no right!"

Myla hugged her herb bag in front of her like a shield. Now? He wanted to fight about this now? "I'm sorry, but he said he'd burn my books."

Beran threw up his hands in disbelief.

"I don't care if he burns every stoning tree in this stoning forest." Delur prodded Kaven, sending a trickle of blood down his neck. "Everybody back off, or I'll kill him."

"Go ahead and kill him," Zale said. "He kidnapped my bride."

"I will *never* marry you," Myla said. "And I will never help you overthrow Lord Corin and King Thien, so you might as well go home."

"Overthrow?" Beran sounded as if he were choking.

"I just said I never would," Myla cried.

Zale pointed his sword at Delur. "You and your man can keep Kaven and the grassland boy, but we're taking Myla."

"Get him, Lanal!" Delur urged, still clutching Kaven.

With a heart-stopping shout, Lanal scooped up a handful of dirt, flung it into Zale's eyes, and rushed him. Da jumped away from the fight, alarm in every line of his body.

"Open that door," Delur shouted at her as he dragged Kaven toward the tomb. Myla slapped her hands onto the door and read the words carved around it. The door slid open. "Come on, Beran!" she cried before darting inside, with Delur hauling Kaven in after her.

"Wait for me!" Lanal's voice came as she led Delur and Kaven in a headlong rush down a crumbling flight of stairs. She heard the tomb door grind shut behind them and twisted to see if Beran had made it inside, but the curve of the staircase blocked her view.

"Go." Delur ordered, and she went cautiously down the last few steps over which the right wall of the stairwell had shed not just pebbles but chunks of stone on the steps.

She stumbled into the first room to see an empty pedestal clearly designed to hold a coffin but covered only in dust and leaning sharply because the floor had broken under one end. On the far wall, the altar to Silvit had crumbled to a heap of rubble. Silvit save them. What was happening in this tomb?

"Where are the offerings?" Delur dragged Kaven to the altar's other side.

"I don't know." Myla didn't recognize her own voice. "I thought Jorn's coffin would be right here. Maybe his people moved him when the floor gave way."

Rubble bounced down the stairs behind her. "Lanal?" Delur said. When no one answered, Delur jerked Kaven closer and put the knife to his ribs. "Show yourself," he said with a sigh.

Myla was unsurprised, but deeply relieved, when Beran edged into the room. Better he should be here to ally with her and Kaven, rather than alone with Lanal, Da, and Zale.

"Stone you," Delur swore. "You are as persistent as lice. I'd heard your father's wrath was bad, but you have to be worse. Drop the rock." Delur reinforced the order with a jab sharp enough to make Kaven stifle a cry. With a grimace, Beran peeled his fingers away from a rock and let it bounce to the broken floor. A shard broke off and hit Delur in the ankle, and when ..e hopped away, Kaven wrestled against his grip. Myla lunged toward them, glimpsing Beran doing the same thing, but before they could act, Delur had Kaven under control again. Breathing hard, he said, "Come here, sweetheart."

Myla stiffened, but eyeing the knife in Kaven's side, she closed the gap between her and Delur. With a quick shove at Kaven, Delur moved his grip and his knife to Myla. Her heart burst into a gallop. Delur's arm across her chest was tight enough to make it hard to breathe. This close, he smelled of some wild feeling, on the edge of losing control.

Kaven jammed to a halt next to Beran, both of them tense. "Hurt her, and I'll hunt you to your death," Kaven said.

"How she fares depends on you and the royal pain here. Which way?" Delur asked Myla, frowning at the three other doorways.

"I'm not sure," Myla said. Which way would give her and the boys a chance to escape?

Delur motioned for Kaven and Beran to precede him and Myla down the steps leading from the leftmost doorway. At least he shifted his hold to her arm so she could breathe. Like the entry stairs, these stairs were a trap, littered with debris from the failing walls. Myla felt a twist of worry, but assured herself this place had been here for centuries. Why would it collapse now? Sweat dampened her armpits nonetheless.

The room they emerged in had two more doorways, one across it and one just a yard to their right. Three thickly dusted coffins stood in the room's center. Delur dragged her toward them while Beran ran a hand over the large stone half-blocking the closer door, as if worried about whether it was balanced enough not to crush them on those stairs.

"What is this useless trash?" Delur poked at the remains of a leather quiver and stringless bow. "Where's the gold? Where are the jewels? Is this all that'll be in here?" Face flushed scarlet, Delur pushed the knife tip close under Myla's chin. The prick of pain lifted her to her toes, his hand still tight on her arm. "Have you been leading me on?"

Kaven stepped closer. He kept his voice even, but his fists were clenched. "Take it easy, Delur. Some of the other coffins will have what you want."

Beran gestured toward the half-blocked doorway. "This way looks promising."

"Delur?" Kaven said.

"Come on, Kaven," Beran said. "Let's try this way."

With the part of her brain not concentrating on the knife under her chin, Myla hoped Beran's bossy tone meant he had a plan and wasn't just being royal.

Beran slid carefully around the rock at the stairway top and started down. After an instant's hesitation, Kaven followed but kept his head turned enough to see Myla. She judged he'd heard the same hint in Beran's voice she had.

"Hey," Delur called. "Stay close or she gets cut."

"Let's go after them, Delur," Myla said. "There'll be plenty more coffins."

Delur's hand trembled. Then he took the knife away. "Go."

She started down, lowering herself over a step that had crumbled entirely. Below her, she heard Beran and Kaven murmuring to one another. The light at the stairway bottom glowed brightly. The moment Myla entered the room, she saw why. Firelight bounced off the gold cups and jewels piled on the two coffins, shining even through the dust that blanketed them. Beran glanced back toward the stairway, the room's sole way out. "A dead end," he said, holding her gaze as if willing her to understand.

"Yes!" Delur cried. "You weren't lying after all, sweetheart. Lucky for you." He rushed to the treasure, dragging Myla with him fast enough that she tripped and rammed her hip painfully on the pedestal. For a moment, Delur juggled the knife, then he let go of Myla but held the knife close to her. He glanced at Beran and Kaven. "Believe me when I say I can stab her faster than you can take this knife."

Myla watched for the slightest tic of movement from either boy.

Delur slipped his pack off one shoulder and then the other and flipped the top open. He picked up a jeweled chain, blew the dust off, and crowed when green and red gems emerged from the filth. He stuffed it in his pack. A gold plate made him lick his lips and widen his eyes like a boy with a cake all to himself.

Beran gave the tiniest of nods toward the stairs, and Kaven soundlessly inched that way. With his hand held low next to his thigh, Kaven crooked a finger at her. She darted her gaze from Kaven to Beran and back. The knife hovered a hand's span from her side.

"What's that?" Beran pointed to a wooden chest at Delur's elbow.

"At the Steeprise tomb, a chest like that held gold coins," Myla said. Delur leaned to work at the chest's latch, and Myla shoved him hard.

"Up!" Beran cried, and pelted up the stairway. Myla jumped toward the stairs, seizing the hand Kaven held out to her. They tore up the stairway, leaping the missing step, to find Beran with his shoulder and hands braced against the rock balanced at the top. She and Kaven were still flying through the narrow space between the rock and the side of the doorway when Beran gave his first shove. The rock didn't move. Almost blind from panic, Myla leaned against it with all her weight. Kaven braced his back against the wall and pushed with his feet.

Delur pounded up the steps with a cry of wordless rage.

The rock tipped over the edge of the top step and rolled, slowly at first, then gathering speed. It filled the narrow stairs, crashing into steps and walls. A blow sent the right side of the stairwell sliding down like a sled descending a hill. Dizziness swept over her. Everything seemed to be moving, and she realized the wall next to them was sliding slowly downward.

"Move," she cried. Dust boiled through the room, choking her. Chunks of rock flew past, one clipping her shoulder.

With Kaven and Beran, she scrambled into the shelter of the coffins holding the ancient bow and quiver Delur had scorned. The floor shook. She huddled against Kaven as rocks rained down on them. The light strips went out, leaving a blackness so complete it stuffed her mouth and ears. Her heart thundered. They were as dead as Delur.

The noise ebbed, and to Myla's intense relief, the lights glowed on. A last pebble bounced off the back of her hand. She stood, grit pattering off her, and looked where the stairwell had been, or where she thought it had been, but she couldn't be sure because that whole side of the room had collapsed. The stairway to the dead end had vanished.

So had the one by which they'd entered, the one back to the outside world.

Chapter 23

Myla gripped the edge of the coffin to steady herself, then realized the floor had finally stopped rumbling so she must the one shaking. "We're all right," she panted. "We're all right. I can't believe we're all right." Kaven put an arm around her shoulders, and she felt him trembling. She let the arm stay.

Beran staggered toward where the stairs had been. "Is there another way out?"

"I don't know." She gulped, trying to swallow her panic, but choking on dust. "There's only one door to the outside, but the rooms might connect to make another path to it."

Beran put a hand on the stones blocking the way out, then moved to the dead end and stretched, trying to see around the barrier. When he lifted a smaller stone, more pieces of wall crashed to the floor.

"Leave it alone!" Kaven cried.

"I want to see what happened to Delur," Beran said.

"He's dead." Myla heard what had to be her own voice echo off the walls, sharp and high. "Him and Rickard. Both dead."

Beran brushed his fingertips across a rock. "I need to be sure." He glanced at Kaven. "I'm sorry about your uncle, Kaven. I should have acted sooner."

"He wasn't a good person," Kaven said, though Myla heard the catch in his voice. His uncle was family, after all, and had been stabbed right in front of him.

"He was better than Delur," Beran said, "and he had a right to live until the king's law judged him."

Dust grayed his hair and skin. He'd look like that as a middle-aged man, Myla thought. She glimpsed his face, set blank in a look she'd come to recognize as his mask, and shuddered. It was how he had looked that day in Green Valley's tomb when he'd told her rulers not only couldn't act on what they felt, but sometimes couldn't even allow themselves to feel. Not a middle-aged man, she decided. A middle-aged king, grim with the weight his role laid on his shoulders.

"Come away from there, Beran," Myla said. "We have to…" She wasn't sure how to finish the sentence. She was still breathing like a bellows, finding too little air in this closed-in underworld. Her heart thudded with the desire to run, to race along all the stairs that led up, to find a way out. But if they fled the tomb—their tomb?—she'd run right back into Da and Zale and have taken every risk for nothing. An instant later, she realized she'd just judged that she'd have nothing if she and Kaven didn't pledge themselves to one another. Her heart turned over. "We have to find Jorn."

Kaven's breath caught. "Are you sure?"

"It's the only way Da won't kill you. What's more, it's the only way to make Da give up his plans, so it's the only way the Forest will survive. Besides, I want to."

"Don't argue, Kaven." Beran sounded disgusted. "Any fool could see she was working her way up to forgiving you."

Kaven's face glowed. "Then what do you know about how the tomb is likely laid out?"

"Nothing really. The Forest makes them all different, opening rooms as manors need them."

"We can't just wander at random," Kaven said.

"We could look for older and older coffins. That should lead us to Jorn."

His hand tightened on hers, but his voice was steady. "That's as good a plan as any."

Beran still lingered by the rock slide, frowning and twisting a finger of his right hand. He looked at the bare finger, fished a ring from his belt pouch, and pushed it over his knuckles. His signet ring, she realized. A shadow rippled over the rocks beside him. Was that a cat? Finally, Beran came to join her and Kaven, and they moved toward the second doorway.

"We should mark the places we've been," Kaven said. "Does either of you have anything to write with?"

Since Beran had come after them with just the clothes on his back, he didn't bother to answer. Myla pawed through her herb bag. No charcoal. No chalk. She pulled out the pot of salve Kaven had put on Beran's wrists. "This is green," she said doubtfully.

Kaven uncorked it and smeared a small arrowhead on the doorframe, pointing the way they were headed. She inhaled the clean smell of the herbs she'd used to make it, and her galloping heart slowed.

"At least, we won't wander in circles," Kaven said, so she knew he had the same fears she did. They started down the second stairway.

"Tell me about the circlet, Myla," Beran said.

Something in his voice sent alarm lancing up her spine. "Da said he'd burn my books if I didn't get it for him."

Beran shook his head. "Don't try to explain yourself. Just tell me what happened."

So she did, all the while choosing the doors leading to coffins with the simpler gifts of leather and wood. Some of the coffins were carved with sigils of long-gone manors, and some of the walls had been painted with lifelike trees or animals. She scanned every coffin and wall for a sign that Jorn lay there. Surely his people had wanted to remember the resting place of the first chieftain. Forest dwellers needed to know where they came from, what had shaped life in the Forest to be what it was. If they forgot, they might strip the trees from a hillside.

When she'd finished her tale, Beran said, "So Zale and your father are planning rebellion?" He sounded so different she looked to be sure it was him speaking, though who else it would be, she didn't know. Kaven had been silent, holding and occasionally squeezing her hand. She'd already told him all this before they'd left Lady Isadia's.

"If I don't marry Zale, I don't believe he'll help Da," Myla said. "I'm the thread that weaves their plan together because opening tombs supposedly shows I'm chieftain."

"They're mad," Beran said. "The king would crush them at a terrible cost to the Forest."

"I know," she said. "I tried to stop them."

"You should have told me," Beran said.

"I didn't know you."

"You do now."

She wasn't sure she did. She groped for what had changed in him. It wasn't that he was angry. He'd been angry since his guard was killed, maybe before for all she knew, but he'd mostly kept his fury tamped down while he tried to act as the distant king would like. Now he seemed to claim his anger as his right.

The search went on and on. Myla had never imagined a tomb with so many rooms, nor one so close to collapsing. Maybe the tomb was going because its manor was gone. Even the echo of their footsteps was enough to send bits of wall showering down. Three times, they found coffins crashed to the floor, spilling a mix of bones and coins. They climbed a stairway missing a third of its steps, but could go only a yard inside the room at the top because the rest had collapsed. Myla squeezed to one side, but couldn't find a way through.

"Come, Myla," Kaven said. "We'll go a different way."

"What if Jorn is beyond here?" Myla asked.

"Then we may have to leave without seeing him."

"No!"

"We need to rest."

"We have to keep on."

"We'll be better for a rest and some food," Kaven insisted.

She recognized the tone. He'd made her rest before on long days in the woods when she was so deep in her feeling for the Forest she hadn't known she was tired. They climbed carefully back down the steps to a mostly intact room, where Myla kicked stones out of the way and slumped cross-legged against a wall.

As the boys settled on either side of her, she dug for the packet of dried apples at the bottom of her herb bag. Her fingers brushed something stiff. Puzzled, she pulled it out and found it was a piece of parchment with a drawing of a tomb's green exterior. It must have been the loose page she'd rescued from the floor of the herb room at home. When she had hidden her books, this must have stayed tangled with the pouch of medicines.

She offered the apples to Kaven and Beran, then scanned the words below the drawing while she chewed on a sweet slice. She already knew that when they found Jorn, both she and Kaven would have to drink an infusion of tomb moss so Jorn could enter their visions and approve of their binding themselves to marry when they came of age. Given her first, spine-wilting experience with moss tea, she'd been silently worrying about the effects the moss might have on Kaven. Maybe this page would tell her how to use the moss more safely. She was pretty sure the words said the moss would increase a person's power, or maybe restore a person's power. At home, she'd left another book with a drawing of the moss plant in fine detail that said the same thing. This one just showed the curve of a tomb with a door half open.

"Drink, Myla," Kaven said.

Some notion slipped away. She drank from her water skin, washing away the dust scratching her throat. She passed the skin to Beran.

"How much do we have?" He hefted the skin and grimaced as he figured out the answer to his own question. "We've been in here longer than I realized." He sipped and gave it back to her. The blood-stained edge of his sleeve pulled back from his raw wrist. When she reached for the salve, he shook his head. "Save it for the doors. There can't be much of it left either. What's that?"

"A page from my books." She turned to face him more fully. "You say I should have told you what Da was up to, but he really did threaten to burn them. You saw him taking them from Isadia's herb room the day of the

Thread Feast. The knowledge in those books saved your life, Beran. It could save other people too, in the Forest and grasslands alike. I couldn't let Da destroy it."

His eyelids drooped. "Assuming we get out of here, I don't intend to let Lord Talun destroy anything."

The Forest save her from having him ever speak of her in that menacing growl. "We'll get out." They had to. She thrust the page back in the bag and rose, dusting the seat of her trousers.

They continued their search, light rolling along or sometimes skipping broken walls. Myla's head kept nagging at her, wondering what she could have done differently so she and Kaven and, it turned out, Beran wouldn't have wound up caught in this tomb. She'd tried to do right by the Forest, to keep it from war, to preserve its knowledge. She'd tried to cling to Kaven, too, still looking for a way to get what she wanted. Good and bad reasons were hard to untangle sometimes. Da loved the Forest. He just loved power more. She thought again of the cat shadow she'd glimpsed over Beran's shoulder. Silvit was the living embodiment of the Forest. Did he see her and her father as better for it than Beran and his father? Only a fool would think that. Still…

"You know, Beran," she said, "your father hasn't exactly done himself proud in looking after things here."

"You have advice?" he said dryly.

"The books will matter only if the Forest isn't destroyed, because some of the plants are rare. You should tell the king or Lord Corin to make laws protecting them."

To her surprise, he laughed. "That's a good idea, though I'm unlikely to 'tell' my father anything. I have to say, Myla, that knowing you has taught me why it's stone-hard to make laws for the Forest."

She smiled at him. "Knowing you has taught me that a few grasslanders must have a seed or two of sense, but then, Forest wisdom always did say we'd be better off together." An affectionate touch brushed across her back, but when she turned, Kaven was a yard away, painting a salve arrow. Was the air moving in here? That would be promising for their eventual escape.

They entered a room with the simplest offering of all, a jar that had probably once been filled with herbs. She leaned over the jar and breathed deeply. The faint scent of the Forest filled her head with a sense of it stretching wide and alive above ground, and also deep into this tomb and her people's past.

"We must be getting close." Kaven sounded a little desperate as he moved toward the only door other than the one they'd come in by.

At the doorway, Myla stopped abruptly. She felt as if she'd walked out of the tomb and into the woods. The room held only one coffin. There were no rich offerings, though a faint thickening of the dust suggested a loop of something had once rested on the coffin and had long since crumbled. But the walls bloomed with painted life. Trees raised leaf-thick branches to a blue sky. Birds and butterflies darted through the greenery, spots of red, blue, and yellow. Vines twisted along the room's edges.

"Jorn," she breathed.

"How do you know?" Beran asked.

"It has to be. Don't you think so, Kaven?"

He was spinning, sending wide-eyed looks at every part of the wall. He turned back to her, face serious. "I don't know, but there's one way to be sure."

Her heart kicked into a gallop. "We try the Asking." She unshouldered her herb bag and pulled out the two-handled cup. When she lifted its lid, the moss inside seemed to glow. She hesitated, wishing she knew more about it. She pinched some off and laid it on the coffin. "A blessing for you, Lord Jorn," she murmured.

"What's involved in this Asking?" Beran said. "What are you going to do?"

"I'll ask Jorn for his permission to bind myself to Kaven." Myla poured the last of her water over the plant in the cup. "Kaven could do that because, if you go far enough back, this is his family tomb too, but he doesn't need to because he already has—had—his uncle's permission. Then we'll both drink, and we should each have a vision. If we have the same vision, that means Jorn approves of our joining." She eyed her brew, waiting for its green to deepen.

"It's good you're here, Beran, because we'll need a witness to convince my father of what happens. We'll each tell you our vision, and you'll be able to swear we had the same one."

"Assuming you both tell me the truth," Beran said. "As I've learned on this little jaunt into the woods, you're both capable of twisting your tongues."

"This will be truth," Myla said. "It's too important."

"Treason wasn't important?" Beran regarded her soberly enough to make her pause and weigh her words.

"It was," she said. "I should have told you the truth then. I swear I'll do it now. Now and always," she added impulsively.

Beran shifted his gaze to Kaven. "Truth?"

"Now and always," Kaven said.

When Beran nodded, Myla faced the coffin. An instant of doubt surprised her. This had to be Jorn, didn't it? And he'd give permission, right? She'd been so sure all she had to do was find his resting place because of course he'd approve of anything she wanted. But why should he?

"Lord Jorn," she said, "I come to you as one of your children's children. I ask permission to follow my heart and choose Kaven of Sweet Stream Manor. Grant me a vision of the path I should take."

Mindful of the way she'd fainted the last time she'd swallowed a mossy drink, she sat down and patted the floor next to her. Kaven too sat, his hip warm against hers. Gripping one of the cup's handles, she held the other out to him. He took it, and sharing the weight between them, they drank at the same time. She tried to strain the moss out with her teeth, but it tasted how she imagined a swamp would. The stuff was at least wet, and her throat was grateful. The angle was odd, and a dribble ran down her cheek. Kaven wiped it away with callused fingers.

In an eyeblink, Kaven was gone. She was walking through the woods, unwinding a ball of yarn as she went. She knew the end reached back to her herb room at home, so she could find her way back there any time she liked, but the ball was shrinking, so she had to decide soon whether to go forward or back. Ahead, she heard a rush of water, and she came out along the bank of a stream. To her delight, Kaven waited on the stream's other side. Then her heart tripped. The streambed was a dozen feet down. She sidled along the bank, looking for a narrow spot she felt safe enough to jump.

Something moved to her right, and she realized Beran was there, watching the treetops ripple in the wind. He turned toward her and put out his right hand for the end of the yarn. She closed her fingers around it and looked again at Kaven, waiting on the other side. She was going to have to jump. If she held on to the yarn, she could pull herself up if she fell. Or maybe not. The yarn might break. That would be too bad. It was dyed bright green, quite beautiful and worth preserving.

She swung her gaze over the trees, the stream, the underbrush, the birds, the web of life in the Forest, and, her heart swelling with joy at all of it, she made her choice. Smiling at Beran, she tied the end around his wrist. He smiled back, but she didn't linger. Instead, she ran to the stream bank and leaped across into Kaven's waiting arms. As he held her against his solid warmth, a vine shot out of the earth and twined around them. It sent out two shoots, and one of them touched a spot under her left collar bone. The spot burned as if a spark from a fire had jumped there. She cried out.

"Myla?" Kaven spoke in her ear, his arms tightening around her.

She was back in Jorn's tomb, with Kaven truly there, holding her.

Beran crouched next to them. "Are you two all right?"

She blinked at him and sat up. "Let me tell you."

He held up his hand to stop her. "Kaven first."

"There wasn't much." Kaven sounded doubtful. "I was in the Forest near a stream. Myla and you were on the other side, her tying something on your arm. Then she jumped across to me." Frowning, he fingered a spot under his collarbone. "A vine bound us together."

"You didn't see me before that?" Myla said. "I walked out the woods unspooling yarn that was anchored back at Da's manor. That's what I tied to Beran's wrist."

"You tied me to your father's manor?" Beran's forehead wrinkled.

"To my herb room."

"That's better." Beran twisted his ring. "So Kaven didn't see you until the very end of your vision. How alike are these visions supposed to be?"

Myla opened her mouth and words almost fell out, words saying the visions were alike enough, and if Beran couldn't see that, his brain had root rot. But something in Beran's steady gaze made her hesitate. She supposed she should be glad he was taking this as seriously as any Forest dweller would.

"I'm not sure," she admitted. "The old teachings just say the visions should be the same."

"These were the same," Kaven said. "Myla and I wound up in the same place, and we both saw you. That can't be an accident."

Slowly, Beran smiled. "So. What happens now?"

Myla's heart leaped. She spun to face Kaven. "We say the pledge." Kaven breathed as quickly as she did. She started to reach for Kaven's hands, then looked over at Beran. "It's important you witness this. Usually, our families would tattoo marks to show we were promised. We have to rely on your word instead."

"I understand," Beran said.

Once again, she faced Kaven. They were trapped in a tomb, and if they ever got out, Da and Zale would be waiting, and yet, happiness bubbled in her chest. She and Kaven joined hands. Myla spoke first, the way Forest women had done all the way back to the beginning.

"Kaven of Sweet Stream Manor, I bless you and promise when the time is right, I will be your lover and your partner. I will treasure you and not harm you. I will join with you to be part of the web of Forest life."

Kaven's hands shook a little. He drew a deep breath. "Myla of Oak Ridge Manor, I bless you and promise when the time is right, I will be your lover and your partner. I will treasure you and not harm you. I will join with you to be part of the web of Forest life."

In the whisper of space between her palms and Kaven's, something quivered. A buzz spread up her arms and through her body. Kaven's eyes widened and she knew—*knew*—he felt it too. The buzz gathered in her chest, and then, in the vine-touched spot below her collar bone, heat flashed. Her hands spasmed on Kaven's, as he gasped and his hand jerked. The feeling faded. They stared at one another. Her gaze caught at the edge of his shirt. She nudged his collar away. A tiny red oak leaf looked as if it had been branded into his flesh.

Kaven slid a trembling finger into the neck of her shirt and pulled it aside. She craned her head to see two wavy blue lines, the sigil of Sweet Stream Manor.

For an instant, neither of them moved. Then Kaven bent and kissed the mark. She put her hand to his cheek and lifted his mouth to meet hers. His kiss was sweet and gentle, like the boy himself.

From far away, Beran said, "Excuse me. I'll be at the top of that last stairway."

She never heard him leave, but when she looked, he was gone. For a time, life blossomed with warmth and joy, and the desperate hope they might have a day after this, and one after that, and a long string of others after that.

Chapter 24

Huddled against the wall under a light strip, Beran tried to convince himself he felt its heat. His stomach growled, but he was *not* thinking of roast venison, of fresh bread, of tart apples.

As had happened twice before, a chunk of wall slid to the floor and sent pebbles rolling toward him. He held still and watched them come. How had Delur felt when he saw those rocks rolling down the stairs? As he pictured it, Beran's parched mouth went dryer. Delur had deserved to die. In killing him, Beran had avenged Ander. So, good. Good.

When he wrapped his arms around his knees and gripped his wrists, pain bit the left one. The rope wounds were scabbing over, but they were still plenty sore. He held both wrists up to the light to see how they were doing, then squinted at the right one. Its skin was completely healed. When had that happened?

Footsteps sounded on the stairs, and Myla and Kaven strolled into the room, holding hands and looking as serene as Beran had ever seen them. *Not* thinking about any possible reason for that, either.

He rose and sipped gratefully from the water skin Kaven offered. "Ready to get out of here?" he asked as confidently as he could. As he waited for them, he'd begun to be plagued by twinges of guilt over what would happen to Rinland if its king's natural heir went missing in the Westreach. Protecting Kaven and Myla had been the right thing to do, he assured himself a little desperately.

"It's safe to meet Da now," Myla said. "When he knows Kaven and I are pledged, he'll have to see sense."

In Beran's opinion, Lord Talun wouldn't see sense if it perched on his nose, but he'd worry about what to do with Talun once he was sure he, Myla, and Kaven wouldn't join the dead in this tomb. He chose a doorway they hadn't been through before and entered a room with two more doors, one leading to a stairway going up, the other to a stairway going down. Beran started toward the ascending stairs, but something warm nudged against his leg, pushing him the other way. Heart pounding, he spun to search for what had secretly slipped up so close.

"What's the matter?" Myla had one foot on the bottom stair.

"I don't know. I thought…Nothing." He took a step toward her and felt the nudge again. Less in his ears than in his head, he heard a soft growl. The image of a wildcat sprang into his mind. The Powers help him. The howling storytellers would love this if he were ever fool enough to tell anyone. "Let's go the other way."

"Down?" Kaven said doubtfully.

Unable to explain why they should go deeper into the earth, Beran simply clattered down the stairs. After a moment, he heard Kaven and Myla follow. The room at the bottom had two more doors. Beran chose the left one at random. At least, if Kaven or Myla asked, he'd say it was at random, though he'd felt another nudge. He found yet another room with two more doors. Again, he went left.

Halfway through the doorway, he stopped, staring at a green salve arrow pointing out of the room. As Myla and Kaven came up behind him, Beran dodged around them and ran to the right door. It, too, was marked with an arrow, this time pointing in.

"Silvit save us," Kaven said. "We've been here before. We're wandering in circles."

Beran was already by the third door, the one they'd just used to enter the room. No arrow. "Don't you see?" he cried. "We've been here before, but not by the same route. The rooms connect in more than one way."

Kaven and Myla stared at Beran and then at one another. "There could be more than one way to the door out," Myla said.

"But the connection to outside isn't through here because we've been here before." Kaven frowned.

"Don't think of that. We skipped a bunch of doorways." Beran plunged across the next room and chose an unmarked doorway. He hurried across a room and up some stairs.

"The air here feels warmer to me." Myla trotted after him.

"To me, too," Kaven said, "and warmer still through there." He pushed Beran toward a door. They ran across a room, up more steps, and through the door at the top. And there, waiting for them, were Silvit's broken altar, the tilting stand from which Jorn's coffin had been moved, and the stairs curving up to the door out.

Beran had to stop because his knees softened like they might give way. He realized he hadn't fully believed they'd ever escape the tomb. Rather than rush past him, Myla and Kaven halted too, as if it would be wrong for any of them to leave one of the others behind. Beran grinned at both of them. "Is this where I say, 'the Forest be thanked?'"

"You'd better say that, grassland boy." Myla grinned back, then stretched to kiss Kaven's cheek.

Maybe not purely grassland, Beran thought, rubbing the spot on his thigh where he'd felt the last push. At the edge of his vision, something moved. He had time only to think Silvit might truly have come to life when a hard, heavy body crashed into his side, flinging him into the stone wall. A chunk of rock broke loose and bounced off his already screaming shoulder. Hot breath puffed into his ear.

"You little stoner. Thought you were done with me, didn't you?" Delur drew back his elbow, ready to thrust in the knife.

Beran caught the man's wrist and heaved, shoving Delur back the fingerwidth he needed to wriggle away. His heart punched his ribs. It couldn't be. Delur was dead.

Breathing hard, a very much alive Delur backed to face them all and wave his knife in an arc. "Thought I was trapped, didn't you? But when that wall came down, there was a room on the other side. I wasn't caught there, and I'll be hanged if I'll be caught here either."

Quick as a snake's tongue, he grabbed Myla's arm and dragged her away, putting himself and his knife between her and Kaven and Beran. He staggered when he moved, as if his pack weighed almost more than he could carry. He'd probably stuffed it with every precious object he'd been able to find between where they'd left him and here. Gesturing with his knife, he ordered, "You two get over there. Sweetheart here is going to let me out." He bared his teeth. "And you two will rot since, as I recall, useless Kaven never could figure out how to open a tomb door. Neither one of you has the power."

Beran heard Myla suck in her breath. "Power," she breathed.

Fury tightened every muscle in his body. Like a nightmare he couldn't shake, Delur threatened two of Beran's people, and Beran was going to have to stoning kill the man *again*. He launched himself across the room and drove his shoulder into Delur's gut. Letting go of Myla, Delur toppled backward, pulled by the weight of his pack. He landed on the stairs, and the edge of one step crumbled under his and Beran's combined weight.

They slid to the rubble on the tomb floor where Beran pounded Delur's wrist on a rock. "Drop the knife. Drop it!" He glimpsed Myla caught on the side of the room away from the exit and Kaven on a step flexing his knees to jump on Delur, but Delur staggered away, hauling Beran with him.

"Myla!" Kaven cried. "Go! Open the door! You hear, Beran? She'll open the door."

A fierce growl forced its way out of Beran's mouth. Delur grunted and leaned back as if something had clamped its jaws around the pack on his back.

"I can't get near," Myla cried. "You open it, Kaven."

"I can't. You know I can't."

"You can! It's the moss, Kaven. The book said the moss gives power."

Delur fell back still more, eyes white-edged with fear. Beran shoved him against the slanting tomb stand. The floor under the collapsed end gave way entirely, and the whole thing slid slowly down. Cracks zigzagged across the floor, widening as they went.

Claw marks slashed across Delur's cheek, and his knife clattered to the floor and spun away, but he managed to rip loose from Beran's grip and run for the stairs, where Kaven had vanished around the curve. Beran scooped up the knife and went after him, the sound of Myla on his heels.

The stairs crumbled as they climbed, but Beran caught sight of the door sliding open under an open-mouthed Kaven's hands. Shoving Kaven aside, Delur lunged for the doorway. No! The man was not escaping again. Beran leaped, got hold of Delur's pack, and tightened his grip. They erupted out of the tomb in a tangle, Beran landing on top. In a move the training master had drilled into him, he drove the knife up into Delur's diaphragm, up under his ribs. He felt the skin and muscle give way, felt the heat of the blood running over his hand, knew that this time, there was no doubt.

A roar of noise and a cloud of dust billowed over him. He looked up to see Kaven and Myla scrambling away from the tomb entrance as the door frame gave way behind them and the tomb collapsed in on itself. Beran froze, paralyzed by the thought of what would have happened if they'd been a few heartbeats slower.

"Beran!"

The unexpected voice made him roll off Delur's body and sweep his gaze over the clearing. He almost couldn't take in its normalcy. Mid-day sunlight flooded it. Fish threaded on green sticks roasted over a fire. At the fire's edge, circles of flat bread cooked on rocks. Lord Zale and Lord Talun sat on one side of the clearing across from a group of Isadia's men-at-arms, all leaping to their feet and drawing their weapons.

And, of course, Carl. He grabbed Beran's arm and pulled him erect. "Sweet Powers. What's going on?" He looked down at Beran's bloody hand, glanced toward Delur's body, and clamped his mouth shut. Behind him, every man in the clearing looked with wide eyes in the same direction.

Lord Talun took a step back, then spoke in a shaky voice. "Grassland murder is what's going on. I'm taking my daughter and leaving right now." Some of Isadia's men shifted their uneasy looks to the circlet Talun still wore.

"I'm not going with you, Da," Myla said. "Kaven and I are pledged."

"You're not," Talun squared off to face her, and Beran was struck by their identically set jaws. "My daughter is not going to waste her life tied to a failing manor. Besides, I haven't given permission."

"Jorn did," Myla said. "We used the Asking."

"I don't believe you," Talun said.

Myla tugged on her shirt collar, exposing a blue mark. "Then how do you explain this?"

"You did it yourself somehow," Talun said.

"Enough." Beran shook off Carl's hand. "They're pledged, Lord Talun. I myself stood witness for the Asking."

Talun hesitated, then touched the circlet. "I still don't believe it."

Beran walked away from the body he'd made, toward Talun and Zale. Zale's face was cautious, but he held his ground while Myla's father took a step back. "Are you questioning my word, sir?" Beran asked in a tone that even to him was startlingly like his father's. He could hear Myla still arguing and Talun answering, but he let the words wash around him unheeded because he was done.

"We really are pledged, Da," Myla said. "And I have a thanksgiving gift for the Forest—I know how people can open their own tombs, so they won't need me to do it which means I have no claim on anyone's land."

"No," Talun said.

Isadia's men all came to attention. "How?" one asked.

"With plant medicine," Myla said, "and as soon as I'm sure of the recipe, I'll send it everywhere."

"I said *enough!*" Beran stalked closer to Talun. "I repeat. Are you questioning my word?"

Talun looked again at Beran's gory hand, which had begun to shake ever so slightly. Beran was close enough to see Talun's throat knot bob.

"Of course not," Talun said.

Zale snorted, then shouldered a pack that had rested on the grass next to him. "I should have known. Come, Talun. We might as well go home."

Before Talun could move, Beran snatched the circlet from his head, leaving a smear of blood in his hair. "I've had a bad last few days, Lord Talun. Don't test me. Don't test me now. Don't test me ever." He handed the circlet to Carl, who hastily passed it to one of Isadia's men, then returned his freed hand to the hilt of his undrawn sword.

"Da! Myla!" a new voice cried, and Beran turned to see Galen emerge from the woods to gape at them. He clutched the arm of a limping Lanal, who had a bloody bandage around his thigh. Beran felt like he'd been climbing a ladder and missed a step. He'd been concentrating on Myla's presumptuous father to such an extent that he hadn't noticed Lanal was gone.

"Where have you been, Galen?" Talun asked. "I wanted you, and you weren't at home. And who is this man?"

"This is the one who ran when we got here, right?" Carl said. When Zale nodded curtly, Carl swung to face Galen, making it clear that he, too, wanted an answer.

"I was…I heard the True might be tearing up the north end of the new road," Galen said. "I was telling them to stop, and this man snuck up and tried to steal my pony. I put an arrow in him, but then had to chase him for miles. I'd only just caught the little insect when we heard voices here." As Galen spoke, his tone grew more and more indignant. He shoved Lanal toward one of Isadia's men-at-arms. "I've done most of your job for you. Now get rid of him."

"He stole more than a pony," Beran said. "He's the thief who attacked Myla." Lanal stared past him to where, without looking, Beran knew Delur's body lay. Again, he felt Delur's flesh give way under the knife. He blinked away dancing dark spots.

"I stopped the True and caught one of the thieves?" Galen turned a hopeful look toward his father, then shifted it to Beran when Talun ignored him. "So like you said, Thien or Corin will say I'm a hero."

Beran pictured himself explaining this to his father. Stone it. He'd talk to Corin.

"Aren't you proud of him, Da?" Myla asked.

"Of course we Forest dwellers had to take care of the thieves ourselves," Talun said. "I'm not surprised. Leave the grassland thieves, Galen. We're going."

Beran suspected Talun meant to include him among the grassland thieves, and he was through being polite to this would-be, but inept, traitor. "Delur was a grasslander, but Rickard and Lanal are from the Forest."

Talun shrugged. "Grassland bad influence."

"Da, won't you stay and get to know Kaven?" Myla's anxious tone made Beran want to grab Talun by the throat.

Talun swayed toward her, some unexpectedly soft emotion wrinkling his eyes and mouth.

"Come, Talun," Zale said.

Talun's face hardened. "You made your bed, Myla. When you regret how hard it is, come home." He and Zale vanished into the forest with Galen trailing after them, sending a wide-eyed, horrified look back at Myla. Her face crumpled, and she buried it in Kaven's chest.

As Isadia's men tied up Lanal, Carl pointed to Delur's body and then to two more men. "Bury this one with Rickard. And you," he said, picking out another, "get back to Lady Isadia's and tell her and Kaven's mother that these three are safe."

Men scattered, all of them, Beran noticed, giving him a berth as wide as the one courtiers gave his father in a temper. Even Myla and Kaven settled a distance from Beran—or anyone else, to be fair—arms around one another, faces sagging with exhaustion.

The trembling in Beran's hands had grown too strong for him to hide any longer. "Excuse me," he said to no one in particular, then walked far enough into the woods to be out of sight, braced a hand on a tree so ancient it was holy, and vomited all over its trunk. From his empty stomach, he spewed up every drop of bile until his throat was raw, and sweat slicked his forehead. He closed his eyes, and a memory opened. He'd been about ten. His parents had gone to a reception for some visiting lord, and Beran had spent the evening in Ander and Lyren's rooms. They had no children of their own, something he'd been glad of when he was little and grown sorry for only when he was older. He'd fallen asleep on the rug in front of the fire, and then stirred with the sense someone had spoken his name.

"He's such a nice, little boy," Ander's wife had said. "I could weep when I think of what they'll make of him."

"Don't fret, Lyren," Ander said. "It can't be helped, and he'll keep hold of his true self too."

"Don't you see how being both will bring its own dose of bitterness?" Lyren had said. "He'll always be at war with himself."

At the time, Beran had drowsily wondered what they were talking about.

His breath caught in his throat, but to his shame, it wouldn't stay there. Instead, it came out in a sob. Pressing his fists to his mouth, he sank to his knees, then rocked with his shoulders shaking, horrified at what power allowed and demanded, at what he could and maybe already had become.

A booted foot stirred the leaves next to him, and Carl crouched at Beran's side. For a moment, he hesitated. Then he put an arm around Beran's shoulders and pulled him close. "Shh. It's all right."

"I did the right thing." Beran's snot smeared onto Carl's shirt, but he didn't seem to be able to stop his humiliating crying.

"You did. But sometimes your head knows that, and your heart can't forgive you anyway."

Helplessly, Beran leaned against Carl and wept. At last, he managed to get hold of himself. Maybe he'd washed the grief and horror away, or maybe he'd just stuffed it into a dark hole in his head where it would lurk, waiting for his weak moments. He straightened, scrubbing his face with the heels of his hands. "Myla told me about Balar, Carl. I'm sorry."

When Carl turned away, Beran feared he'd touched a spot that was too sore and should have shut up. Then Carl said, "He was brave. He was a fool. He should have had long years yet. He should have had a life."

"I'm sorry," Beran repeated, knowing it wasn't enough, but then, what words would be?

Carl looked Beran up and down. "You want to clean up before you go back?"

When Beran nodded, Carl led him to a stream and waited while Beran rinsed his hands and splashed water on eyes that were no doubt swollen and cheeks probably streaked with Delur's blood. Beran rose, drew a deep breath, and slipped his court face into place.

"I'm ready now," Beran said and walked toward where his people waited.

Chapter 25

Myla frowned over the drawing of a plant she'd never seen. The book said it would ease old folks' joints, but to her puzzlement, the book also said the plant came from the grasslands. The books had never mentioned a grassland plant before, and she'd swear she'd been through them all a dozen times. She moved to the bookshelf to look for some other account of the plant.

It always made her feel stronger to see the books here in the Green Valley herb room. Beran had rolled his eyes and retrieved them after Myla proposed she and Kaven should sneak in and steal them back. "Myla can use them to do good," Beran apparently told Da. "I'm sure you'd never want to harm any part of Rinland, Lord Talun. Given the warning Lord Corin gave you, the consequences would be painful." Da had taken the hint, let Beran dig them out from the places Myla told him to look, and gone back to killing butterflies instead of plotting treason. Butterflies didn't bite.

Myla wished she'd been there to see Da's face. On second thought, no, she didn't. Her heart still twisted when Da refused to notice her, even in the same room. Kaven said Da never really had noticed her, but she liked to think he couldn't look because the loss of her was a grief.

She opened a book, found a blank first page, and recognized the book she'd first looked at in the attic at home. The vanished words ran through her head. *It takes a child to see beyond looking, to risk a first step and weave the web of life back into being. The Forest provides.*

She stared out the open door at the autumn trees blazing over Silvit's long back on the Green Valley roof. Was it possible the verse spoke of her?

She'd been a child when she found the books and made the first medicine it described. Then she'd learned how to reopen closed tombs, though that didn't work the same in everyone. After drinking the moss tea, Kaven could open the Sweet Stream tomb, but not the Green Valley one, and Beran could do the opposite, but Myla could open both. And yet she'd done nothing on her own, just drawn on the books and the Forest. Something soft rubbed against her leg. She jumped but only a little. She was growing used to it.

The mark on her chest grew warm, and she turned to the doorway, already smiling. A moment later, Kaven strode in. She saw too little of him these days because he spent most of his time at Sweet Stream, working to undo the damage Rickard had done, a healing that was going faster, now that Kaven had opened the tomb. She ran to the door and stretched to press her mouth to his, her heart pounding and her body softening.

With a moan, Kaven lifted his mouth away. "There are people in the yard, Myla. Is Magistrate Halid here? I thought I saw his pony in the stable."

Grinning, Myla stepped back. "He is."

"I'll wait a while to go in then," Kaven said dryly.

"He came to talk about Galen, I think because he wanted to see my reaction. He showed Galen a wolf mask that Beran gave him, then promised mercy in trade for the names of the other True. Galen couldn't talk fast enough."

"Good. Sweet Stream needs an intact road."

"Kaven, don't you think Galen would be happier at Sweet Stream? Maybe your mother would foster him now that Corin proclaimed him a hero."

Kaven didn't quite hide his flinch. "Your father would never agree." He rushed on before she could argue. "I heard something yesterday that will interest you. You remember my talking about Markel, the grasslander who'd been given a manor west of Sweet Stream?"

"The one who treats the trees with reverence? Silvit only knows how he learned."

"I hear a new tomb opened in the center of that manor."

Her jaw sagged. "Not possible."

"Maybe. I haven't had a chance to look for myself."

"He's a grasslander!"

"Who's a grasslander?" Lady Isadia stood in the doorway, her hand full of folded parchments. "Has Sweet Stream already heard about Beran, Kaven?"

Myla's breath caught. "The Council voted?"

Isadia smiled a little sadly.

"They named Beran heir!" Kaven said.

"They voted unanimously in his favor. Corin actually spoke on his behalf, saying Beran is fierce and loyal. And Thien's Battle Leader took Lieutenant Lith into the meeting with him. Apparently, Lith was impressed by Beran's care of Ander."

"I'm so glad!" Myla cried. "He'll be good for the Forest."

"He will." Isadia handed her one of the parchments.

Myla unfolded it to find fancy lettering and the Tower of Rinland impressed in a wax seal at the bottom. She read aloud so Kaven could hear. "On the occasion of being named King's Heir, I do hereby give to the City of Rin the coin to build a fountain at the corner of Crookback Lane and Alehouse Alley so that the people of the Shambles will have water for themselves and their households and for the use of the City Watch in battling fire.

Signed in the nineteenth year of the reign of King Thien on the Feast of Lightdark,

Beran, by the grace of the Powers, Prince and King's Heir of Rinland." Blinking, Myla gave the parchment back to Isadia. "Good for Beran."

Isadia was silent a moment. Myla knew she'd been hoping the Council would reject Beran, and he'd come back to rule Green Valley, but when he'd returned the circlet to the tomb, Myla had known he wouldn't stay. She still felt guilty when she thought of the stricken look on Isadia's face when she realized the circlet wasn't where it belonged.

"Do you think he's happy?" Myla asked.

"If he isn't, he'd never tell me. And he doesn't write often." Isadia cleared her throat and opened a second parchment. "You did more good than you know when you sent a bundle of medicines home with Beran, Myla. Thien has issued orders that the Forest be treated in a way that preserves the plants you used in the cures."

Myla nearly missed the stool when she sat down. "Silvit save us."

"You've done a great service to the Forest, Myla," Isadia said.

"I'd have saved Beran's life without a reward," Myla said. "Healing is a Forest gift. It would be wrong to reject it."

"Thien wouldn't change the rule of the Forest just because Beran is his son," Isadia said bitterly. "There was blister plague in Rin when Beran got there, and he carried your remedy. That's why the Forest plants are to be preserved. But Thien has tried to reward you for what you did for Beran." Isadia held up the last parchment. "He's offered to pay for your training with the finest herbalist in Rinland."

The only sound in the herb room was the rustle of leaves outside. Frowning, Kaven turned away so Myla couldn't see his face. Her throat contracted. "Do I have to go?"

"Of course not. Beran chose his path," Isadia said, a hitch in her voice. "You can choose too. Ailith didn't have that chance, but I'll rot before I see you forced anywhere."

She wouldn't go, Myla decided with relief. Then she looked at the book on the table, open to the picture of the grassland plant that eased old folks' pain and felt a sudden treacherous longing to know what other plants grew in the places she'd never been. A heavy, warm body seemed to lean against her knee. Claiming her? Or encouraging her?

Kaven turned to face her. "You should do it."

"What?" She scanned his face. Regret showed in the lines of his mouth, but the set of his body was sure.

"You should go and learn everything you can. We have time, and I know you'd come back."

"Of course I'd come back!" She rushed into his arms again and pressed herself against his chest. "But how can I go?"

Laying his cheek against her hair, he said, "You can go because for you, it's right."

"You don't have to, Myla," Isadia said. "You can stay with me as long as you like."

Myla turned to look at her. There was no mistaking the anguish in Isadia's face. Stay at Green Valley Manor? Myla felt the safety in that. She'd grown here in ways that kept surprising her every time she stumbled over them. She opened her mouth, but Isadia raised a hand to silence her.

"I'll rejoice if you stay, but I'll rejoice for you if you go too." Isadia smiled tremulously. "As Kaven says, I know you'll come home again."

Kaven put his arm around Myla's shoulders. A furry head nudged her hip. She drew a breath. "I'll go."

She would go. She would come home. She would lie forever, safe in the arms of the Forest.

Originally from Detroit, Dorothy A. Winsor has lived in the Iowa cornfields since 1995. She has taught technical writing at Iowa State University, edited the Journal of Business and Technical Communication, and taught at GMI Engineering & Management Institute, along the way winning six national awards for research on the communication practices of engineers. She lives with her husband, a tractor engineer, and has one son, who first introduced her to the pleasure of reading fantasy. Finders Keepers (2015), her first novel, was a finalist in the e-book fiction category of the Eric Hoffer Awards.

CPSIA information can be obtained
at www.ICGtesting.com
Printed in the USA
FFOW02n1548171016
28536FF